THE MAN WHO WASN'T ALL THERE

THE MAN WHO WASN'T ALL THERE

David Handler

SEVERN
HOUSE

First world edition published in Great Britain and the USA in 2021
by Severn House, an imprint of Canongate Books Ltd,
14 High Street, Edinburgh EH1 1TE.

Trade paperback edition first published in Great Britain and the USA in 2022
by Severn House, an imprint of Canongate Books Ltd.

severnhouse.com

British Library Cataloguing in Publication Data
A CIP catalogue record for this title is available from the British Library.

ISBN-13: 978-0-7278-9248-5 (cased)
ISBN-13: 978-1-78029-769-9 (trade paper)
ISBN-13: 978-1-4483-0507-0 (e-book)

All Severn House titles are printed on acid-free paper.

Typeset by Palimpsest Book Production Ltd.,
Falkirk, Stirlingshire, Scotland.
Printed and bound in Great Britain by
TJ Books Limited, Padstow, Cornwall.

This one's for Diana, who was forced to home shelter with me 24/7 for way too many months yet never lost her gentle, serene nature.

ONE

I was *me* again.

For six glorious weeks I'd been living my dream, the one that I'd been clinging to for more than a decade – ever since the *New York Times Sunday Book Review* proclaimed me 'the first major new literary voice of the 1980s.' Ever since Joe Papp's loveliest and most gifted discovery, Merilee Nash, and I were anointed as the Big Apple's It Couple. Ever since I got writer's block, snorted my career up my nose and Merilee drop-kicked Lulu and me back to my crappy fifth-floor walk-up on West 93rd Street, where I was relegated to scratching out a non-distinguished living as a ghostwriter of celebrity memoirs.

But now? Now I had my voice back. Not to mention residential privileges in the place I'd once called home. Every morning I was awake before dawn in that king-sized bed in Merilee's opulent sixteenth-floor apartment on Central Park West, my head exploding with ideas. I was there but I wasn't there. My body was living in the autumn of 1993. My heart and soul were living in the summer of 1975 – 'My Sweet Season of Madness,' as I was calling my new novel. I was back in *my* New York, the grimy, graffiti-strewn, rodent and drug-infested *Ford to City: Drop Dead* New York. The New York of CBGBs, the Mudd Club, Max's and those after-hours dance clubs in Spanish Harlem that the Walt Whitman Award-winning poet Regina Aintree, my first great love, and I would go roaring up to at four a.m. on my big, bad black Norton. The New York of the Chelsea Hotel, where we were making crazy monkey love in Reggie's third-floor room the night Sid Vicious of the Sex Pistols stuck that knife into Nancy Spungen's stomach in Room 100. Allegedly. He OD'd before he came to trial.

I was so into what I was writing that while Merilee's espresso machine did its thing I'd skip my morning shave and put on a white T-shirt, torn jeans, Chippewa boots and my 1933 Werber leather flight jacket just like I used to. An author is a method actor who works alone on paper. And I was totally in character. The one I'd been in '75, who shaved twice a week and chain-smoked unfiltered Chesterfields. I'd bought a carton of them and allowed myself one smoke a day after dinner. I'd even had Grandfather's old Ronson Varaflame lighter resuscitated at a cigar shop on Madison. All it had needed was a new flint spring assembly, the stooped, ancient repairman said.

While I drank my espresso I'd devour a toasted baguette with blackberry jam from Merilee's farm while I put down Lulu's breakfast of 9Lives mackerel for cats. She has rather unusual eating habits for a basset hound and, trust me, the breath to prove it. Then I'd head straight for my solid steel 1958 Olympia portable, which was parked on the genuine signed Stickley library table set before the windows overlooking Central Park in the office that Merilee had custom furnished for me, complete with a leather Morris chair and an Edward Hopper landscape painting of the craggy Maine coastline. Not a print. The actual painting. I'd crank up *Rockaway Beach* by the Ramones, which I listened to every morning – on vinyl, the way it was meant to be listened to – and I'd time travel back to that sweet season when I was so young, talented and brilliant, so high on life and an array of psychedelics that I was utterly convinced no one had ever lived a life like mine or possessed the ideas and insights I possessed or shared the passion that Reggie and I shared.

It was all brand new.

I soaked up the music and wrote my novel, which was turning out to be a darkly funny valentine about two gifted young New York artists who are in love with each other, with their work, with *life* – and the price they'd paid to make their dreams come true. Certainly the price that I'd paid.

Every day, the hours flew by as I heard the sounds, smelled the smells, experienced the joy and the agony all over again. My skin tingled as the words flowed through me. I had no idea what was coming out next. Just that they were words that demanded to be read. For a writer it's the greatest feeling in the world.

The only missing element was Merilee, who was in Budapest playing Lady Brett Ashley in a lavish remake of Ernest Hemingway's *The Sun Also Rises* opposite Mel Gibson. But, in the immortal words of Meat Loaf – or Mr Loaf as the un-failingly hip *New York Times* insisted upon calling him – two out of three ain't bad. Besides, we'd made amazing progress over that past summer, my celebrated ex-wife and I. When I'd told her I might have an idea for a novel she'd generously offered me the guest cottage on her eighteen-acre farm in Lyme, Connecticut. I'd written my first three chapters there while she was busy directing a revival of Noel Coward's *Private Lives* at the historic summer playhouse in nearby Sherbourne. A couple of people got murdered. Maybe you heard about it. I'd returned to the city Labor Day weekend. She'd followed me soon thereafter because Paramount had agreed to finance *The Sun Also Rises* and, after our first night of atomic passion in more years than I can remember, she'd invited Lulu and me to stay in her apartment while she was away. Since the calendar said it was still summer and the temperature averaged a muggy triple digits in my crappy fifth-floor walk-up on West 93rd, I'd leapt at the chance. So had Lulu, who enjoys her creature comforts almost as much as she enjoys anchovies, preferably chilled because the oil clings better. Did I mention she has unusual eating habits?

As much as I was missing Merilee, maybe it was better this way. I was zoned in seven days a week, morning, noon and night. Spoke to no one. Saw no one. I'd shown those first three chapters I'd written over the summer to the Silver Fox, my literary agent, who'd not only pronounced them 'thrilling' but had landed me a hefty advance from a top-flight publisher. I'd produced more than a hundred new pages since Merilee had left. I would write from dawn until noon, take Lulu for a brisk walk in the park, then mark up that morning's work and rewrite it until I was satisfied. Evenings we'd stroll down to Tony's on West 79th and Amsterdam where I would scribble notes in my notepad while I devoured linguini with homemade sausages and drank Chianti. Lulu would put away a small plate of calamari. After dinner I'd fire up my nightly Chesterfield, dragging contentedly on it as we strolled home. I'd climb into bed, review my notes for tomorrow, savor a few pages of Mrs Parker, who is someone I like to re-read every few years just to remind myself what good writing is, and then drop off, raring to get back to work in the morning.

I was so zoned in I was barely aware of what was happening in the world around me. I knew that the Toronto Blue Jays and the Philadelphia Phillies were playing in the World Series. I knew from my weekly trek up to West 93rd to collect my mail that the hottest movie packing them in at the Loews on Broadway and West 84th was a riotously funny feature film remake of *The Beverly Hillbillies* staring the riotously funny Jim Varney as Jed Clampett. I knew from standing in line at the grocery store that Vanna White, the remarkably gifted letter turner on TV's *Wheel of Fortune*, was pregnant. So was Marla Maples, mistress of that puddle of ooze the tabloids called The Donald, as in Trump, who was considering marrying her but wasn't entirely sure she was worthy of his greatness. I also knew that the New York I was writing about, *my* New York, was so much more vivid and meaningful than the one I was living in now, which was why it was so vital for me to get it down on paper. And get it right. And I was. I felt sure of it. I also felt sure that the end of Nancy Spungen's life under that bathroom sink in the Chelsea Hotel would signify the end of 'My Sweet Season of Madness,' although I had absolutely no idea how I was going to get there. *I didn't know*. That's part of the adventure. Or, as a very drunk John Gregory Dunne told me one night at a cocktail party: 'I sit down to write the book to figure out why the fuck I'm writing the book.'

After sticking to my Spartan work routine for those six glorious weeks I'd reached a major crossroads in my plot and had no strong instinct telling me which road to take. Just a vague itch that something was missing. So I decided to treat myself to a change of scenery. Merilee had not only given me the keys to the apartment but to the 1958 red XK150 roadster that she was awarded in the divorce settlement, and had urged me to make use of her farm at the top of Joshua Town Road in Lyme, the bucolic Yankee Eden situated at the mouth of the Connecticut River on Long Island Sound, halfway between New York and Boston. She kept chickens there, had a duck pond, apple and pear orchards. I'd drive out for a few days and take in the splendor of late October in New England. The autumn leaves would be turning. The night air would be crisp and clean. I'd take long walks in the woods with Lulu. Put the vegetable garden to bed that I'd tended over the summer. Collect some baskets of apples and pears. Make a fire every night in the stone fireplace, sip Macallan, and think non-deep thoughts. It would be just what I needed.

At the copier shop around the corner I made a Xerox of the hundred new pages I'd written and messengered them to the Silver Fox for her feedback. She was an old-school agent who'd represented the likes of Steinbeck, Cheever and O'Hara and was *the* savviest reader in town. And then I packed. My Olympia went into its travel case. My manuscript and several notepads went into my Il Bisonte briefcase. My shaving kit went into Grandfather's battered leather suitcase. I would need warmer clothes. The antique farmhouse was not exactly toasty. Some Viyella shirts. A six-ply shawl collar cashmere cardigan. My heavy barley tweed Norfolk jacket that I'd had made for me in London at Strickland & Sons. Also the Gore-Tex trail hikers that a little man on West 33rd Street had made for me many years back. I phoned old Mr MacGowan, Merilee's neighbor out there, who fed the chickens and looked after the place, and told him Lulu and I would be coming out for a few days, which he was delighted to hear. Lastly, I wrestled Lulu into her Fair Isle wool vest. She's susceptible to colds and snores like a lumberjack when she gets them. I know this because she likes to sleep on my head. After I'd locked up the apartment we rode the elevator down and strolled over to the garage on Columbus where Merilee kept the Jag. I stashed my bags, checked the oil and gassed her up. Lulu curled up on a blanket on her biscuit-colored leather seat, since the vintage British ragtop has little in the way of heat. Make that nothing in the way of heat.

We left mid-afternoon under threatening skies. By the time we'd reached New Haven on I-95 it was pouring rain and droplets were starting to leak in on us. The ragtop isn't what I would call an impenetrable barrier. It was not only pouring but pitch black out when I got off the highway at Old Lyme and headed up Route 156 into the rolling hills of Lyme with my high beams on.

Joshua Town Road is narrow, twisting, hilly and there are no street lights out there. Not an easy drive in the best of conditions. In the dark of night with the rain pouring down on so many fallen leaves it was hard to even find the pavement. But I finally made it to the open gate at the end of the road and sped my way up the gravel drive that led to the darkened nine-room farmhouse that had been built in 1736 by Josiah Whitcomb, a prosperous shipping magnate. Merilee had installed motion-detector lights, which were a huge help as I pulled into the courtyard, where the chickens had retreated from their wire coop into the nice, dry barn. I parked as close to the front door as I could. Dashed to the front door, unlocked it and turned on a few lights. Lulu darted inside while I came back out for my Olympia, briefcase and suitcase.

Mr MacGowan, being a lifelong Yankee, had set the thermostat for the furnace at a thrifty, gelid fifty-five degrees. I jacked it way up to a hedonistic sixty-five and built a big fire in the parlor's stone fireplace. Happily, he'd laid in a stack of dry seasoned hardwood and plenty of kindling. After the fire started crackling and popping I went into the huge farmhouse kitchen with its double work sink of scarred white porcelain and gallantly hideous yellow and red linoleum floor. I fed Lulu her 9Lives mackerel and checked out the refrigerator. Mr MacGowan had thoughtfully stocked it with a few essentials like fresh milk, orange juice, butter, cold cuts, a loaf of bread and a package of English muffins. Also a carton of a dozen eggs with a note taped to it: *Just got laid*. The man's a savant when it comes to barnyard humor. I dug some thick-cut bacon out of the freezer and got several slices going in the Lodge cast iron skillet while I carried my suitcase into the master bedroom suite, which was not only freezing cold but had no covers on the bed. I built another fire in the fireplace in there, then made up the bed with flannel sheets, a Hudson Bay blanket and down comforter before I fed the fire in the living room, moved the bacon around in the skillet and unpacked my clothes.

By then Lulu was curled up contentedly on the parlor sofa in front of the fire and the bacon was ready. I removed it from the skillet, poured off the fat into an old coffee can, popped an English muffin in the toaster and cracked four of those fresh laid eggs into the skillet. Their yolks were an incredibly bright orange. When the English muffin was done I buttered it and put it on a plate with the bacon and eggs. Found a bottle of Bass ale, put some Erroll Garner on the stereo, joined Lulu on the sofa and devoured my dinner while the fire crackled and the rain poured down and the Little Elf had his way with *Misty* like no one ever has or ever will. When my plate was clean I fished a Chesterfield from the pack in the pocket of my leather flight jacket, tapped both ends of it on the coffee table and lit it with Grandfather's lighter, dragging on it gratefully as I drank the last of my Bass and felt my muscles unwind from the long drive.

After I'd smoked my cigarette I tossed the butt into the fire, cleaned the kitchen, turned off the stereo and lights and made my way to the bedroom, where I fed the fire before I took a hot shower. By the time I was ready for bed Lulu had already staked a claim to considerably more than half of it. I climbed into the cozy flannel sheets under the blanket and comforter and listened to the rain pour down and the fire crackle as Lulu burrowed close to me with her head on my tummy. She doesn't exactly love the farm. She's afraid of the coyotes and bobcats. She's afraid of the wild turkeys, raccoons, possums and woodchucks, the chickens in their chicken coop, the ducks in their duck pond. Afraid of the duck pond. She can't swim. Only dog I've ever met who can't. Just sinks straight to the bottom *glug-glug-glug*. But wherever I go, she goes. We're a team, like Dickens and Fenster. So I held her as I lay there in the firelight, fully intending to read Mrs Parker for a while. Never happened. I was fast asleep before I knew it.

By early morning the storm had passed. Quasimodo, Merilee's rooster, was crowing his head off and the sky was a shade of blue you seldom see in New York City. Actually, make that never see. I lay there gazing out the French doors at the autumn leaves on the maple trees and at the open pasturage that tumbled down to Whalebone Cove, where six acres of freshwater tidal marsh were home to one of the state's last remaining stands of wild rice, not to mention several rare marsh plants. Also great blue herons, long-billed marsh wrens, ospreys and the occasional bald eagle.

I threw on a T-shirt, torn jeans, a toasty black and white Tattersall Viyella shirt and my Chippewas. Put on the coffee, fed Lulu, toasted an English muffin and slathered it with Merilee's blackberry jam. While I ate at the big kitchen table, which originally had been a washhouse table at a Shaker colony in Mount Lebanon, New York, I made a fall chores list. Attending to seasonal chores is a great way to clear your head. It's a trick that's worked for me many times before. Actually, it's a trick that's never worked for me before but why let a small technicality get in the way?

After I'd drained my second cup of coffee I dug a pair of pliers and Phillips screwdriver from the tool drawer, went outside by way of the mudroom, discovered from the thermometer mounted outside of the door that it was forty-six degrees, went back inside for my flight jacket and headed out again, taking deep breaths of the clean air as Lulu waddled along with me in her vest at my insistence, grumbling. She would have been much happier staying in bed, but if she doesn't get a proper amount of exercise she puts on weight and she doesn't really have anywhere to put it – except even nearer to the floor. So she joined me as I fed Quasimodo and the girls, making sure she kept a safe distance from their wire coop.

The guest cottage wasn't winterized and needed to be closed-up for the season. I unscrewed the screen door from its hinges, carried it inside and propped it against the wall. Latched all of the windows shut. Used the pliers to shut off the water under the bathroom sink and turned on the faucet and shower to bleed the pipes. I also flushed the toilet twice to empty it so that no water would be left in it to freeze and crack the porcelain. Then I stood there gazing at the plain pine writing table and narrow white iron bed, smiling. I had many fond memories of working on my first three chapters in this cottage on summer mornings when the breeze that came through the screen door was cool and fragrant from all of the flowers that were blooming.

I closed the door and moved on.

Chopping kindling was next on my chores list, but you don't want to chop kindling the morning after a rainstorm. You want a dry, frosty morning when it hasn't rained for several days. So I fetched a spade and pruners from the barn and led Lulu around the duck pond to my vegetable garden. Specifically to my shriveled, yellowing tomato plants, which needed to be cut back, pulled out by the roots and buried somewhere far, far away since they harbor blights.

I'd just started in on the job when a Connecticut State Police Ford Crown Vic cruiser eased its way up the gravel driveway and parked behind the Jag. It wasn't the standard silver State Police Crown Vic. It was a dilapidated rust bucket of no particular color tricked out with a humongous black demolition derby front bumper, as well as an array of spotlights and antennae. Lulu let out a low growl of warning, which surprised me. She's usually happy to greet sworn personnel. And absolutely nothing makes her happier than riding around in a police car.

The trooper who climbed out was in his mid-forties and didn't have the bearing of a typical state trooper. He was exceedingly short and roly-poly, not to mention unshaven and unwashed. His body odor was so strong I could smell him from ten feet away. He wore no Smokey hat over his unusually large, balding head, and was dressed in what appeared to be a state trooper's uniform except it wasn't. His slate-gray long-sleeved shirt was adorned with no nameplate, badge or official insignias. His navy-blue trousers had no royal blue and gold stripe, and he wore Adidas sneakers, not polished black brogans. He did have on a black garrison-style belt equipped with a hickory nightstick and holstered weapon, but he carried no two-way radio. And his weapon wasn't the Sig Sauer semi-automatic that state troopers were carrying now. It was an old-school revolver.

The round little man stood there gazing admiringly at the historic farmhouse and barn and orchards. His eyes were set unusually close together, as if they were both on the same side of his nose. Then he hitched up his trousers, swaggered over toward me, raising his chin in the air authoritatively. 'This is Merilee Nash's place, isn't it?' His voice sounded oddly boyish and petulant. His breath was foul enough to make my eyes water.

Again, Lulu growled at him.

I shushed her before I said, 'Yes, it is. But she isn't here right now. May I help you?'

'And who might *you* be?' His manner wasn't what I'd call courteous.

'How about you go first? May I see some ID, please?'

He opened his wallet and produced a dog-eared card that identified him as Austin Talmadge, a member in good standing since 1988 of the Connecticut State Police Booster Club.

'Correct me if I'm wrong, but you're not an actual state trooper, are you?'

'I'm auxiliary state police,' Austin said defensively. 'I provide vital assistance in rural areas like this one.'

'I'm Merilee's ex-husband, Stewart Hoag. I was out here all summer yet I don't recall seeing you around providing vital assistance.'

'I was . . . away,' he said, reddening, before he abruptly switched gears. 'I sure did love her in that Gulf War movie where she counseled vets with PTSD. She has so much genuine heart. Really, really relates to people who are hurting. I have lots of movie ideas myself. I've written more than forty scripts. Romantic comedies, heist pictures, westerns.' His speaking manner was rapid fire and disjointed. 'I'd love to show them to her.'

I tugged at my ear, wondering if he was a celebrity stalker, a country oddball or what. 'She's not here, like I said.'

'But she'd read them, wouldn't she? She isn't the sort of snob who'd just throw them in the garbage.'

'It's her agent's job to read any submissions that are made to her. She doesn't have the time to read them herself.'

He tilted her head at me curiously. 'Are you in movies, too?'

'I'm a novelist.'

'I've written those, too. Dozens of them. I've got them in a trunk somewhere. Want to read one?'

'I'm in the middle of a book of my own right now. If I read someone else's work it can affect my voice. Thank you for the offer, though. Tell me, what else do you do?'

Austin furrowed his brow at me. 'What do you mean?'

'When you're not writing screenplays, novels and helping provide the state police with vital assistance in rural areas – do you have a regular job?'

'This *is* my job.'

Country oddball it was. Lyme had quite its share of them. It was a remote, rural area that had been settled by a very small number of families more than 300 years ago. Many of the descendants still lived there. I also wondered if Austin was a stoner. But if he were high on weed, would he be driving around playing Officer Krupke?

'If you're her *ex*-husband, how come you still live with her?' he demanded, peering at me.

'That would fall under the category of none of your business.' As I circled around his tricked-out cruiser I noticed that the entire back seat was a toxic waste dump of greasy fast food wrappers, pizza boxes and plastic jugs of Coca-Cola. I stopped when I got to the front of the car, studying it.

'What are you doing?' he demanded.

'Memorizing your license plate number.'

'What for?' A whiny quaver had crept into his voice.

'It's a mental exercise. My short-term memory's a work in progress. I dropped a lot of acid when I was in college.'

'Oh, I get it. You're a wise guy, huh?'

'And I get paid a lot of money for it, too.'

He reddened again. 'A word of warning. You don't want to get on my bad side.'

'That's funny, I didn't realize that totally round objects *had* sides.'

He shook a stubby finger at me. 'You're going to be sorry you said that. And you still haven't shown me *your* ID. Hand it over right goddamned now!'

'That's not going to happen, Austin. You have no authority to make me show it to you. I think we're done here now, so why don't you get in your toy car and go back the way you came?'

He stuck his chin out at me, his hands parked on what would have been his hips if he'd had hips. 'You don't seem to understand. I'm conducting a criminal investigation.'

'A criminal investigation of what?'

'Trespassing, possible breaking and entering . . .'

'OK, that does it. I've tried to be patient with you but you've exhausted my reserves of goodwill. I'm going inside the house now to phone the resident trooper and lodge a complaint that *you're* trespassing and harassing me.'

'You don't want to do that,' Austin warned me.

Lulu let out another growl, this one considerably more menacing. I told her to let me handle it. 'I don't want to do what, Austin?'

'Make me angry. I can cause you more problems than you already have.'

'Actually, there are no problems here – except for you. So why don't you make the problem go away by leaving?'

He glared at me some more with those close-set eyes of his, shoving his pouty lower lip in and out. 'Fine, I'll go. But I want it understood that I don't care for your attitude. Next time you see me you'd better show more respect.'

'And here I was hoping I wouldn't have to see or smell you again.'

'That was a really nasty thing to say.'

'I'm so sorry. I deeply regret it if I hurt your feelings. You have until the count of ten to get back in your car and off of this property. If you don't I'll sic Lulu on you.'

His eyes widened in fear. 'She's an attack dog?'

To be honest Lulu had been in exactly one fight in her entire life – with a Pomeranian named Mr Puff Ball in Riverside Park. She came out on the losing end. But there was no need for him to know that. 'Let's just say she's highly protective of me. I'm going to start counting now. Ten . . . nine . . .'

His eyes blazed at me as he hurried toward his Crown Vic. 'You'll regret this,' he vowed.

'This is me quaking in my boots. Eight . . . seven . . .'

He jumped back in his car, started it up and went tearing

off down the gravel driveway. Lulu chased after his car for about fifty feet, barking, until she ran out of pep and pulled up, gasping.

'Atta girl. You sure showed him who's the boss around here. He won't dare mess with *us* anymore.'

It took less than five minutes for old Mr MacGowan to come speeding up the driveway in his battered Dodge Ram pickup. Lulu ambled over to greet him when he got out. He bent over to pet her, or at least did his best to. He was well into his seventies and barrel-chested with an arthritic back. The MacGowan family had farmed the neighboring land since the early 1800s, and Mr MacGowan knew everything there was to know about farming, although he'd also taught math at the high school for forty years in order to pay his property taxes. Like so many of the old-timers in Lyme he came across as chilly and abrupt – a Cranky Yankee – until he decided you were OK. He'd decided in no time that Merilee was plenty OK. I'd eventually managed to win him over, too.

'Awful nice to see you again, Hoagy,' he said, patting Lulu's head.

'Likewise, Mr MacGowan. Thanks for stocking the fridge. Those provisions came in mighty handy last night.'

'No trouble at all. I was at the A&P anyway.'

'How are my girls doing?'

By 'my girls' I meant Joanie and Sandy, who'd started working there as cashiers in high school, had never left and were now in their late forties. They'd taken a shine to me that summer, possibly because I enjoyed flirting with them.

'Still full of piss and vinegar.' He furrowed his brow at me with concern. 'Hoagy, I would swear I just saw a rusty old Crown Vic go tearing down Joshua Town past my place. Did you by any chance have a visitor?'

'I sure did. A smelly, unpleasant little fat man who claimed he was an auxiliary state trooper. Celebrity stalker is more like it. He was very upset that Merilee wasn't here and demanded to know who I was and what I was doing here. Said his name was Austin Talmadge.'

Mr MacGowan paled, swallowing. 'So he's out again . . .'

'Out again?'

'Hoagy, if I were you I'd get your things together and drive straight back to New York.'

'But I just got here.'

'Trust me, Austin's not someone you want to trifle with,' he said, his voice rising with urgency. 'Especially if he's got Merilee in his sights. He's a major nut case who's been in and out of psychiatric hospitals his whole life. You should call the state police right away. Don't bother with Jim Conley. He's a fine resident trooper but you need somebody who has a lot more pull.'

I studied Mr MacGowan curiously. 'Are you saying this guy's dangerous?'

'I'm saying I wouldn't feel safe here if I were you.'

'You sound awfully serious about this.'

'Only because I am.'

'I do know someone who I can call.'

'Will you promise me you'll call him right away?'

'I promise.'

'Then I'll leave you to it.' Mr MacGowan climbed back in his truck and drove off, leaving me there feeling totally bewildered.

I went inside and leafed through the phone book in my briefcase for the number of Pete Tedone, whom my lawyer had put me in touch with last summer when things got super messy with a former Yale Drama School classmate of Merilee's. Pete took care of it and kept it out of the papers. He'd been deputy superintendent of the Connecticut State Police until his wife got caught shoplifting several valuable items from the Gucci store on Fifth Avenue while Pete was right there by her side, clueless, or so he'd claimed when store security landed on her. He took early retirement and became a private detective – a private detective who was related to half the hierarchy in the state police.

I called him and left Merilee's unlisted business number with his answering service.

He called me back in five minutes. 'Hoagy, what a nice surprise. I thought you'd gone back to Gotham City to work on the great American novel.'

'I did. I am. Just came out for a few days to take in the fall color. Merilee's shooting a movie in Budapest. I'm out here by myself.' Lulu coughed. 'Which is to say it's just Lulu and me.'

'Something I can help you with?'

'I don't know, to be honest. Her neighbor out here, an old-timer, seems to think I'm in the middle of a situation.'

'What kind of a situation?'

'A strange sort of guy just showed up here in a tricked-out old Crown Vic wearing a fake state trooper's uniform and carrying a nightstick and gun. He was in his forties, short, fat and smelled like a homeless person. Called himself an auxiliary state trooper. Also a huge admirer of Merilee's work, as in my idea of potential stalker material. Me, he didn't like at all. Told me I'd better show him more respect the next time we see each other.'

'Got a name for me?' Pete was unable to hide the dread that had crept into his voice.

'Austin Talmadge.'

'Are you going to be around this morning?'

'That's the plan.'

'Good. I'll be there in less than an hour.'

'Super. Thanks, Pete.'

'A word of warning, Hoagy . . .' Pete Tedone cleared his throat. 'I won't be alone.'

TWO

It was actually a small convoy that arrived forty-five minutes later. Heading up the convoy was Pete Tedone, who still drove a standard-issue silver Crown Vic just as he had when he'd been deputy superintendent. Pete was a chesty fireplug in his early fifties with a shaved head and a twenty-inch neck who was partial to cheap, shiny black suits that were just a bit too snug in the shoulders.

He'd barely had time to greet me with a grim nod and a firm handshake before the gravel driveway was overflowing with men exiting their vehicles. Each of them greeted me with that same grim nod and firm handshake when Pete introduced us, one by one. The first was Jim Conley, resident state trooper of Lyme and Old Lyme. Resident troopers are common in rural Connecticut towns that are too small to fund a police force of their own. Conley carried himself with a great deal of calm authority. He was maybe fifty, tall, lean and broad-shouldered. Wore a wide-brimmed Smokey hat and a trimly tailored uniform. A genuine one, unlike Austin Talmadge's. His superior was Captain Donovan Rundle of the Troop F Barracks in Westbrook – or 'F Troop' as the locals called it in mocking homage to the '60s TV sitcom about an inept cavalry troop that starred Ken Berry, Forrest Tucker and the one, the only Larry Storch. Rundle was in his mid-fifties, a jowly, paunchy, deflated accordion of a man who looked incredibly unhappy to be pulled away from his primary job, which was sitting at his desk counting the days until he could retire and play golf in Boca Raton. Moving on up the food chain, Pete introduced me to Buck Mitry, the man who'd succeeded him as deputy superintendent. Mitry was a stern-faced black man who was a good two inches taller than I am – which would make him six feet five. He was dressed in a sober gray suit and muted tie and possessed the largest hand I'd ever shaken in my life.

Lastly, I met Colin Fielding, a slightly built man in his late forties with thinning sandy hair and piercing eyes. Pete Tedone described him as a 'personal envoy' from the governor's office.

'I'm here but I'm not here,' Fielding said cryptically. He wore a navy-blue suit and a silk tie of bold orange and black stripes that identified him as a Princetonian.

I led them inside where we sat around the big kitchen table. They declined coffee. They weren't there to drink coffee. Or to fuss over Lulu. Didn't pay the slightest bit of attention to her.

She curled up at my feet with a sour grunt. She doesn't like to be ignored. 'Forgive me for jumping to conclusions, gentlemen,' I said, 'but I get the feeling I've just had a close encounter of the weird kind.'

'That you have, Hoagy.' Pete Tedone nodded his shaved head.

The table fell silent after that. And stayed silent.

Resident Trooper Conley cleared his throat. 'Forgive us, we're waiting for one more member of our team to arrive,' he explained as I saw a Volvo station wagon pull up outside. 'Ah, here she is.'

'Come on in!' I hollered when there was a tap at the mudroom door.

In strode a strikingly attractive woman. She was in her early-forties, I'm guessing, with penetrating brown eyes and a lush, untamed mane of chestnut-colored hair streaked with silver. She was about five feet seven and had the kind of lean, muscular body that only comes from working out like a total demon eight days a week. She wore a tight-fitting black cashmere turtleneck sweater, tight-fitting black fine-wale corduroy pants and a pair of trail hikers. No make-up or jewelry, other than a plain gold wedding band. No perfume either, which was a blessing because Lulu is highly allergic to most of them.

'Sorry I'm late,' she said in a low, cool voice as she joined us at the table. 'Had to wait for my mother to get here from Guilford. My youngest is home with the sniffles. Forgive me, but what's this all about? You said it was urgent.'

I said, 'Excuse me, you are . . .?'

'Oh, sorry,' Pete Tedone said. 'Stewart Hoag, say hello to Dr Annabeth McKenna. She's on the faculty at the Yale School of Medicine. Her field is child psychiatry. She's in private practice, too, and for the past several years she's attended exclusively to the needs of one very special patient.'

I tugged at my ear. 'Going out on a limb here – would that one very special patient happen to be named Austin Talmadge?'

'Correct, Mr Hoag,' she replied, running her fingers through her hair.

'Make it Hoagy.'

'As in Carmichael?'

'As in the cheese steak.'

She arched an eyebrow at me curiously. 'On the surface, Austin might strike you as a bit of a departure for a child psychiatrist. But allow me to assure you that while the calendar may say he's forty-two, Austin is a highly unstable, anti-social delusional psychotic who has the emotional maturity of a ten-year-old boy. Did he threaten you? Is that why we're here?'

'He said, and I quote, "You'll regret this." Is that your idea of a threat?'

'Why don't you tell us what happened?' she suggested as Captain Rundle kept sneaking admiring looks at her, no doubt picturing her in a bikini lounging by the side of his pool in Boca.

'He showed up here anxious to speak with my ex-wife.'

She smiled at me, brightening. 'That would be Merilee?'

'Do you two know each other?'

'We were on a committee together last year. Blocked a developer from building sixteen McMansions on Selden Cove Road. She's a real fighter.'

'That she is. Austin seems to feel she's also deeply caring and understanding based on a role she played in a movie last year. That sort of thing happens to actors. It's an occupational hazard.'

Deputy Superintendent Mitry cleared his throat. 'I don't like it that a celebrity of her stature is on Austin's radar screen. He might start watching the house, tailing her when she leaves . . .'

'We're in luck in that regard,' I said. 'She's on location in Budapest shooting a movie.'

'Did you tell Austin that?' Resident Trooper Conley asked.

'All I said was that she wasn't here.'

'Meaning he has every reason to believe that she was just out running an errand. I don't like it,' Mitry repeated, glancing pointedly at the governor's special envoy, who was there but not there. 'He's already been harassing a number of residents lately. And now we've got celebrity stalking to sift into the mix. This is trouble waiting to happen.'

'He must be off of his Thorazine again,' Annabeth McKenna said unhappily. 'He hates taking it because it makes him fuzzy headed and contributes to his weight gain. I should point out that he's also missed his last two sessions with me, which I consider mandatory.'

'Do you think we should pull the ripcord?' Captain Rundle asked her.

'Already done,' Mitry informed him. 'I pulled it as soon as I got Pete's call.'

'The *ripcord*? Forgive me if I sound a bit testy,' I said, 'but I came out here from the city to clear my head. Instead, I've run into a nut case with intergalactic B.O. who likes to pretend he's a state trooper, a special envoy of the governor who's here but not here, a Yale School of Medicine child psychiatrist who treats exactly one middle-aged patient, and a table full of official people who are speaking in code. Will someone kindly tell me what the hell is going on?'

They exchanged an uncomfortable look.

On Mitry's nod, Annabeth McKenna said, 'Austin is something of a special case.'

'Trust me, that's already been made abundantly clear. Special as in . . .?'

She gazed across the table at me, her mouth tightening. 'He may not look or smell like it, but Austin Talmadge is a billionaire who owns a thirty-one-room riverfront estate on Elys Ferry Road. He's one of *the* Talmadges, who were among the original British royal land grant families to settle this state in the 1600s. Unlike the Pecks, Beckwiths and other founding families, the Talmadges worked tirelessly generation after generation to expand upon their original holdings of land and timber into shipping, banking and the construction of New England's first rail system. As a result, Austin happens to be the second richest man in the entire state of Connecticut. And there are a lot of rich people in the state of Connecticut. The only person in the state who's richer than Austin is his older brother, Michael, an attorney who is his trustee.'

'The state police have been under a long-standing, explicit order from one governor after another to treat Austin with kid gloves,' Deputy Superintendent Mitry explained. '*Unless* he creates a situation. Which, I regret to say, he has begun to do.'

Resident Trooper Conley nodded unhappily. 'A few weeks ago, he decided to dedicate himself to restoring proper law and order around here, which he feels has become woefully lax under my watch. Purchased a reconditioned Ford Crown Vic, fashioned a uniform of sorts for himself and bought a used Smith and Wesson revolver at Old Tom's Guns up on the Boston Post Road. Fortunately, Tom alerted me and I made certain that he removed the firing pin without Austin's knowledge. It's essentially a toy gun. Doesn't present a genuine threat. But Austin does. He's taken to going out on patrol. Last week he broke up a late-night bonfire party on White Sand Beach. Just showed up down there, waving his gun, and confiscated a case of Coors from the Hardy Boys.'

'Frank and Joe?' I asked.

'No, Antoine and Gaston, better known as Tony and Gas. They plow driveways, do odd jobs. They're actually Austin's second or third cousins from the non-moneyed side of the family. Their grandmother married a French-Canadian house painter. You run into a lot of haves and have-nots with these old families around here. Tony and Gas are members of the volunteer fire department. Decent, hard-working guys. They were furious. Austin has no authority to do what he did. He for darned sure has no authority to pull drivers over in the wee hours for the purpose of interrogating them. Night before last he stopped a Cornell University graduate student named Donna Willis on Old Shore Road, ordered her out of her car, frisked her in a highly inappropriate fashion and demanded to know if she was currently . . . menstruating.'

I looked at him in disbelief. 'And you can't arrest him?'

'Ought to be a snap. I've got him dead to rights for impersonating a police officer, harassment, breach of peace . . .' The resident trooper puffed out his cheeks. 'But, like the deputy superintendent said, we have to let Austin be Austin *unless* he presents a credible, legitimate threat to the public's safety. Believe me, there's no love lost between Austin and me. I grew up with him. He used to taunt my kid sister, Becca, because she had a weight problem. Taunt her until she'd cry. When we were twelve I punched him in the nose and told him if he bothered her again I'd do a lot worse. He never got the chance. After school that very day Becca threw herself in front of an Amtrak train.'

I shuddered inwardly. 'How awful . . .'

'It wasn't pretty,' he said tightly, his mouth barely moving. 'And now that evil little bastard's trying to rile me again with that patrol car of his. Make it seem as if I'm not doing my job properly.'

'Nothing could be further from the truth,' Rundle spoke up on his behalf. 'You do a heck of a job, Jim. We all know that. Lowest crime rate in New London County.'

'Thank you, sir,' he said quietly.

'What about his older brother, Michael?' I asked. 'What's his story?'

'Michael does not exactly enjoy a warm, fuzzy relationship with Austin,' Annabeth McKenna replied. 'In fact, he's had a pathological fear of Austin ever since Austin shot him in the head with a pellet gun back when they were kids, leaving him permanently deaf in his left ear. Michael remains convinced that Austin's deepest wish in life is to murder him. As a result, he lives in a walled, high-security mansion on Mitchell Hill Road where he's guarded by four ex-Green Berets as well as a trained attack dog. Michael adamantly avoids any private physical contact with Austin. On those rare occasions when he'll consent to be in the same room with him, he'll do so only if I'm there with them, along with one of his ex-Green Berets, who carries a gun that is *not* a toy.'

'As Dr McKenna mentioned,' Jim Conley continued, 'Austin owns a huge place on Elys Ferry Road that he inherited from his father. But he rarely goes near it. His habitat of preference is a remote, densely wooded section of Talmadge State Park, which was once part of the family's original land grant from the British crown. The ruins from their earliest settlement – fieldstone foundations, chimneys, kilns, root cellars – can still be found up there if you're willing to make a rugged seven-mile hike. So can a number of caves that Native American dwellers called home long before the Talmadges arrived. Austin has been known to camp out up there for weeks at a time searching for family artifacts. He hated it when Michael donated the Talmadges' original settlement to the state. He considers it *his*. But Talmadge State Park is of great interest to historians and archeologists as well as botanists, who've found many rare species of native plants that have grown there practically undisturbed for centuries.'

'I've heard about it,' I said. 'Everyone calls it Mount Creepy.'

'And with good reason,' Annabeth McKenna acknowledged, studying me across the table with those penetrating brown eyes of hers. 'I've hiked it many times and, while it's beautiful up there, it also has an eerie aura. It's not something you can explain. You just *feel* it.'

Resident Trooper Conley nodded in agreement. 'I'm not the sort of person who goes in for scary campfire stories but, I swear, it's as if something evil happened up there long ago. Mind you, there's an *otherness* about the Talmadges dating all of the way back to the original settlers. They were a secretive clan who refused to join up with the other founding families at the mouth of the Connecticut River. Instead, they chose to settle several miles upriver in the hills way, way off by themselves.'

'Sounds to me as if Austin is the living, breathing product of multiple generations of incest.'

'You'll get no argument from me,' Annabeth McKenna said.

'So you can't bust him,' I said to Deputy Superintendent Mitry, 'because he and his big brother have way too much financial pull – judging by the presence at this table of Mr Fielding, the governor's special envoy.' Which drew no response whatsoever from Fielding. 'What *can* you do?'

Mitry folded his giant hands on the table before him. 'There is a protocol in place for dealing with Austin when he strays too far outside of the lines. It involves the services of Dr McKenna and the team of former Green Berets employed by his brother, who are tasked with escorting Austin – with or without his consent – to his estate on Elys Ferry Road, which also functions as a private sanitarium. He's detained there while Dr McKenna works with him one-on-one until she's able to determine whether or not he's stable enough to be released as an outpatient.'

'This would be the aforementioned "ripcord?"'

'It would.'

'And this has been going on for how many years?'

'Seven,' she answered, her voice barely a whisper.

I shook my head at them. 'Can I be candid with you? I belong back in New York City, where life makes sense.'

The deputy superintendent treated me to a frosty look. 'I take my orders from the superintendent. He takes his from the governor, whose largest campaign contributor happens to be Michael Talmadge, who should be arriving here momentarily with his security detail. Let's be clear about something, Mr Hoag. I don't like it one bit that Austin Talmadge gets privileged treatment. I believe that the law should be enforced equally no matter what your tax bracket is. Unfortunately, that's not how our world works. I'll also have you know that we're not the ones who set up this protocol. Austin has been the recipient of special treatment since he was ten. That's how old he was when he poisoned his cousins' dog.'

'Would this be the Hardy Boys again?'

'It would, yes,' he responded. 'Not long after that he shot his own brother in the head and drove Jim's sister to throw herself in front of a moving train. And those are merely the things we know about. God knows what else he did. None of it was ever recorded as a criminal offense.'

'Michael told me that their father sent Austin away to any number of residential treatment schools after the horrid event with Jim's sister,' Annabeth McKenna said. 'None were able to help him. And Austin has been in and out of psychiatric hospitals for virtually his entire adult life. I've been forced to check him into McLean Psychiatric Hospital up in Massachusetts numerous times, including most of this past summer, because he's needed more around-the-clock supervision than I could give him.'

I heard cars speeding up the gravel driveway.

'That'll be Michael,' she said.

I went to the mudroom door with Lulu tagging alongside of me in time to see one, two, three humongous black Chevy Suburbans pull up in a row.

One of Michael Talmadge's extremely muscular ex-Green Berets climbed out of the first car wearing camouflage pants, a snug-fitting black crewneck sweater and a semi-automatic handgun in a shoulder holster. With him, on a tight leash, was a huge German Shepherd that immediately barked ferociously, baring a set of two or three hundred teeth.

Lulu let out a yelp and skedaddled in wide-eyed terror across the linoleum kitchen floor toward the master bedroom, where I expect she hid in the closet.

Michael's lead bodyguard stood there with the dog, his eyes taking in the barnyard, guest cottage, chicken coop, duck pond and, lastly, me as I opened the mudroom door and stepped outside.

The middle of the three Suburbans was driven by another ex-Green Beret wearing aviator shades. Someone whom I couldn't quite make out sat alone in the back seat. They remained inside of their vehicle as two more bodyguards wearing camouflage pants, black crewnecks and shoulder holsters stepped out of the rear vehicle, scanning the area behind them for any potential danger. All of them were young, as in no more than thirty.

I approached the lead guard, his German Shepherd snarling at me as I got closer. 'I have a somewhat timid basset hound in the house. Would it be possible for you to keep your dog in the car?'

He sorted through my question. 'You telling me he's going to scare your dog?'

'That's the general idea.'

'Sure, no prob. In the car, Pinkie,' he commanded the Shepherd, which immediately jumped back in the Suburban.

'His name is Pinkie?'

'Yeah, what of it?'

'Kind of a wussie name, isn't it?'

He raised his granite chin at me. 'What's wussie about it?'

'Not a thing. It's a fine name. Truly.'

He turned to the middle car and nodded. The driver in aviator shades got out, opened the back door and out stepped the richest man in the entire state of Connecticut.

Michael Talmadge could not have been more differently proportioned than his short, roly-poly brother. He was a tall, gaunt, stooped man who looked at least ten years older than Austin and moved very slowly and unsteadily as he started across the courtyard toward me. Possibly the permanent hearing loss he'd suffered when his kid brother shot him in the left ear with a pellet gun had also affected his balance. He wore no hearing aid, or at least none that was visible. Michael was not exactly the sort of flashy jet-set billionaire whom TV viewers had come to expect lately from gorging on Robin Leach's *Lifestyles of the Rich and Famous*. The drab gray suit he wore shouted J.C. Penney's – with at least five years of wear in it. It also shouted that he'd lost weight. The shoulders sagged, the collar rode up in back and his trousers were baggy in the seat. As he made his way closer to me I noticed that the collar of his white button-down shirt hung loose around his neck, as if he needed to start buying a size smaller. Not to mention more often – the white had a yellowish tinge to it and the collar was fraying. His black necktie was one of those pre-knotted clip-on ties that young boys wear. I couldn't remember the last time I'd seen a grown man wearing one. As he continued to make his way slowly toward me I was struck by how monochromatic Michael Talmadge was. It was difficult to tell where his ashen-gray complexion left off and his limp, ashen-gray hair began. His eyes were gray. If he were to smile I had no doubt his teeth would be gray, too. But I doubt he'd smiled in a long, long time. He was much too frightened. So frightened that he trembled visibly.

He looked at the mudroom door with dread. 'I'm to go in there?' he asked the lead bodyguard, his voice thin and reedy.

'Correct, Mr Talmadge,' he responded. 'I've been assured that there are three state policemen in there and one former state policemen, all of them armed.'

Michael Talmadge didn't bother to introduce himself to me as I led him into the kitchen through the mudroom. Didn't so much as look at me. Merely sat down with the others, positioning himself at the far end of the table so that his good ear, the right one, would be able to take in the conversation.

The governor's special envoy, Colin Fielding, who was there but not there, said, 'Mr Talmadge, this is Stewart Hoag, ex-husband of Merilee Nash, the movie star. It seems Austin showed up here today and got rather nasty.'

Michael gave me a brief nod as he sat there, trembling. 'So he's on the warpath again, is he?' he said to no one in particular.

'He's been on the warpath for several days, sir,' Deputy Superintendent Mitry said. 'He's adopted a new guise as an auxiliary policeman, complete with a refurbished cruiser and a uniform of sorts, and has exhibited confrontational behavior toward several townspeople.'

'Is he armed?' Michael asked, his voice quavering.

'He's carrying a weapon, though Resident Trooper Conley made sure the firing pin was removed. We don't believe he presents a danger in that specific regard, but I'm afraid he has pulled over a young lady and subjected her to physical and verbal harassment, and now he's crossed over the line into potential celebrity stalking. He also threatened Mr Hoag.'

'And he's failed to show up for his last two mandatory therapy sessions,' Annabeth McKenna pointed out.

'How do you intend to proceed?'

'For starters,' Captain Rundle said, 'we'll keep a trooper stationed at the foot of the driveway here just in case he decides to come back.'

'He won't come back,' Michael said with gloomy certainty. 'He'll head for the old family ruins up on the mountain. We'll find him camped out up here. My security team and that big attack dog of theirs . . .'

'Do you mean Pinkie?' I asked him.

He waved me off like I was a house fly buzzing in front of his ashen face. 'They'll track him and reel him in within twenty-four hours. It's what they're trained to do, and they're very good at it.' He glanced at Annabeth McKenna. 'You'll be informed when they've got him and can bring him home for treatment. You'll be ready for him?'

'I'll be ready,' she assured Michael. 'My first priority is to get him back on his medication. Then he and I will need numerous sessions together before I can determine if he will stabilize. If I'm not convinced that he can, then we'll have to hospitalize him at McLean again. But it's my hope that he'll settle down and feel grounded again. On several occasions he has.' To me she added, 'I've always believed it's a good idea for him to be productive, too. For several stretches of time – not lately, unfortunately – he's been employed at the Old Lyme A&P. He's not suited to being a cashier or bag boy. The interaction with customers overwhelms him. But as long as he's left alone to open cartons and stock the shelves, he's steady and reliable. It's done him a world of good to have the job. He has a schedule and responsibilities. And the manager has been quite understanding.'

'For a price,' Michael pointed out aridly. '*I've* been paying *him* to employ the little bastard.'

'Still, you must admit that working there has been a boost to Austin's self esteem.'

'I "must admit" not one damned thing when it comes to Austin, Dr McKenna, other than to acknowledge that I've been cursed with being responsible for him my entire adult life – and shall continue to be until the day I die.'

'I thought Austin was doing very well after his stay at McLean this summer,' she said. 'He was taking his medication, showing up for his sessions. He was even talking about going back to work at the A&P.'

'So what happened?' Captain Rundle asked her.

'What always happens,' she said with a sigh of resignation. 'As soon as he starts feeling good he stops taking his medication. Doesn't think he needs it anymore. And then, inevitably, his demons return.'

'Hence my full-time security detail, because Austin intends to murder me some day,' Michael stated with utter certainty. 'He just hasn't tipped his hand as to how or when. It's his way of tormenting me. He hates me, you see. You're probably asking yourself why. I've been asking myself that very question for the past forty years. I don't know why. I only know that I've never had a moment's peace in my entire life. I've never married. Never so much as gone out on a date. I'm too afraid of what he might do to any woman to whom I show the slightest interest. So I live a bachelor's life in a home that could easily be mistaken for a high-security prison. I manage the family's financial affairs. And I manage my acute anxiety and panic attacks as best I can by taking the combination of drugs that my physician has prescribed.' He glanced down at his trembling hands. 'As you can see, they're not wholly effective, but I'm at maximum dosage. He told me I'll risk liver damage if I exceed it.' Michael paused, breathing raggedy. 'But that's enough about me. We're here to discuss Austin. My team will reel him in, as I said. After that, the ball is in Dr McKenna's court, though his recent behavior would seem to indicate that he needs to be re-admitted to McLean.'

'We'll see,' she said placatingly. 'Let me have a sit down with him.'

'I think that settles things for now,' Deputy Superintendent Mitry concluded. 'We'll give you your kitchen back, Mr Hoag. And, as Captain Rundle said, we'll keep a trooper parked at the foot of your gate until Austin has been found. If you spot him hanging around, do not hesitate to let us know.'

'Of course.'

He got up from the kitchen table, as did Captain Rundle,

Resident Trooper Conley and Colin Fielding, the governor's man. Michael Talmadge stood up as well, slowly and gingerly. They all filed out by way of the mudroom door. Pete Tedone and Annabeth McKenna stayed behind with me at the table. We sat there in silence as one car after another started up and headed off down the long gravel driveway.

Pete ran a hand over his gleaming dome. 'If I were you, my friend, I'd pack up and go back to New York right now. Just get the hell out of here.'

'No one chases me off of my property. Well, Merilee's property.'

'Do you have a gun?'

'No.'

'I have a spare in my glove compartment. If you're going to insist on staying I'll loan it to you.'

'I'd rather you didn't. I hate guns.'

'Why?'

'Because they go off.'

He puffed out his cheeks. 'I forgot what a pain in the keester you are.'

'I must be slipping. Most people remember right away. Besides, the resident trooper said that Austin's gun is basically a toy, remember?'

'Lots of people said lots of things. I'm not sure how much of it I believed. We're dealing with a billionaire fruitcake here. Listen, if you get so much as a whiff of him I want you to call me right away. You've already managed to piss him off once. There's no telling what he might do. Promise me you'll call me?'

'I'll call you, Pete. Scout's honor. And thanks for your help.'

'No problem.' He turned to Annabeth McKenna and said, 'Nice meeting you, Doc.' Then he barged his chesty self out the mudroom door and drove off.

She seemed in no particular hurry to leave.

'Can I offer you some coffee?'

'That would be lovely. Please forgive me if I seem a bit awestruck. I'm a huge fan of your novel, *Our Family Enterprise*. I've read it three times.'

'Really? That puts you in very select company. The only

other person I know of who's read it that many times is my mother, and her I'm not so sure about.' I put the coffee on and called out, 'You can come out now, Lulu!'

I could hear her nails on the old oak plank floor as she came inching in warily from the bedroom and stretched out on the kitchen floor, eyeing Annabeth suspiciously.

'Your dog doesn't seem to like me.'

'No, it's nothing like that. She's just very protective of me.'

'Do you give her reason to be?'

'Afraid so. Trouble is not my business, but it manages to find me no matter how hard I try to avoid it. I've spent the past decade ghosting celebrity memoirs. Rich, famous people have a lot of dark secrets and a whole lot of enemies. I've had more than my share of close calls. In fact, if it weren't for Lulu I would have ended up with a toe tag at the LA County morgue or the New York City morgue or the—'

'I get the idea.'

'But I can't tell you anything about rich people that you don't already know, can I? You're working for a billionaire. Or I should say two billionaires.' I poured us each a mug of coffee. She took hers black, as do I. 'Do you mind if I ask you how it came about?'

'Not at all.' She sipped her coffee cautiously. 'Ahh, good and strong. Just the way I like it.' She put her mug down and ran her hands through her gorgeous mane of hair, which I was beginning to think was more of a nervous gesture than intentionally provocative, though it was definitely provocative and I had definitely been without attractive female companionship since Labor Day. 'Michael phoned the dean of the Yale School of Medicine seven years ago and asked him for the name of the faculty's top child psychiatrist.'

'That would be you.'

'It would, as it happens.'

'In that case you must know my old pal T.J. – Tommy Joshua. We were classmates when I was up at Cambridge.'

'Dr Thomas Joshua?' Annabeth's eyes widened slightly. 'Why, yes, I know him quite well. His office is right down the hall from mine. He's a highly respected psychoanalyst and teacher.'

I let out at laugh. 'Positively *the* last guy who I imagined I'd ever hear described that way. When I knew him he had exactly three interests in life – rugby, women and Moosehead beer.'

'And yet he has a razor-sharp mind, as he'll be the first to tell you,' she said, smiling faintly. 'Also a lovely wife, Beth, and four beautiful children. We evolve, Hoagy. We grow up.' Her face darkened. 'Except for those unfortunate few of us who don't.'

'I take it you're speaking of Austin now.'

'I am. As I said, Austin is still very much a ten-year-old boy and he and Michael are still locked in the exact same relationship they were in when they were children. Michael remains pre-adolescent himself. I don't believe either of them has ever had a sexual relationship with a woman. They're quite an unusual pair, as you've no doubt observed. Also a tremendous drain on my time. To be honest, not a day has gone by that I haven't regretted agreeing to take Austin on. He's made it impossible for me to see other patients and to continue my research at Yale's Child Study Center. But Michael pays me one million dollars a year to treat him and I'm a widow raising three teenaged kids. I simply can't afford to say no, although I do donate a healthy chunk to the Study Center.'

'May I ask what happened to your husband?'

Her face darkened. 'I live a few miles down Joshua Town Road from here. You've driven by my house a million times on your way to Route 156. It's the yellow saltbox on the right that's sliding ever so gently off of its foundation because I have no time to devote to it. Realtors would say it "needs TLC." Five years ago, Paul was sideswiped by a hit-and-run driver when he was out jogging early one Sunday morning. He pitched headfirst into a fieldstone wall and died instantly. He was a Greek scholar at Yale. We were classmates and best friends. He was my soul mate. And he'd encouraged me to take on Austin as a patient. Not just because of the money. He thought it would be a fascinating challenge for me.' Annabeth paused, sipping her coffee. 'When I lost him I didn't think I'd make it. But I've survived. *We've* survived. Max is seventeen now, Sarah's fifteen and Gloria is thirteen. We're a sturdy bunch. We've had to be.'

'Do you have a man in your life?'

She smiled faintly. 'Other than Austin, you mean? I have no room in my life for a man. That's assuming I actually met one worth bothering with, and I haven't.'

'Well, you certainly take good care of yourself. You look extremely fit, if I may say so.'

'You may. I run five miles every morning and do an hour of weight training. That's *my* therapy.'

'Was that a regular habit of Paul's? Taking an early Sunday morning jog, I mean.'

'It was, yes.'

'Did they ever catch who hit him?'

'No, they didn't, and I know exactly where you're going with this. Austin was hospitalized at McLean when it happened, so it couldn't have been him. Besides, why would he want to kill Paul?'

'Because he wanted you for himself. You're an attractive, compassionate woman. Are you telling me he's never shown any interest in you?'

'None. As I said, Austin is still pre-adolescent.'

'Could it have been Michael? The driver who hit Paul, I mean.'

Annabeth shook her head. 'Michael isn't capable of something that aggressive. He's much too frightened. However, unlike Austin, he takes his meds diligently and handles the family's business affairs very effectively.'

'And, yet, he still trembles.'

'And, yet, he still trembles,' she acknowledged. 'He's totally overwhelmed by the stress of being responsible for Austin.'

Her cup was empty. I refilled it for her.

She ran her finger around the rim of her cup, tilting her head at me slightly. 'You'd make a good therapist. You're easy talk to.'

'Ghosting is a bit like being a therapist. You spend your time trying to get people to tell you things they've never told anyone else. The only difference is that you have to write a book when you're done.'

'I've actually thought about trying to write one about the Talmadge brothers. They're such a peculiar, fascinating pair.' Her brown eyes met mine briefly, then darted away. 'If it wouldn't be a gross imposition I'd love to get your input on how to go about structuring it.'

'Of course. I'll be happy to sit down with you.'

'That would be great. First, we have to get Austin settled down.'

'So you believe that you will?'

'Of course. When it comes to Austin this is really nothing very out of the ordinary, hard as you may find that to imagine. How long will you be out here?'

'A week or two. I've been grinding hard on a new novel. Thought a change of scenery would help. You'll have to come over for dinner some night. I'm a pretty fair cook, and you'd be doing me a huge favor. I haven't spoken to anyone for the past six weeks other than Merilee's doormen, the waiters at Tony's, and Lulu, who has a limited vocabulary.' Never one to miss a cue, Lulu rolled over on her back and made that argle-bargle noise she makes when she wants her belly rubbed. I bent over and rubbed it. 'Seriously, I'd enjoy your company.'

'In that case I'll be happy to join you for dinner.' She studied me curiously. 'So are you and Merilee back together?'

'We're working at it. We still have a lot of healing to do. Totally my fault. I put her through hell when I couldn't come up with a second book after *Our Family Enterprise.* It turns out that I needed ten years to come up with an idea, but that's not exactly how the publishing industry works. I was handed a huge advance and put under a tremendous amount of pressure to deliver an even bigger book instantly. I crash-landed and was living on reds, vitamin C and cocaine.' On her blank gaze I said, 'Not a Grateful Dead fan, I take it.'

'No, Brahms is more my style. But you're doing well now. You're at ease and exude great confidence in the book you're writing.'

'I'm back doing what I was born to do.' I gazed across the table at her. 'Tell me, is Austin dangerous?'

'In his present state of mind? He absolutely is. Why do you think all of those men came rushing over here?'

'If that's the case then why wasn't he institutionalized years ago?'

'Because the super-rich live by a different set of rules than the rest of us, as Deputy Superintendent Mitry so aptly put it.'

'I'm curious about what sort of parents Austin and Michael had. Since no one mentioned them, I'm assuming they're both dead.'

'They are. Their father, Cyrus, was a hard-driven business titan who didn't marry until he was well into his fifties. The woman he chose was his secretary, who was still in her twenties. She committed suicide one year after Austin was born. Jumped into the Connecticut River and was washed out into Long Island Sound. It took the Coast Guard five days to find her body. She left no suicide note, but I gather from some of the older townspeople that Cyrus was plenty peculiar himself, as in pathologically fearful of being kidnapped and held for ransom. He rode to his office every day in a bullet-proof limo driven by an armed chauffeur. He also installed a ten-foot wall around his property and topped it with razor wire. That's the house Michael lives in now.'

'Sounds as if the apple didn't fall far from the tree.'

'Cyrus had very little to do with either boy, especially after their mother's suicide. They were raised by a succession of nannies. Michael was sent off to boarding school, prep school and Princeton. Austin, who became disruptive at the Lyme elementary school at a very young age, went from one special needs school to another, never with any success.' She stared down into her coffee mug. 'As I said before, not a day has gone by when I haven't regretted the deal I made with Michael to treat Austin. But I have to live with it. Give him the soundest possible treatment that I can and make sure that he isn't a threat to the community.' She finished her coffee, studying me over the rim of her cup. 'Not exactly what you had in mind when you came out from New York to get a fresh perspective on your book, is it? Sorry about that.'

'Don't be. I'm relieved.'

'Relieved? How can you possibly be relieved?'

'Because I'm the one who was out here all alone when Austin decided to show up.' I took a deep breath, letting it out slowly. 'It could have been Merilee instead. That's something I don't even want to think about.'

THREE

The bright morning sunlight gave way to clouds by early afternoon and there was a late-October chill in the air. As promised, a genuine Connecticut State trooper was stationed in his genuine cruiser at the foot of the gravel drive. He had a large blocky head, a blond crew cut, and appeared to be reading a comic book. Forgive me, but I still have trouble adjusting to the idea that lawmen are now significantly younger than I am. He'd closed and latched the gate, which Merilee seldom did. It made me feel like I was imprisoned there, but it also made sense until Austin was found by brother Michael's ex-Green Berets and delivered to his own private sanitarium.

I finished uprooting my tomato plants, which was what I'd been doing when the roly-poly billionaire lunatic had shown up in the first place, toted them into the woods and gave them a non-denominational burial. By then the sun was getting lower and the temperature was dropping. I changed into a turtleneck and my tweed Norfolk jacket before I took a long walk in the woods beyond Whalebone Cove with Lulu, ruminating over where I wanted the plot of 'The Sweet Season of Madness' to go next. The story had flowed so incredibly naturally and easily so far. Yet here it was – what I like to call my first Jack Finney Moment, as an homage to 'The Third Level,' his brilliant short story about a commuter who gets lost in a maze of corridors below Grand Central Terminal and somehow stumbles upon a third level that no one had ever known existed down there. Writing is instinctive. My instincts were telling me that I was having trouble deciding what happened next because there was still another level of depth that I had yet to discover. I would just have to be patient until I found it. And I would. I had total confidence. My only concern was that my fictional world was in the process of being hijacked by the real one. I seriously considered taking

Pete Tedone's advice and going back to New York right away. I couldn't allow the likes of Austin Talmadge to interfere with my literary mission. But I also couldn't leave. Even though the farm was technically Merilee's, it still felt like my territory and I was not going to abandon it while that nut job was on the loose. I needed to be here. And so, as the sun lowered behind the trees and a gorgeous sunset beckoned, I headed back to the farmhouse, Lulu ambling along ahead of me, nose to the ground, snuffling and snorting.

By the time we'd made it back, darkness was beginning to fall. I built a fire in the parlor fireplace, warmed my insides with two fingers of Mr MacGowan's Connecticut calvados and fed Lulu. Dug a container of four-alarm chili from the freezer and dumped it into a saucepan on low heat to thaw.

The unlisted phone rang. It was Pete Tedone. 'Just checking in,' he said. 'Want me to stop by on my way home?'

'Thanks, Pete, but there's a teenaged trooper guarding the gate. I'm fine.'

'Sure you are. And, believe me, Michael Talmadge's Green Berets know what they're doing. They'll reel Austin in before he knows what's hit him.'

'I'm sure they will.'

'Listen, we can be men with each other, can't we?'

'I'd like to think so.'

'If you'd rest easier tonight having an armed bodyguard around I'd be happy to stay over in one of your guest rooms.'

'I appreciate the offer, Pete. I really do. But I'll be fine.'

'Fair enough. Just thought I'd put it out there. Have a good night.'

After we'd hung up I gave the chili a stir as it began to thaw. Lulu had finished her dinner but didn't curl up contentedly in front of the fire like she usually did. Instead, she paced the house uneasily, going from room to room. She was unsettled. Knew something was wrong. Again, I thought about returning to New York. Again, I decided to stay put. I wasn't going to let Austin Talmadge chase me away.

The unlisted phone rang again.

'Hi, Hoagy, it's Annabeth McKenna. I hope you don't mind

me calling you on this number. Merilee gave it to me when
we were on that committee together.'

'No, not at all. What's up?'

'I wanted to let you know that I haven't heard from Austin.
He hasn't called me.'

'Were you expecting him to?'

'I was, actually. When he gets frightened he usually
calls me.'

'I don't see how he can if he's camped out on his mountain.
Or has he installed a phone booth up there?'

'He calls me from a pay phone at the gas station on the
Boston Post Road. Do you often ask such silly questions?'

'Yeah, it's pretty much a full-time thing. Why, does it
bother you?'

'Noo, I just need to recalibrate. You're such a serious
author I didn't realize you'd be so . . . so . . .'

'Juvenile?'

'Well, yes. Are you doing OK?'

'OK as in . . .?'

'You're not worried, are you?'

'I'm not, but Lulu is. She's keeps pacing around.'

'That's because she senses you aren't as calm as you think
you are. Dogs have very strong instincts about such things.'

'So you're a basset hound psychiatrist, too?'

She let out a surprisingly loud honk of laughter. 'My God,
I can't remember the last time I did that.'

'Honked?'

'Giggled.'

'I'm familiar with giggles. That was no giggle. You honked.'

'Didn't.'

'Did.'

'OK, you win. I should know better than to spar words with
a writer. I'll let you go. I just wanted to assure you that there's
really no need to worry. Austin gets highly unstable when he's
off his meds but he's never actually hurt anyone.'

'Aside from the time he shot Michael in the head with a
pellet gun, you mean.'

'That was a long, long time ago.'

'Thanks for checking up on me, Annabeth'

'You're a neighbor. That's what we do in Lyme.'

Then Dr Annabeth McKenna said goodnight and hung up, leaving me to wonder whether she was a) more concerned than she'd let on or b) was developing a crush on me. I do have that effect on women, and that's not just me bragging. In its July, 1983 issue *Cosmo* came right out and called me attractive 'in a devil-may-care way that is reminiscent of Hollywood leading men of the 1930s.' And, being honest, if it weren't for Merilee I could imagine myself developing a crush on Dr McKenna. She was smart, interesting and very attractive. Although there was absolutely no way I'd ever be interested in a package deal that included three teenaged kids *and* Austin Talmadge.

I opened a Bass ale and sat on the sofa in front of the fire with my bowl of chili and a couple of those discus-shaped hardtack Nabisco Crown Pilot crackers that Merilee always kept stored in an airtight tin. A venerable Yankee tradition. Lulu joined me on the sofa, grumbling and fussing. I tried to reassure her but she wasn't buying it. I opened up 'About Time,' my well-worn volume of Jack Finney short stories, and re-read 'The Third Level' while I ate. After I'd finished it I set it aside, even more convinced than I'd been on my walk that there was still another layer of depth to 'The Sweet Season of Madness' that was waiting for me to find it.

'I sit down to write the book to figure out why the fuck I'm writing the book.'

I washed the dishes and got a fire started in the bedroom fireplace. Before I turned out the lights I locked the doors and latched the windows, which isn't something Merilee usually bothers to do. Lyme is a place where no one locks their doors or windows. By the time I'd brushed my teeth and willfully neglected to floss them, the fire in the bedroom fireplace was casting the entire room in an inviting orange glow. Lulu, however, was not curled up on the bed waiting for me. She'd gone back to pacing the house. She was guarding the fort. How did she know it needed guarding? Maybe Annabeth was right. Maybe she could sense it from me. Whatever the reason, she was definitely on patrol. Since bassets are world-class scent hounds – only bloodhounds outrank them – I wondered

how close to the house Austin would have to be for her to get
a whiff of his feral man scent. A hundred yards? A quarter-
mile? I hadn't a clue. All I knew was that if he was determined
to come back and talk to Merilee – whom he did not, repeat
not, know was in Budapest – then that teenaged state policeman
at the gate was serving as nothing more than an ornament.
Austin could hike his way through the woods to the farmhouse
from three other directions. I climbed into bed with the heavy
blanket and down comforter over me, turned off the bedside
light and lay there in the darkness, watching the reflection of
the flames dance across the ceiling. I told myself there was
absolutely no way that Austin was anywhere other than camped
out high on Mount Creepy. That he wasn't about to come
crashing through the master bedroom's French doors, chainsaw
in hand, like a ski-masked spree killer in a horror movie.

And yet, Lulu would not stop pacing the house.

When Quasimodo woke me at the crack of dawn Lulu still
hadn't come to bed. I found her perched on the parlor sofa,
wide awake. I put the coffee on and fed Lulu her mackerel,
then climbed back into bed with my steaming hot mug of
coffee. She climbed her step stool on to the bed and joined
me there, her head on my tummy, as I savored the view of
the autumn sun rising over Whalebone Cove. Then I stropped
Grandfather's razor, shaved and threw on a warm Viyella shirt
over a T-shirt, jeans and my Chippewas. After I'd put on my
flight jacket I went outside and fed the girls. There was a thin
coating of frost on the roof of the barn. I went back inside,
put away a toasted English muffin with blackberry jam
and my second cup of coffee, checked my fall chores list and
decided it was time to begin installing the farmhouse's storm
windows, a labor-intensive job because the fourteen downstairs windows were not the standard modern-era aluminum
over-under variety that simply involve sliding the storm
window down and latching it in place, which takes all of
ten seconds. No, the downstairs windows were old-fashioned
mullioned wood casement windows that swung open outward.
The wooden screens, which were hinged on the inside, had to
be unscrewed and removed one by one before I could install

the storms. Those were made of hard, two-inch-thick yellow pine, latched in place over the windows from the outside and hooked tight on the inside with hooks and eyes. The parlor storms were three feet by five feet, weighed a good forty pounds apiece, and I had to climb a ladder to install them. It was no ten-second job.

And then there were the farmhouse's old wood storm doors, which weighed nearly a hundred pounds apiece and had to be hoisted into their slots *just so*. Those would require an extra set of hands – Mr MacGowan's – to install.

I grabbed a Phillips head screwdriver from the tool drawer in the kitchen, found an empty jam jar and got busy unscrewing the downstairs screens, storing the screws in the jar for safe-keeping. Then I carried all of the screens, which had collected a summer's worth of dirt, pollen and cobwebs, outside. The morning sun had warmed the air well into the forties by now. I filled a bucket with soapy water and took a stiff scrub brush to them. Hosed them down and propped them against the side of the barn to dry. Lulu sprawled in the sun and dozed. I don't think my guardian had slept a wink all night.

When I went back inside the house she followed me until she realized I was going down into the cellar, which was where Merilee stored the storm windows for the summer. Did an abrupt U-turn and scampered on to the parlor sofa. Mice. She's terrified of mice. When late October arrives they start to burrow their way in for the winter. Her keen ears could hear them skittering around down there.

I carried the storms up the steep, narrow cellar stairs one by one and propped them in the mudroom. Each one's destination was marked on the inside in a workman's neat, tiny handwriting because they were not interchangeable. No two window frames in a 1736 farmhouse are the same exact size. No two of anything are the same exact size. When I'd brought all fourteen of them upstairs and closed the cellar door I examined them and discovered that the glazing compound that seals the glass to the wood had dried out and cracked on several of them. That meant I'd have to remove it with a putty knife, re-glaze, prime and paint them before they'd be ready to hang.

That fall chores list? Total pain in the ass.

I was starting my way out to the barn in search of glazing compound when the unlisted phone rang.

It was Resident Trooper Jim Conley. 'Just wanted to share some good news with you,' he said in his calm, steady voice. 'Michael Talmadge's Green Berets and their dog found Austin camped out in one of the caves near the ruins of the old family settlement shortly after dawn.'

'Glad to hear it,' I said, feeling my stomach muscles relax.

'You and me both. He offered no resistance and was transported directly to his home, where he's been sedated and is now under Dr McKenna's personal care. Michael's guards are staying put there for now. A nurse is on duty as well.'

'Did you impound that bogus state police cruiser of his?'

'No, we did not,' he said tonelessly. 'It was returned to his house.'

'Even though he's been using it to harass people?'

'Captain Rundle's decision to make, not mine. The car is Austin's property and Austin is—'

'A Talmadge, I understand.'

He responded with tactful silence before he said, 'You can relax and put this whole business behind you. There's absolutely no way that Austin will bother you again. We've removed the trooper who was staked out at the foot of your driveway.'

I thanked him for letting me know and hung up, pleased that I could go back to thinking exclusively about my book instead of that fat little lunatic.

Lulu was parked in front of the refrigerator staring intently at it. She wanted an anchovy. I gave her one and realized that my own stomach was growling. It was nearly noon and I'd been up since dawn. I made myself a sandwich out of the Black Forest ham and Swiss cheese that Mr MacGowan had kindly laid in for me and poured myself a glass of milk.

I was just about to bite into my sandwich when I heard a car come speeding up the gravel drive and screech to a halt. Its door creaked open and slammed shut. I looked out of the kitchen window and standing there beside his rust-bucket Crown Vic cruiser was none other than Austin Talmadge wearing his make-believe uniform and waving his toy gun in the air. Sedated? Guess again. He was red-faced and wild-eyed. Tears streamed down his face, snot from his nose.

Lulu started barking at him from the mudroom door. She has a mighty big bark for someone with no legs. I shushed her.

'MISS NASH?' Austin hollered as he stood out there, choking back tears. 'CAN I *PLEASE* TALK TO YOU? *PLEASE*, MISS NASH . . .?'

I opened the mudroom door, sandwich in hand, and started my way across the courtyard toward him with Lulu on my heel, a low growl coming from her throat. As I approached him I noticed that he was clean-shaven and smelled a whole lot better. His shirt and pants had been laundered.

'*You* again.' He wiped his eyes, sneering. 'The ex-husband.'

'What brings you by, Austin?' I asked, munching on my sandwich. 'Are you OK?'

'No, I'm *not* OK!' he erupted in response.

'Come on inside and tell me about it. You hungry? Want a sandwich?'

'Are you deaf or something? I *need* to talk to Miss Nash. She's the only one who cares.'

'Don't you think Dr McKenna cares?'

His close-set eyes blazed at me. 'Dr McKenna's an evil bitch. She wants to chain me to a bed in a psycho ward somewhere.'

'Why would she want do that?'

'Because she does whatever Michael tells her to do. I hate her. And I *need* to talk to Miss Nash!' Tears were streaming down his face again. 'Can't I *please* speak to her?'

'I'm afraid she's not here, Austin.'

'Well, when's she coming back?'

'Not for several weeks. She's in Budapest filming a remake of *The Sun Also Rises* by Mr Ernest Hemingway. Ever read it?'

He glowered at me. 'When I was here before you made it sound like she was out running errands. You were bullshitting me.'

'No, I wasn't. I simply told you she wasn't here. And she's not.'

'You're a bullshit artist!' he blustered angrily, pointing his toy gun at me. 'A no-good bullshit artist!'

'And here I thought we were getting along better.'

'Not a chance. I don't like you.'

'I'm very sorry to hear that, Austin. I'm a pretty nice guy once you get to know me. Why don't you come inside while I finish my lunch? You want some ice cream? It's from Salem Farm.'

'Miss Nash has to forgive me!'

'Forgive you for what?'

He took a deep breath and let it out raggedly, lowering his eyes. 'I . . . I just did something terrible.'

'Well, come on in. Let's talk about it.'

I headed back inside with Lulu following close behind me. Sat back down at the kitchen table and started in on the other half of my sandwich. After a long moment, a really long moment, Austin followed me inside, toy gun in hand, and stood there watching me eat as Lulu huddled at my feet with that same low growl coming from her throat. I took a gulp of milk, maintaining a calm exterior. I've worked with crazed celebs high on coke threatening to kill themselves, kill their loved ones, kill *me*. Austin was a whole new classification of crazy. I hadn't a clue what he was capable of. But based on prior experience my best play, my only play, was to act as if nothing out of the ordinary was happening.

'Have a seat, Austin. Sure you don't want some ice cream? I've got rocky road.'

'Will you *shut up* about the ice cream?' he screamed at me. 'Did you just say rocky road?'

I got the half-gallon container out of the freezer, a spoon from the drawer and put them on the table in front of one of the chairs. He sat, setting the gun on the table next to him. Pried open the ice cream, lowered his face to the container and started shoveling away like a piggish little boy.

I finished my sandwich and sat back in my chair, watching him. 'Want to tell me what happened?'

'Idiots thought they could keep me there,' he said around a giant mouthful of ice cream.

'Which particular idiots are we speaking of?'

'Those soldier boys Michael hires to keep me away from him. When they got me home they stripped off my clothes and threw me in the shower,' he said, continuing to work on the ice cream. 'One of them, Joaquin, kept staring at my pecker. He's hinted to me a bunch of times that he'd like to have sex with me. Guy's a homo.'

'And you?'

'What about me?'

'Are you gay yourself?'

'You shut up about that!' He turned bright red again. 'I'm *not* gay! That's why I need to see Miss Nash, don't you get it?'

'I'm afraid not. I still don't know what's happened, remember?'

'Oh, right, right. You weren't there.'

'I wasn't where, Austin?'

He didn't respond. Just kept shoveling his way through the carton of ice cream.

'How did you get away from your house?'

He smirked at me. 'I just left, that's how. Dr McKenna has a downstairs bedroom set up like a sanitarium, OK? After the soldier boys had cleaned me up they gave me a pair of pajamas, got me into bed and her nurse, who wasn't my usual nurse, gave me a pill to knock me out. Told me I needed to get some rest, like I'm an idiot boy.' He smirked at me again. 'What she didn't know is I've spent so many years in hospitals taking pills that I'm an expert at hiding them between my cheek and gum. I pretended to swallow it and then spit it out after she'd drawn the curtains and left me there. Chilled for a while so they'd all think I was asleep and pay no attention to me. Then I sprang into action. They'd locked me in but get this – I have a key to unlock the door. Dr McKenna's never known that because I've never needed to use it. But I had to use it today. Had to get back out on patrol. I mean, I have a mission now, understand?'

'Sure, I understand.'

He finished the carton of ice cream, scraping the bottom of the empty carton with his spoon before he shoved it away. 'I keep it hidden in the desk. The key, I mean. I tiptoed to the door, unlocked it and snuck a peek outside. Dr McKenna was on the phone in the living room with her back to me. The soldier boys were playing poker in the dining room. Their lame guard dog was fast asleep under the table. Didn't so much as stir. What a joke. The nurse was rustling around in the kitchen. Nobody was paying any attention to my room. Didn't think they had to because they're so smart and I'm so stupid.'

'So what was your next move?'

'I tiptoed into the laundry room and found my uniform in there, freshly laundered and folded. My wallet, money, sneakers and everything were piled right there. So was my belt, with my weapon and my nightstick, which the soldier boys didn't even bother to confiscate. That's how seriously they take me.' He cackled at me shrewdly. 'Well, I showed them. Got dressed quick as can be, slipped out the laundry-room door and jumped in my car, which was sitting right there, keys in the ignition. I was gone before they knew what hit them.'

'They must have heard you drive away. Are they out looking for you?'

Austin's face fell. He started blinking back tears again. '*Everyone* is out looking for me. I–I did a bad thing.'

'Are you going to tell me what you did, Austin?'

'See, I–I started feeling hungry while I–I was out on patrol . . .' He began breathing so raggedly he was almost panting. 'So I stopped at the Old Lyme Beach Club, which was co-founded by my great-great-grandfather. I have privileges there for life. It's mostly closed up for the season but they still serve lunch out on the deck and make *the* best lobster roll on the shoreline. I–I parked and went around to the take-out window to order one. While I was waiting I looked out at the deck and guess what I see? Two young guys sitting at a table holding hands, hugging and . . . and kissing. At the beach club. *My* beach club.'

I listened, nodding. He seemed just a teeny bit obsessed about the gay thing. I'm no shrink, and I don't play one on TV, but I couldn't help wonder if he was a repressed gay himself. Annabeth McKenna would no doubt have an opinion about that. 'What did you do, Austin?'

'I approached them and ordered them to leave the premises at once. In response they laughed at me in a highly disrespectful manner. I drew my weapon and ordered them once again. When one of them advised me to "go screw myself" I discharged my weapon and blew a hole in his friend's left shoulder.' Austin started to weep again. 'God, there was blood *everywhere*. I–I didn't mean to hit him, I swear. I just wanted to scare him. But I *missed*.'

'Good thing you didn't miss a few inches to the left or you would have killed him.'

'God, don't *say* that!'

'Resident Trooper Conley said he'd made sure the firing pin was removed from your gun.'

Austin nodded readily. 'He had. It was. But I took it back up to Old Tom and got him to restore it for me.'

'How much did that cost you?'

'Why do you care?'

'Because Old Tom knows perfectly well why it was removed. I'm curious what his price was. I'm a writer, remember? Details interest me.'

'Ten thou in cash.'

'You carry that kind of cash around?'

'Always. I don't trust banks.'

'He could have asked you for much more than that.'

'Probably, but that's what he asked for and that's what he got.'

'The man's disreputable but not greedy. Fascinating, isn't it?' On his silence I said, 'So what happened after you fired the shot?'

'People went crazy, what do you think? Everybody was running around screaming their heads off. I–I made a mad dash for my car and got the hell out of there fast. The one thing I knew for sure was I *had* to see Miss Nash. She's the only person who can help me.' He sat there in stricken silence, shaking his somewhat largish head. 'Except now you tell me she's in Czechoslovakia.'

'Hungary.'

'Can you phone her? I have to explain to her what happened. *She'll* understand. *She'll* help me.'

'I hate to disillusion you, Austin, but Merilee was just playing a character in a movie. In real life, she can't help you. It's Dr McKenna who can, and I'm guessing she's really worried about you right now. I think we should phone her and let her know that you're OK. What do you say?'

Austin's chest heaved, his eyes bulging at me. 'What do I *say*?' He jumped to his feet so abruptly that he kicked over his chair. 'I *shot* someone! If I tell her where I am she'll notify the state police and they'll lock me away for the rest of my life. That's what Michael wants. That's what Michael's always wanted. But it's not going to happen, hear me? I've got one chance – head for my family's mountain and make damned sure they won't dare come after me.'

'Why won't they?'

'Because I'll have hostages.'

'By hostages you mean . . .?'

'You and your little dog.'

'She's not little. She's short.'

'Shut up!' He reached for his gun on the table and pointed it at me. 'I want you outside right now. You *and* your dog. Let's go!'

I stayed put, crossing my arms in front of my chest. 'We're not going anywhere, Austin. Not going to happen. So just put that idea out of your head.'

Austin responded by shooting a hole in the kitchen wall about two feet over my head. The gunshot was so incredibly loud that I wondered if Mr MacGowan had heard it in the country quiet. Wondered if he was home. Hoped and prayed he was home.

After a brief deliberation, my ears ringing, I said, 'Well, OK. We'll join you if you feel that strongly about it.'

I got up and started toward the mudroom door. Lulu joined me, making low, unhappy noises. Austin followed me closely, prodding me in my back with his gun as we went outside.

'You don't have to keep doing that. I get the idea.'

'Shut up!' he snarled. When we reached his Crown Vic he popped the trunk. 'Get in there. Both of you.'

'What on earth for?'

'Because I say so! Get in the trunk!'

Lulu needed an assist, which is to say I had to pick her up and hoist her in before I climbed in after her, curling myself into a fetal position. Austin immediately slammed the trunk shut on us.

Total blackness.

It also didn't smell particularly fresh in there. He started up the engine with a roar and took off. The ride was jarringly bumpy as he sped down the gravel drive and on to Joshua Town Road, tossing us this way and that as he screeched his way along the narrow, twisting country road. Lulu was whimpering in fear. I fished Grandfather's Varaflame lighter from my jeans pocket and fired it up. Being able to see calmed her a bit. She huddled close to me, her nose nuzzling my neck. I put my arm around her, glancing about for a tire jack or some other form of weapon. I found nothing except for a heap of dirty laundry, hence the non-fresh smell. Before I flicked off the lighter I hid my wallet underneath the laundry for the state police to find should they locate Austin's car.

After a stomach-churning drive that seemed to go on forever and made me sorry I'd finished my sandwich, Austin finally came to a stop, backed up, moved forward and then backed up again before he finally turned off the engine, got out and popped the trunk.

I glanced around us, blinking at the bright autumn sunlight. He'd hidden the Crown Vic behind a tangle of tall, wild brush near the parking lot to Talmadge State Park. Or so he seemed to believe. My guess? It would take the troopers a tidy thirty seconds to locate the car once they came looking for it. But, as you may have figured out, Austin wasn't thinking super clearly.

I climbed out, arching my aching back before I hoisted Lulu out. 'Now what?'

He slammed the trunk shut. 'Now we hike,' he responded, grabbing a black canvas duffel bag from the back seat.

'What's in the bag, Austin?'

'Cheetos, Doritos, Slim Jims, Baby Ruth bars, some three-liter bottles of Coke. I always keep supplied. I come up here a lot and I don't like to get hungry or thirsty.'

'Yes, I can see that.'

He flared at me. 'I'm warning you. Don't push me with your wise-guy attitude.'

'What are you going to do, shoot me?'

'No, I'll shoot your dog.'

Lulu immediately let out a yowl of protest.

He gaped at her. 'Am I crazy or does she understand English?'

'English and Spanish. Forget French. Her French is terrible. But, since you ask, you *are* crazy.'

Austin narrowed his close-set eyes at me. 'I don't like you.'

'I'm sensing that, and I'm real broken up about it. Maybe we should try couples counseling instead of this kooky hostage scheme of yours.'

He drew his gun and pointed it at me again. 'Move, asshole.'

We started into the park, where we immediately encountered a huge map behind glass of the park's color-coded trails. There were five trails in all. I didn't need to ask which one we'd be taking. It was the green trail – the steep, seven-mile climb that led all of the way up the mountain to the ruins of the historic Talmadge family farm. Mr MacGowan hadn't been exaggerating. The original Talmadge settlers must have been quite a peculiar, stand-offish clan to choose to live in such a remote locale instead of at the mouth of the Connecticut River with the other founding families.

We started our way up the leaf-strewn trail with Austin bringing up the rear, muttering under his breath but saying nothing. Or at least nothing that I could comprehend. We'd been hiking for about a half-hour when Lulu came to an abrupt halt, raised her head and sniffed at the air several times. Then she tilted her head slightly, listening. She can smell and hear things that I can't. Her nose and ears are extremely valuable assets when I get myself into the messes like, well, this one. They're the main reason I kept Her Earness around. That and the whole glam thing.

'Why's she standing there like that?' Austin demanded, gasping for breath.

'She smells someone. Hears them, too. We're not alone.'

Austin turned and looked back down the trail, listening for a long moment before he said, 'She's imagining things.'

'She's a dog, Austin. They don't imagine things, except in cartoons. And this isn't a cartoon. You do know that, right?'

'What I know is this mountain – better than anyone else alive. And I'm telling you there's no one back there. Come on, get going.'

We got going. It was a nice, brisk day for a hike in the autumn woods. Just not a nice day for a seven-mile march up Mount Creepy with a deranged psychotic pointing a loaded gun at my back. He had to stop periodically to catch his breath, what with being overweight and lugging his duffel bag filled with junk food and Coke. I didn't stop. Just kept putting one foot in front of the other as the trail grew steeper.

I heard a river rushing somewhere nearby when we finally arrived at the ruins of the remote Talmadge family settlement. There were the fieldstone walls, stone foundations, chimneys, kilns and root cellars that Jim Conley had spoken of. Also deep indentations in the stone ledge that had once been the caves where Native Americans had lived a long time before the Talmadges arrived. It was a special place. I saw the most vivid, electric-green moss growing there that I'd ever seen in my life. All sorts of wild mushrooms, lichen. And yet, as both Annabeth McKenna and Mr MacGowan had told me, it was not a peaceful place. Creepy was just the word for it. Evil things had happened here. I could feel it. So could Lulu, who let out a low, unhappy moan.

'Why's she doing that?' Austin demanded.

'I don't know. She doesn't always tell me everything.' I came to a halt near the remains of a dug root cellar, glancing at Grandfather's Benrus. It was just past three o'clock. 'OK, now what happens?'

'Now you take a nap,' Austin answered, whacking me over the head with his hickory nightstick so hard that I saw purple and green stars bursting before my eyes as I felt him shove me down into the cellar.

I heard him yell something at Lulu. No idea what. I was somewhere else by then. I was gone.

Total blackness.

Again.

This time I smelled damp earth and I was very cold. I seemed to be lying on my side. The back of my head hurt like hell. I reached my fingers around to touch it and felt tender flesh and wetness. My hair was matted with blood. I had no idea how much time had passed since Austin whacked me. No idea of much of anything. I was in such a daze that I kept slipping in and out of consciousness. At one point I thought I heard voices off in the distance, though I might have imagined them. My ears were ringing and . . . then I was gone.

No idea how much more time passed before I came to again. Now my face was all wet and smelled like fish. Someone was licking me. *Lulu.* My hand found her in the darkness. I stroked her. She whimpered.

'It's OK, girl,' I whispered to her. 'We're OK.'

Although I had no idea if we were. No idea of much of anything. All I knew was that I was lying there in total darkness with an awful headache. My Varaflame lighter. I dug it out of the pocket of my jeans and flicked it on.

We were trapped down in that shallow root cellar. The one I'd been standing next to before Austin whacked me. He'd moved a pair of flat, heavy stones over it to close it off like a tomb. It wasn't airtight. We could breathe. But he must have used a pry bar to lodge them into place because when I reached up to push at them they didn't so much as budge.

Lulu hadn't been idle. She'd been digging at the soft, moist ground to widen the cellar and create a way out. Digging so furiously that she'd bloodied her paws. Now that she'd awakened me she went back to work, panting from the exertion. I wriggled over to her. Could see a crack of daylight in the space she'd created next to one of the flat stones. It was morning. I remember I'd checked my watch before Austin knocked me out. It had been around three p.m. That meant we'd been down there, what, sixteen, eighteen hours? I started digging with her, first with my bare hands, then with a sharp stone that I found. Working together, we managed to widen an opening between the damp earth and the stone that was just large enough for us to squeeze through. Lulu first, then me.

It was early morning. Chilly. The ground up there on the mountain was coated with frost. I saw no sign of Austin. I was incredibly dizzy. Lulu limped her way on her bloodied front paws to a small stream nearby and drank from it, thirsty from her labors. She was no doubt hungry, too, but there was nothing I could do about that right now. I fell to my knees next to her and drank. The water was ice cold. I splashed some on my face, climbed back up on to my feet and everything started spinning. I had to lunge for a tree limb to stay on my feet.

The trail before us was marked with a green arrow. If I remembered correctly from the big map at the park's entrance it would lead us through the rest of the Talmadge settlement, then take us back down the mountain to civilization – hopefully without encountering Austin again.

We started walking, neither of us doing particularly well. I'd never seen Lulu hobble so slowly and painfully. My poor, brave girl could barely walk. And I was so dizzy that I had to grab on to any tree I could find to keep from toppling over. I did find a stout stick that helped steady me a bit as we made our way slowly along the trail. I could hear a waterfall now. Then I saw it as the green-arrowed path took us directly alongside of it. A wooden safety railing on the edge of the trail kept hikers from straying too close and falling. There was a deep stone gorge at the base of the waterfall. It was quite a breathtaking view. I'm sure I would have appreciated it keenly if I hadn't been on the verge of passing out again. As I paused there, leaning my full weight against the safety railing, Lulu nudged my shin with her head.

That's when I saw him.

Austin was lying on his stomach way down there on a large, flat stone in the gorge. He wasn't moving. The tormented billionaire had chosen suicide as the only way out of the mess he'd gotten himself into. Did a Brody off of the top of the waterfall. He was dead, it appeared, but I had to be sure. I climbed over the safety railing, my head spinning, and crawled, slid and tumbled my way down the hill to the base of the gorge as the waterfall roared and the spray soaked me. Soaked us, I should say. My faithful, fearless partner had managed to climb her way over the railing and was right there next to me as we waded into the river and I turned Austin over and . . .

He hadn't jumped.

Someone had gone at him with a knife. There were deep, savage gashes in his throat from ear to ear. His jugular vein and carotid artery had both been severed. There are those who think of death as a state of eternal peace. The second richest man in Connecticut wasn't at peace. He died angry, his wet face scrunched in a permanent scowl, his eyes bulging furiously.

Murdered. Austin had been murdered.

Meaning Lulu hadn't been wrong when she'd gotten that whiff of somebody as we were hiking our way up the mountain. Not that I for one second thought she had been. Somebody *was* tailing us. Somebody who knew the mountain. Somebody who was a reasonably fit hiker.

Somebody who had a reason for wanting Austin dead.

As I knelt there in the chilly water, gazing down at him, Lulu began barking furiously. She'd heard faint voices off in the distance. I could hear them myself now. Husky male voices. Volunteer rescuers. Lots of them. And a couple of dogs started barking in response to Lulu's bark.

Slowly, I climbed to my feet and waded my way back toward the riverbank. 'Over here!' I called out as loud as I could before I pitched over on to the bank and was gone again.

FOUR

When I came to I was no longer up on that mountain. I was in a bed in a hospital room with the lights dimmed. The sky outside of my window was a night sky. Had I been out cold all day? My head still ached and my ears were ringing. I had a needle in my arm and was hooked up to a couple of bags so I wouldn't dehydrate, starve or any of those sorts of things. Lulu was lying on the bed next to me fast asleep with her face between two heavily bandaged paws. Dozing in a chair next to the bed in a creamy white turtleneck, herringbone slacks and ankle boots, was Merilee Gilbert Nash, trademark high forehead, magnificently sculpted cheekbones and all – who I could have sworn was supposed to be in Budapest playing Brett in that remake of *The Sun Also Rises* with Mr Mel Gibson.

'May I have your autograph, Miss Nash?' I asked hoarsely.

She blinked at me with those mesmerizing green eyes of hers before her face broke into a huge smile and she practically flew out of the chair to hug me and lay her head against my chest. I stroked her silky, waist-length golden blond hair and inhaled the scent of her Crabtree & Evelyn avocado oil soap before she raised her face to mine and kissed my mouth softly. 'I've never been so scared in my life. I was afraid you weren't going to come back.'

'I always come back. I'm like Arnold in *The Terminator*. But where am I?'

'Middlesex Hospital in Middletown. Let me get the doctor. I just saw her out in the hall a second ago.' She darted out the door and was gone.

Lulu wormed her way up the bed toward me and nuzzled my neck. I put my arm around her and told her what a brave, brave girl she was. She let out a weak whimper and snuggled even closer to me.

A crisply efficient young Asian woman, Dr Cynthia Eng, strode briskly in, trailed by Merilee. 'Welcome back.'

'Thank you. Nice to be back.'

'How do you feel?'

'Dizzy.'

'I'm not surprised. You've suffered a concussion. Miss Nash informs me that you're alert and aware but just for my own satisfaction, can you tell me what your name is?'

'Maitland W. Montmaurency.'

'Hoagy, be serious,' Merilee said.

'Stewart Stafford Hoag. You can call me Hoagy.'

'Can you tell me what your address is?'

'Um, that one's actually rather complicated right now . . .'

'OK, then who's the president of the United States?'

'William Jefferson Clinton of Hope, Arkansas.'

'Good answer.' She paused to check my pulse and blood pressure before she said, 'That was quite some blow you took to the back of your head. What did he use?'

'A hickory nightstick.'

'I was concerned you might have a fractured skull in addition to your concussion and scalp laceration so I ordered an x-ray. It came back negative. You, sir, have one very hard head.'

'Yes, he does,' Merilee said. 'I can assure you.'

'It bled quite a bit. We had to staple it.'

'Sorry, did you say *staple* it?'

'I did. That's what we use now instead of stitches. Surgical incisions and lacerations heal faster with staples.'

I fingered my head for the first time and found metal staples there. Also premature male baldness. They'd shaved off a section of my hair before they'd stapled the laceration shut. 'At least it doesn't hurt.'

'That's because I've shot you full of novocaine. It'll hurt like hell when the novocaine wears off. Sorry about that. Take Tylenol for the pain. Wash and dry the wound thoroughly every day and cover it with a fresh bandage. We'll give you some to take home.' I noticed now that some of my fingers were bandaged. I held them up before me, looking at them.

'They were all scratched up,' Dr Eng explained. 'And your nails were broken. The nurses cleaned you up and gave you a free manicure.'

'Black nail polish would have made for a nice surprise.'

'I'll be sure to let them know. You can probably lose the bandages tomorrow. No deep wounds, unlike your little friend there.'

Lulu's tail thumped on the bed next to me.

'You don't by any chance have any anchovies on the premises, do you?'

Dr Eng's brow furrowed with concern. 'I think we may be losing him again, Miss Nash.'

I shook my head, which was a big mistake. It felt as if a large marble was rattling around in there. 'Anchovies are Lulu's favorite treat.'

'Oh, I see. I suppose I can ask at the nurse's station, but . . .'

'No need,' Merilee assured her. 'I brought a jar from home.'

'What a good mommy you are,' I marveled as she pulled the jar from her purse, extracted one and fed it to Lulu, who gobbled it down gratefully. 'Why, some day, I can even imagine the pitter patter of little feet around the old Whitcomb place.'

'We already have an ample supply of those, darling.'

'I mean *other* than the mice.'

Dr Eng studied us curiously, slowly coming to the realization that we weren't like other people. 'Mr Hoag . . . Hoagy . . . have you had a tetanus shot lately?'

'I . . . can't remember.'

'I'm going to take that as a no. You shall have one, because he said you were pawing around in rubble.'

'"He" being . . .?'

'Resident Trooper Conley. He's been very anxious to talk to you as soon as you regained consciousness. I've phoned him and he's on his way, but right now you still belong to me.' She shone a pen light into my eyes to test the responsiveness of my pupils. 'How's your appetite?'

'Haven't got one.'

'That's typical. The dizziness will do that. Have you suffered any prior concussions? It's important that I know, because the effects can be cumulative.'

'One. Well, two, actually.'

Merilee drew in her breath. 'You never told me that before.'

'I like to be a man of mystery. It adds to my allure.'

'Were they recent?' Dr Eng asked.

'No. I got the first one when I was on the football team my sophomore year of college up in Cambridge. I attended the school that we don't mention by name so that we can draw more attention to it.'

'You *never* told me you played football at Harvard,' Merilee said indignantly.

'It wasn't my finest hour, I assure you. I was our punter. First game of the season we were playing Columbia at Baker Field in upper Manhattan, overlooking the Hudson. Wonderful old wooden stadium, like out of an F. Scott Fitzgerald story. I half-expected to see people wearing raccoon coats and drinking hooch out of flasks. Columbia had a terrible team but they had a punt returner who was a real jackrabbit. I got off a good, high kick and angled it toward the sideline the way we're taught to. Didn't matter. He darted his way through our entire punt defense, which left it up to me to bring him down or he'd score a touch-down. I dove for him and got kneed right in the head. He kept on going and scored six while I lay there on the grass in la-la land. I had no idea where I was until the trainer waved something under my nose, but I had a headache that lasted a week. I decided to quit the team and focus strictly on track and field after that. Dr Eng, it might interest you to know that I was once the third best javelin hurler in the entire Ivy League.'

'And how about the second concussion?' Evidently not a keen fan of Ivy League sports, our Dr Eng.

'That one was four years later . . .' I hesitated, cringing inwardly. 'I got thrown from my motorcycle in Spanish Harlem when I hit a pothole the size of a Plymouth and flew headfirst into a parked car.'

'Were you wearing a helmet?'

'Helmets take away all of the fun.'

'And here I thought you were a smart man,' she said disapprovingly. 'Did you lose consciousness that time, too?'

'Actually, I was in a coma for three days.'

Merilee gasped. 'I can't believe you've never told me this.'

I fell silent for a moment, remembering. 'Reggie walked away without a scratch. I nearly died. Things were different after that. It was as if it signified the end of . . .' I fell silent again, realizing I'd just wandered down a darkened corridor and found my Third Level. All along I'd been thinking that Sid, Nancy and Room 100 of the Chelsea Hotel marked the end of 'My Sweet Season of Madness.' But it was my coma, an experience I try to block out because it terrifies me to recall it, that was the genuine end. I came out of it a different person. No longer the wild and crazy kid whom I'd once been, but a determined young writer who was obsessed with becoming an *important* author. After I got out of the hospital I broke it off with Reggie and got serious about 'Our Family Enterprise.'

Merilee was studying me curiously. 'The end of what, darling?'

'I'm sorry, does one of you have a pad and pen?'

Dr Eng passed me a pharmaceutical company notepad and pen. I began scribbling madly with my bandaged fingers, page after page after page.

'Is he OK?' she asked Merilee.

'He's fine. I take it you've never lived with a writer.'

'No, my husband's an electrical engineer.'

I scribbled like a man possessed for several minutes before I tore the pages from the pad and asked Merilee to put them in her handbag and guard them with her life. She took them from me, smiling faintly. Then I lay back, my head spinning.

'Are you still with us?' Dr Eng asked.

'Right here with you.'

'I want to keep you until the morning. Get you on solid food. You've had quite a blow.'

'Of course. Whatever you say.'

'You'll be sensitive to light. Suffer from headaches and dizziness. The symptoms should subside, but you must take it easy for a few days.'

'He will,' Merilee said.

'Also your balance is going to be impaired. Be careful when you get up out of a chair, go up and down stairs, that sort of thing. And, for God's sake, stay off of ladders. Based on what you've just told me, you do *not* want to get another concussion or you're likely to suffer more severe side effects.'

'Such as . . .?'

'Disorientation.'

'That's something I'm already accustomed to.'

'You haven't lost your sense of humor. That's good. But if you lost your short-term memory that wouldn't be so good, would it?'

'No, I suppose it wouldn't.'

I looked up and saw Jim Conley standing out in the brightly lit corridor in his Smokey hat, looking tall, lean and weathered.

Dr Eng followed my gaze. 'Feel well enough to see the trooper?'

'Sure, but can you give us a minute first?'

'Certainly.' She smiled at Merilee. 'I'm a huge fan of your work.'

'Why, thank you. And thank you for taking such good care of the tall guy.'

She left us, pausing in the hallway to speak to the resident trooper, who made himself scarce as requested.

'Merilee . . .?'

'Yes, darling?'

'Aren't you supposed to be in Budapest?'

'Oh, that. I gave Mr MacGowan a number there where I could be reached in an emergency. And there *was* an emergency, as in he heard a gunshot coming from the direction of the farm.' So I'd been lucky. He had been home. 'He jumped in his truck, drove over and found a kitchen that smelled of gun smoke, an empty ice-cream container and an overturned chair. The Jag was there, but you and Lulu weren't. Plus he'd heard a car go speeding by his place moments after the gunshot. He put two and two together and called Resident Trooper Conley, who filled him in on what had just happened at the beach club. Mr MacGowan was convinced that Austin had kidnapped you and intended to hold you hostage or whatever lunatic scheme he had ricocheting around in his crazy head.'

'That was the second time he'd come by. He was desperate to talk to you. Convinced you were the only person who could help him.'

'Me?' She looked at me surprise. 'Why me?'

'Because of that movie you made about the soldiers with PTSD. You were incredibly compassionate and understanding in it, and he couldn't tell the difference between a movie and real life.'

'So you don't think I'm compassionate and understanding in real life?'

I stared at her blankly, unable to summon a comeback.

'Oh, dear, you're still not completely with us yet, are you? OK, I promise I won't bust your chops for a full twenty-four hours, though it'll be quite a challenge.'

'Did you know Austin?'

'I knew *of* him. Everyone in Lyme knows about the Talmadge brothers. As soon I got Mr MacGowan's call I told our director I had a family emergency and had to catch the first flight home. It wasn't until I got here that I learned that Austin had been found in the waterfall gorge on Mount Creepy with his throat cut, that you were near his body, unconscious, and that Lulu was guarding you, bloody paws and all.'

'Back up a sec. You walked off of the production of *The Sun Also Rises* because you were afraid I was in danger?'

'You're my man,' she stated simply.

'How is the shoot going?'

'It's fine,' she said in that abrupt way of hers that meant it wasn't but that she didn't want to talk about it. 'Have you and Lulu been having a good time at the farm? Until all of this happened, I mean.'

'I'd only been there a day, actually. Thought I could use a break after six good, hard weeks of grinding. I sent a hundred new pages to the Fox before I left town. Put the tomato patch to bed. Bled the pipes in the guest cottage. I was just starting in on the storm windows when he showed up.'

'So I saw. Thank you, darling.'

'A guy has to earn his keep.'

She gave me her up-from-under look, the one that does strange, wonderful things to the lower half of my body. 'There are other ways, you know.'

'Are you getting frisky with me? Because I'm concussed. She told me to take it easy.'

'Celibacy didn't enter into it, as it were. And the resident trooper is cooling his heels out in the hall. Shall I leave?'

'I never want you to leave.'

'You're such a flatterer.'

'Hey, I'm not the one who just flew thousands of miles to be here.'

'I told you, you're my man. And Lulu's my brave girl.' Which got a whimper and a tail thump out of her. Merilee fed her another anchovy before she went to find Resident Trooper Conley.

She was gone long enough for a nurse to come in, take my pulse, check my blood pressure and give me a tetanus shot. When Merilee returned she had Jim Conley in tow. She sat back down in her chair and invited him to pull a chair over. He preferred to stand, removing his Smokey hat in a lady's presence.

'How are you feeling?' he asked me, twirling his hat in his fingers.

'I've had better days.'

'I imagine you have. There's a half-dozen TV news crews downstairs. This will be getting big play. It's not every day that one of the richest, strangest men in America gets himself murdered. I'm guessing your head's still fuzzy, so I won't overwhelm you with a million questions. But I do have a particular one that I'm obliged to ask, and please don't be offended. *You* didn't cut Austin's throat, did you?'

'No I didn't.'

'Carry a folding knife?'

'No, I don't. You're welcome to search my jeans if you want to.'

'Not necessary. I was wondering if you remember anything Austin said that struck you as peculiar.'

'Everything Austin said struck me as peculiar.'

'Allow me to rephrase that. I mean anything that might help point us in the direction of his killer.'

I lay there for a moment, thinking back. 'I do remember that he was extremely homophobic. Seemed obsessed, really. First, he insisted that one of Michael's ex-Green Berets, Joaquin, kept staring at his pecker when they threw him in the shower. And then, after he escaped from his private sanitarium, he went so totally berserk at the sight of two gay men being demonstrative at the beach club that he actually shot one of them.'

Resident Trooper Conley nodded grimly. 'Truman Mainwaring. He's up on the fourth floor with a shattered clavicle. He'll be OK, but it was quite some surgical repair job, I'm told. His friend Skip Rimer is by his side. Truman's family has belonged to the club for two generations. They have a big place on Bill Hill Road, though they're vacationing in France right now. Truman's an architect in New York City. His friend Skip is a magazine editor of some kind. Avid rock climber and mountain biker. Has quite a handshake on him. They live together in the city. Came out for a few days to do some leaf peeping.'

'You explicitly told us that the firing pin had been removed from the revolver Austin was toting around.'

His mouth tightened. 'I know I did.'

'Austin told me that he paid Old Tom ten thou to restore it.'

'So I understand. I paid Tom a visit this afternoon and that no-good rascal admitted it to me. I'll get his business license revoked, I swear.' He glanced down at his hat in his hands, turning it round and round. 'Can you tell me what brought Austin to Miss Nash's farm after the beach club incident?'

'The very same thing that brought him there the first time – he *had* to talk to her because only *she* would understand him. He was a sobbing mess. Highly agitated. When I told him what I hadn't told him the first time – that he couldn't talk to her because she was in Budapest – he totally freaked out. Started babbling about how he was going to make a run for it, and that the law wouldn't dare touch him because he was taking Lulu and me along as hostages. When I told him he could forget that idea he shot a hole in the kitchen wall.'

Conley nodded. 'Angus MacGowan and I both agreed that he would head for the mountain. He'd feel safe there, especially if he had you and your pup along with him. I contacted the volunteer fire department and immediately put together a search and rescue team of a dozen men who know the terrain well, including his cousins, Tony and Gas Hardy. Several of them are hunters who own dogs.'

'What about Michael's ex-Green Berets and Pinkie?'

He frowned. 'Pinkie?'

'Giant German Shepherd with about two hundred teeth. Kind of a wussie name, if you ask me. Don't you think it's a wussie name?'

'They played no part in the rescue operation. Michael ordered them to stand guard at his home in case Austin was planning to come after him next.'

'Which he was not.'

'Which he was not. A trooper located Austin's car behind some brush near the parking lot. When he popped his trunk he found your wallet hidden under a bunch of laundry. Smart thinking on your part, Mr Hoag.' He pulled it from his back pocket. Merilee took it from him and put it in her shoulder bag with my sheaf of notes. 'As soon as our volunteers and their dogs arrived they started up the mountain in the direction of Talmadge Farm, but it was already late afternoon by then and starting to get dark. They didn't get very far before they realized they'd have to call it off and return at dawn.'

'Did you make the climb with them?'

'No, I was tasked with setting up a command post in the parking lot.'

I lay there in silence for a moment, my head aching. 'Lulu stopped and sniffed the air as we were climbing. Someone was following us. He was being real careful about it. Staying far enough back so that we couldn't hear him. But Lulu definitely smelled him. Probably heard him, too.'

'Hmm . . . that's interesting. Remember anything else?'

'I was in and out of consciousness after Austin conked me on the head with his nightstick. Had no concept of time. But I thought I heard voices. Couldn't make out any words or anything. They were very faint. And I didn't recognize the other voice.'

'This was when you were down in that root cellar?'

I nodded. Again, big mistake. Something was definitely loose inside of my skull. 'It was daylight by the time I came to. Turned out that my partner here had been digging while I was unconscious. I helped her finish the job and we managed to squeeze our way out. I was dizzy beyond belief, and Lulu's paws were ripped to shreds. But she started hobbling her way up the green trail, determined to continue on. I followed her, grabbing at trees to keep from falling over, until we reached the waterfall. That's when I spotted Austin lying down there on the rocks, face down. I figured he'd done himself in.'

Conley thumbed his jaw. 'Honestly? That would have been my first thought, too.'

'I slid down the hill to check him out. Turned him over and saw that his throat had been slit. Then I started to pass out again. But I remember Lulu started barking.'

'She did indeed. Brought the rescue team right to you. They found you on the riverbank, unconscious. She wouldn't let anyone near you. But Gas Hardy has a real way with dogs. He coaxed her into letting them help you. Both of you. Gas was real concerned about her front paws. They were ripped to shreds, like you said. A bloody mess. You were unconscious but your vitals were stable. They rigged up the portable stretcher and carried you down the mountain with Lulu riding on your chest. You're pretty slim, but she's, well, one of the guys called her a bowling ball with ears. They had to take turns spelling each other on stretcher detail.'

'I can't thank those men enough.'

'Nor can I,' said Merilee, squeezing my hand.

'No thanks are needed. This is what they train for when they join the volunteer fire department.'

'Nonetheless, I promise them a special treat for this year's Christmas party – Merilee in a shimmering gown doing her imitation of Rita Hayworth singing, "Put the Blame on Mame" from the movie *Gilda*. Trust me, it's a real crowd pleaser.'

'Darling, I'm not sure I can fit in any of those shimmering gowns anymore.'

'Nonsense, you're as svelte as a schoolgirl.'

'I take it you haven't seen many schoolgirls lately.'

'The EMT was waiting in the parking lot to bring you here,' Jim Conley went on. 'And Gas drove Lulu straight to Dr Jen's veterinary clinic.'

'Will her paws be OK?' I asked, stroking her head.

'Dr Jen said if you'd been in those woods another night it would have been touch and go, but she's optimistic. Soaked Lulu's paws in a tub of disinfecting soap and shot her full of antibiotics. Wants to see her in a couple of days.'

'I'll take her in,' Merilee promised.

I glanced at her in surprise. 'Don't you have to go back to Budapest?'

'Not until I'm sure that you're both OK.'

'I contacted the M.E. and Major Crime squad,' Jim Conley went on. 'The M.E. and crime scene technicians had a long drive plus the long climb, so they weren't able to spend as much time up there as they wanted to. But the body's been removed and the techies will return to continue their work tomorrow. A homicide lieutenant's been assigned to the case. He'll want to talk to you when you're up to it. Carmine Tedone's his name. Says he knows you.'

'Yes, we're well acquainted with the lieutenant,' Merilee said sweetly.

'Indeed we are. It'll be just like *déjà vu* all over again. I gather that the M.E. thinks the murder weapon was a folding knife.'

He nodded. 'His preliminary exam indicates a folding knife approximately three and a half inches long, often referred to as a hunting knife. They plan to undertake a thorough search for it at the crime scene first thing tomorrow.'

I suddenly felt the room start to spin again. I tried, and failed, to keep my eyes open.

'I guess I wore him out,' I heard the resident trooper say to Merilee apologetically.

'Not to worry,' she said. 'You had to do your job.'

I wanted to thank him again for his help, but I wasn't there anymore. I was somewhere else.

Gone.

FIVE

Dr Eng said I was well enough to go home the next morning. I'd slept most of the night, awakening once with a terrible headache. A nurse came in and gave me some Tylenol and checked my blood pressure and pulse rate. I was still hooked up to two drip bags, I noticed as I drifted back to sleep. I also noticed that Lulu wasn't there when I reached for her. Merilee must have taken her home with her.

When the early morning light came through the window a different nurse came in to unhook me from the drip bags, slap a bandage on the inside of my forearm and raise my bed so that I was sitting up. She removed the bandages from my fingers, examined them and replaced them with a couple of Band-aids. Then she brought me a breakfast tray laden with two beverages that tasted vaguely like orange juice and coffee, a plate of cold, pale scrambled eggs and cold white toast. I managed two forkfuls of eggs and one bite of toast, but I still didn't have much of an appetite. Plus I'm totally spoiled by the farm's fresh eggs. These tasted like they'd originated in a laboratory, not a chicken. I shoved the tray aside and sat there. I still felt foggy, but at least the room wasn't spinning, which I considered a major improvement.

Dr Eng agreed with my assessment after she'd shone a light in my eyes and peppered me with questions to test my state of mental acuity, such as 'Can you spell "world" backwards?' Honestly, I would have had trouble with that one even on the best of mornings. But when I aced it she told me she was going to discharge me – although she did want to see me again tomorrow.

Merilee arrived soon after that to take me home. 'Good morning, darling!' she exclaimed, brimming with good cheer as she fetched my clothes from their locker. 'How are you feeling?'

'Like I have the Godzilla of hangovers. Where's Lulu? She OK?'

'She's fine, not to worry. Waiting for you out in the car.'

I got out of bed, still feeling rubber legged. Merilee steadied me by the arm as I ditched my hospital gown and climbed into my boxer shorts and torn jeans. I had no problem managing my T-shirt and Viyella shirt by myself. I sat down and put my socks on with no problem either – until I got dizzy from bending over. She knelt and gave me a hand with my Chippewas. After I'd put on my flight jacket the nurse came in with my discharge papers and a wheelchair. Merilee wheeled me to the elevator, chattering about how balmy it felt outside compared to late October in Budapest. As we rode down to the first floor everyone else in the elevator gaped at her – a *movie star* – in total awe.

'I'm afraid that you and the beach club shooting victim made the morning news,' she said, wheeling me to the main entrance. 'I encountered some TV news crews when I pulled into the parking lot here. When they spotted me their interest meter shot way up. I phoned Jim Conley. He promised me he'd station a trooper at the farm's front gate to keep them from bothering us.'

'I wonder if it'll be the same one with the blocky blond head.'

'Sorry?'

'Never mind.'

It was an overcast morning. Not nearly as cold out as it had been when it was crisp and clear. The Jag was parked curbside with a state trooper standing watch over it. Lulu was in the passenger seat, anxious to greet me, although not half as anxious as the half-dozen TV news crews whose vans were parked nearby. The camera crews went to work instantly. Reporters shouted questions that Merilee totally ignored. Photographers snapped pictures. The bright lights made my head start to spin. She hustled me into the car with a generous assist from the state trooper. I maneuvered myself into the passenger seat with Lulu and her heavily bandaged paws in my lap. She whooped and licked my face, her tail thumping. I allowed as how I was happy to see her, too.

Then Merilee jumped in behind the wheel, started up the Jag with a throaty roar and sped out of the parking lot toward Route 9. 'I see that you two made yourselves right at home in the master bedroom suite,' she said drily as she got on to Route 9 and floored it for home. She drives fast but well. There's nothing she doesn't do well.

'The guest cottage isn't heated,' I said as my head mercifully stopped spinning. 'Besides, I turned off the water and bled the pipes. I can move upstairs to one of the guest rooms if you wish.'

'Like hell you will, mister. I'm just doing a yank on your frank.'

'"A yank on my frank?" From whom did you pick up that choice morsel of ribald vernacular? Mel Gibson, am I right?'

'Seriously, darling. How do you feel?'

'Like I have a concussion. I'll be OK in a day or two.'

'Sure you will. You just need some rest and TLC. What's the first thing you want to do when you get home?'

'Put away a plate of the girls' eggs, over easy, and a gallon of your coffee.'

'Consider it done.'

'I should feel much better after that, and I'll get back to my fall chores.'

'Not until Dr Eng says you can. And even if she gives you the green light, you are *not* getting up on a ladder to hang those storm windows. Mr MacGowan has called the Hardy Boys.'

'Frank and Joe?' I asked hopefully.

'Tony and Gas, silly man. I swear, sometimes talking to you is like talking to a twelve-year-old. They're coming over to finish the job.'

'Some of the windows need re-glazing.'

'So they'll re-glaze them. And put in the storm doors. And chop the kindling and everything else on that cute little to-do list of yours on the kitchen table. All of these years and I never knew you made to-do lists,' she said with a cascade of girlish laughter as Route 9 merged on to I-95 at Long Island Sound and crossed the Connecticut River. I heard relief in her laughter. She'd been frightened. Having to endure that long flight from Budapest, not knowing if I was dead or alive, must have been hell.

She got off at Exit 70 and started up into the hills of Lyme on Route 156 before she turned off at Hamburg Cove on to twisting, turning Joshua Town Road for home. When we got there four TV news vans were lining the narrow road at the foot of the driveway. But Jim Conley had made good on his promise. A state trooper was staked out at the gate to keep them out. And, yes, it was the same teenager with the blocky blond head. I wondered if he'd armed himself with a fresh comic book. He backed up his cruiser, opened the gate so we could pass on through, and up the gravel driveway Merilee sped.

'You and Lulu are going to do nothing but sit in front of the fire and relax today,' she informed me. 'But first you're getting a treatment.'

'Treatment? What kind of treatment?'

I found out what kind after I'd put away those fresh eggs with their bright orange yolks, a buttered English muffin and two huge mugs of strong coffee. Lulu, who'd already had her breakfast before they picked me up, stared at the refrigerator until I gave her one, two, three anchovies. It was vital to keep her in good spirits. If she weren't – being a dog – she'd start misbehaving by chewing on her bandages, which meant she would have to wear one of those cones on her head. Not an attractive look for a basset hound, take my word for it.

The phone rang non-stop. Reporters wanting to talk to me, to Merilee. Hell, they would have gratefully grabbed a quote from Lulu if they could have. Merilee unplugged it so we'd have some peace and quiet. Our agents and the state police knew her unlisted business number. If anyone important needed to reach us, they could.

Next it was time for my treatment. Virtually all actresses have deeply held beliefs in the curative powers of exotic herbal remedies that other, somewhat more earthbound people might construe as, well, nutty. But I'd grown accustomed to Merilee's home ministrations over the years. This particular one involved me stretching out in the master bathroom's enormous claw-footed cast-iron tub and soaking for a half-hour in steaming hot water laced with eucalyptus oil, camphor oil, hyssop oil, bloodroot and several other things I can't remember and don't want to.

'The two of you were trapped in that cold, damp root cellar for an entire night,' she informed me as she filled the tub with the hottest water the furnace could produce and added generous droplets of her magic potions from tincture bottles, filling the bathroom with their powerful scents. She'd already closed the door and shoved a towel under it, the better to turn it into a steam room. Lulu was curled up on a pile of towels with a pleased look on her face. She enjoys taking steam. Always has. 'I don't want either of you to get sick. You *know* how susceptible Lulu is to sinus and bronchial problems.'

'Hold on, you're going to keep *her* locked in here with me?'

'I am.'

'But she mouth breathes. It'll be like taking a bath with a seal.'

'Darling, Lulu loves you so much that she suffered serious wounds to her front paws to save your life. Are you honestly going to deny her the care she needs?' I had no comeback for that one. There was no comeback. So I began to undress. Again, Merilee had to steady me. 'You look thin,' she observed fretfully.

'I've written more than a hundred new pages since you left. I've done nothing but work.'

'Have you been eating?'

'I do forget to eat lunch sometimes, now that you mention it. But I have dinner every night at Tony's.'

'Still, you're nothing but ribs and collar bones. You haven't been this thin since . . . you're not snorting nose candy again, are you?'

'Never again, Merilee. I swear to you on my mother's grave.'

'Your mother's still alive.'

'I do smoke a Chesterfield after dinner when we walk home from Tony's.'

'You're *smoking*?'

'Just that one cigarette a day. I'm in character. Totally back to being *me* in 1975. I listen to the same music, dress the same way. Surely you of all people can understand what I mean. I even repaired my old cigarette lighter, Grandfather's Ronson Varaflame. And it's a good thing I did. Otherwise, we wouldn't have been able to see a thing when we were trapped down in that tomb.'

She considered this carefully as the tub continued to fill and the bathroom became steamier and more powerfully scented. 'Are they good?'

'The new pages? They're good.'

'And are you finding your work space . . . satisfactory?'

'Merilee, that office is like a dream, I swear. Every morning I sit down at the writing table, look out at the park and think I've actually become the man I always wanted to be – all except for the part about you being in Hungary.'

'Well, that's not forever. Or at least I certainly hope not.' The tub was full. She turned off the water. 'I may just keep you two company for a few minutes. That long flight dried out my sinuses, and if I catch a cold I'll have to loop all of my Budapest dialogue when we move on to London to shoot our interiors. How's your balance? Do you need help getting in?'

'I can manage,' I assured her as I eased myself slowly into the scalding hot water.

'Breathe deep,' she commanded me, perching on her dressing table chair.

I breathed deep. 'This eucalyptus oil makes it smell like one of those Russian bathhouses on the Lower East Side. We should be playing pinochle and drinking schnapps.'

Actually, it felt great. My head was definitely stuffed up from that damp root cellar, and my body felt stiff and achy. I could have lived without the bonus steamy scent of the Fulton Fish Market, but we do have to accommodate the mouth breathers whom we love.

'So what's wrong with the movie, Merilee?'

'Who says there's anything wrong with it?'

I didn't bother to answer her.

She fell silent for a moment. 'I truly don't know. The script's as tight as a drum. The director is inventive, quick-witted and easy to get along with. We have a terrific cinematographer. The locations really look like photographs of Paris in the twenties. Mel has been a dream to work with. He has great energy. The entire ensemble does. But when I look at the dailies Brett just doesn't feel *real* to me. She feels fake. In fact, it all feels fake.'

'Have you considered the source material?'

'It can't be the source material. *The Sun Also Rises* is one of the greatest novels of the twentieth century. Ernest Hemingway was a giant of American literature.'

'Says who?'

'Says everyone.'

'Who's everyone?'

'Literary scholars, critics . . . *everyone*.' Merilee shook her head of long, beautiful golden hair at me. 'Where are you going with this?'

'There's a precious handful of writers whom I reread every few years just to remind myself what great writing is. Hemingway isn't one of them. He wrote some terrific Nick Adams short stories when he was first starting out. His prose was natural and clean. But then his ego took over and he became a pretentious macho gasbag. His characters bear no resemblance to real people. Try leafing through *For Whom the Bell Tolls* some time. The dialogue's so stilted that it's laugh-out-loud funny. He excelled at being a colorful personality – Papa Hemingway – but to me he's the most overrated novelist of the twentieth century.'

She looked at me in stunned disbelief. 'Are you telling me that *The Sun Also Rises*, which everyone with the exception of you considers a literary masterpiece, is doo-doo?'

'Did you read it when you were in college?'

'Of course. Everyone did.'

'Did you enjoy it?'

'Not really.'

'That's because it's crap. I'm sorry, doo-doo.'

'Darling, why didn't you say anything before I took the role?'

'Because it's an A-list project with a top director and you were incredibly excited. Besides, you never know when lightning will strike. My advice to you is that if Brett doesn't seem real then *make* her real. Don't give up.'

'I won't,' she said with quiet determination. 'But I have a truly bad gut feeling about this one.'

'I'm sorry, Merilee.'

'No need to be. Most of what I pour my heart and soul into fails. That's the nature of my business.'

'Mine too. And there's no joy to be had if we don't take risks.'

She excused herself and returned a few minutes later with a teapot filled with boiling water that she dumped into the tub to generate more steam.

After that, she left Lulu and me in peace to our herbal aromatherapy. It was so soothing that I may have dozed off for a few minutes. When she returned a half-hour or so later she helped me out of the deep tub with a hand under my arm – she's nearly six feet tall and incredibly strong – and steadied me while I dried off and stepped into clean boxers and jeans. I was able to put on a T-shirt, cashmere turtle-neck and socks on my own in the bedroom while she drained the tub. Then I stretched out on the parlor sofa in front of the fire she'd built. Lulu hobbled in and climbed into my lap, her tail thumping.

I heard a pair of pickup trucks pull up outside. Doors open and close. Mr MacGowan came in by way of the mudroom. He didn't bother to knock. Neighbors in Lyme don't.

'Well, now, how are you feeling, young fella?' he asked me as he fed the fire with a hickory log.

'Better than my four-footed companion,' I said, stroking her gently.

He nodded gravely. 'I hear she dug you out of that root cellar practically by herself.'

'Mr MacGowan, I sure am glad you were home and heard Austin fire his gun in the kitchen. I hate to think what might have happened if you'd been . . .'

'Don't think about it. You'll be better off. Besides, I brought you a cure for what ails you.' He fetched a jug from the kitchen table. 'Some more of my hard apple cider.

He called it hard apple cider. I called it Connecticut calvados. It was intensely flavorful and warmed the tummy beyond belief.

'Why, thank you. Care to stay and share a glass?'

'Can't. Too much to do. Tony and Gas Hardy are here to hang those big old storm windows for you. Merilee said you're forbidden to stand on a ladder in your concussed state. Tony has a real good touch with glazing compound. He'll freshen up what needs freshening and prime them for you. They can also put in your storm doors. Those mothers must weigh a hundred pounds apiece. Anything else needs doing, you just ask them. They're good boys.' To Mr MacGowan anyone under the age of fifty was a boy. 'I'll tell them to get started.'

'I'd like to thank them first. Could you ask them to come in?'

He fetched them and led them in by way of the mudroom door and the kitchen. They were both big, husky guys in their forties dressed in heavy wool checkered shirts, jeans and work boots. Tony was fair-haired with a flushed, weathered complexion. Gas's shaggy hair and full beard were black, though his beard had a smattering of gray in it.

Lulu let out a whoop when she saw Gas. He immediately went over and patted her with the gentleness of a true dog lover. 'Hey, girl, you feeling better? She's a sweetie.' He had a hoarse, raspy voice. 'And those paws of hers were an awful mess. After Dr Jen took care of them she started to worry about Lulu's teeth and gums, too, what with that breath of hers. But she said Lulu's gums were in the pink and her teeth are tartar free.'

'They are. She just has unusual eating habits.' I stuck out my hand. 'I wanted to shake your hands. Both of you.' Which I did. It was like squeezing two rough-cut boards of wood. 'If you hadn't hiked into those woods and found us, we wouldn't be here right now.'

'It's what we train for when we join the volunteer fire department,' Tony said. 'No big.'

'It's very big. You're both good neighbors.'

'Which is why they won't accept any money for helping out around here,' Mr MacGowan said pointedly.

Gas nodded his shaggy head. 'That's right.'

'Bushwa,' Merilee said as she breezed in from tidying the eucalyptus spa.

'Hullo, ma'am,' the brothers said, blushing in her presence.

'If you do an honest day's work you get an honest day's pay,' she said. 'And I won't take no for an answer.'

Gas scuffed at the rug with his work boot. 'Well, if you insist.'

'I'm sorry about what happened to Austin,' I said to them. 'I understand you were cousins.'

'He was family,' Tony acknowledged. 'But we hated his guts.'

'Ever since we were kids,' Gas said angrily. 'One summer afternoon me and Tony was running around in the ruins up on the mountain with our pup, Tige, and Austin started throwing rocks at us to make us go away. It was like he considered the ruins *his*. We didn't take kindly to it, so I gave him a bloody nose. Next morning we found Tige dead in the backyard. Our dad took him to the vet. Turned out he'd eaten some hamburger meat laced with rat poison. It was Austin who did it. We never had any doubt.'

'He was an evil little bastard his whole life,' Tony said.

'I hear you had some trouble with him on White Sand Beach a couple of weeks ago.'

Gas nodded. 'You hear right. We were kicking back over a bonfire with friends. That lunatic shows up, playing cops and robbers like he was still a kid, and confiscated our beer. Also a couple of doobies. We, uh, didn't mention nothing about the doobies to the resident trooper. Appreciate it if you'd . . .'

'Not to worry.'

'Time for you boys to get started,' Mr MacGowan broke in. 'Miss Nash keeps her storm doors out in the barn. Hoagy hadn't gotten around to those yet. I'll show you where they are.'

'We can get those in for you right away, Miss Nash,' Tony promised. 'Once these old places get cold they stay cold.'

Merilee thanked them and they filed out the mudroom door toward the barn. I watched the shaggy brothers go, wondering just how deeply held their life-long grudge against their billionaire cousin had been.

Merilee reheated the leftover four-alarm chili that was in the fridge and brought me a bowl of it with some pilot crackers and a glass of milk.

'Aren't you going to have some?' I asked her.

'Brett is supposed to be svelte. Can't have her looking like a hippo. But I'll keep you company,' she said as another vehicle came up the drive and parked. Through the front windows we could see that it was a silver state police Crown Vic cruiser.

The man who got out of the passenger seat was no stranger to us. He was Lieutenant Carmine Tedone of the Major Crime Squad, the homicide investigator with whom we'd been involved that summer in the Sherbourne Playhouse murders. Carmine was Pete the Fixer's cousin. Everyone in the Connecticut State Police was related. Carmine was a chesty fireplug like Pete, with dark, hooded eyes and a head of mountainous, elaborately layered black hair that was reminiscent of John Travolta from his *Saturday Night Fever* disco heyday. He wore a cheap shiny black suit just like Pete did. So did his driver, Sergeant Angelo Bartucca, who was his wife's cousin. I wondered if the family bought them in bulk, like rolls of paper towels at Costco.

Lieutenant Tedone hadn't cared much for me, partly because he thought I was an annoying asshole, but mostly because I'd been the one who'd cracked the Sherbourne Playhouse case, with a generous assist from Lulu. I'm fairly certain he would have been thrilled if he'd never had to see me again.

Merilee got up and opened the front door to save them the trouble of knocking.

'Nice to see you again, Miss Nash,' Tedone said with deferential politeness. 'Sorry it's not under cheerier circumstances.'

'Do we ever meet under cheery circumstances, Lieutenant?'

He frowned. 'No, I guess not.'

'Please, come in. Hello again, Sergeant Bartucca.'

'Hiya, ma'am,' he responded, ducking his head shyly as she closed the door behind them.

Tedone gestured in the direction of the sofa with his chin. 'How's the hero doing?'

Merilee smiled. 'Lulu is being very brave and stoic, aren't you, sweetness?'

She let out a low whoop.

'I meant the tall guy.'

'Oh, him. He's still dizzy. The doctor said he has to take it easy.'

Tedone crossed the room toward me. I started to get up to greet him.

'No, no, stay put.' He checked out my head wound. 'Boy, that's quite some wallop. Concussion?'

'Already got one, thanks.'

'Still have that same mouth, too.'

'In fact, it turns out he's had two prior concussions that I knew nothing about,' Merilee said to him. 'It's strange how you think you know everything about a person whom you're close to, but you don't.'

'You got that right,' Tedone agreed. 'Every investigation I ever work I find out things that the victim's loved ones never knew about.'

'Remember that woman up in Wallingford, Loo?' Sergeant Bartucca said. 'Turned out she was married to two men at the same time.'

'Did one of them kill her?' Merilee asked with keen interest.

'No, she killed both of them, actually,' Tedone said. 'Hoagy, we'll try to make this quick so we don't tire you out. We'll also remove that bullet from your kitchen wall, Miss Nash, if you'll show Sergeant Bartucca where it is.'

'Gladly.'

He removed a pair of latex gloves, a baggie and long tweezers from his jacket pocket and followed her into the kitchen.

'So here we are again,' Tedone grumbled at me.

'Here we are again,' I said, nodding, which was still a mistake. I definitely had something rattling around in there. 'Have a seat, Lieutenant.'

He settled into the wing-backed chair by the fireplace and pulled a notepad from the breast pocket of his jacket, leafing through it. 'Jim Conley ran it for me. Told me that you thought Lulu picked up the scent of someone following you up the mountain. That it was about three o'clock when you reached the ruins, which was when the victim conked you on the head. And that you thought you may have heard voices at some point, though you were pretty out of it by then.'

'Correct. Was the M.E. able to determine a time of death?'

'He told me it's going to be very hard to determine. Austin's body was in full rigor, but it was also lying face down in a forty-five-degree river. My guess? He was killed not long after you got conked on the head that afternoon. Dusk approaches early up in the mountains this time of year. I figure his killer would have wanted to make it back down the mountain trail before darkness settled in. We did find where he bled out – on the dirt path on the path at the top of the falls. Soil's soaked with blood. There were traces of it on the safety railing, too, meaning Austin was murdered there and shoved over the railing. We also found a gazillion shoe prints there from your rescue team, which will most likely make it impossible to isolate the killer's shoe prints. But they had no way of knowing they were compromising a crime scene. All they were thinking about was finding you.' He paused, clearing his throat. 'Deputy Superintendent Mitry has told me to tread very lightly on this one. Austin Talmadge may have been certifiably crazy, in and out of mental hospitals his entire life, but he was also . . .'

'The second richest man in the state of Connecticut.'

Tedone nodded. 'So rich he had the Yale School of Medicine's top child psychiatrist, Dr Annabeth McKenna, on an exclusive personal retainer for a million bucks a year. I just paid a courtesy call on his older brother, Michael . . .'

'Who *is* the richest man in the state of Connecticut.'

'He sure doesn't seem to enjoy his wealth very much. The man was so edgy he was shaking. Have you met him?'

'I have. He may be the most frightened person I've ever come across. He's lived in terror ever since Austin shot him in the head with a pellet gun when they were kids and permanently deafened his left ear. Dr McKenna told me that he suffers from such acute anxiety and panic attacks that not even maximum doses of prescription meds give him a moment's ease. He lives in a high security mansion, employs four ex-Green Berets and a trained attack dog for protection.'

'Yeah, I saw them when I stopped by his place. Right now, they're protecting him from the media people who are swarming his front gate. He likes his privacy, I gather. You know this Dr McKenna?'

'She lives down the road, though I just met her the other day when your higher-ups, including Colin Fielding, the governor's "special envoy" – who was here but wasn't here – decided to "pull the ripcord" and have Michael's A-team capture Austin and escort him to his private sanitarium, from which he promptly escaped, shot some poor guy at the Old Lyme Beach Club, kidnapped Lulu and me, forced us at gunpoint to the top of Mount Creepy, cracked me on the head, locked us in a root cellar for something like sixteen hours and managed to get his throat slit.'

He glared at me. 'Are you done?'

'It was a well-devised operation. I especially like the part where Captain Rundle of Troop F made sure he delivered Austin's toy state police cruiser to his home, keys in the ignition, so that Austin could make a quick getaway. That was really shrewd thinking.'

'*Now* are you done?'

'I guess so, although I reserve the right to get genuinely pissed off again. Annabeth McKenna's in her early forties, a widow with three teenaged kids. The Yale School of Medicine's top child psychiatrist, like you said, which is precisely what she told me Austin was – a child. Michael is, too, in her professional opinion. She described both of them as pre-pubescent.'

'Good-looking woman?'

'What does that have to do with anything?'

Tedone raised his chin at me. 'Just curious.'

'She's quite attractive, as a matter of fact.'

Tedone leafed through his notepad some more, sticking his lower lip in and out. 'As far as persons of interest go, Jim Conley mentioned Austin's cousins, the Hardy Boys . . .?'

'Right. No love lost there. They're here right now putting in Merilee's storm doors and windows.'

'Good. I'll have Ang find out where they were when Austin Talmadge was getting his throat slashed. They're not exactly choirboys, those two. They've had brushes with the law going back to high school – vandalism, criminal trespassing, marijuana possession. They got into a whale of a bar fight a couple of years ago at the Monkey Farm Café. Tony broke a guy's jaw.'

'Have they ever served time?'

'No,' he acknowledged. 'I guess it helps being related to the Talmadge brothers. Even a poor relation.' He glanced back down at his notepad. 'Another person of interest is Donna Noyes.'

'Who is . . .?'

'A grad student in botany at Cornell. She drove down a couple of weeks ago to work on her thesis at her parents' place in Old Lyme. It was pretty late at night by the time she got here. Austin, in his self-appointed role as an auxiliary state policeman, pulled her over, groped her and asked her pervy questions.'

'OK, I heard about this.'

'What you may not have heard is that Donna has a serious anger management problem. Recently had a restraining order filed against her by a guy who she'd been seeing at Cornell. The guy met someone else and wanted to break up with Donna. He claims she physically assaulted him. Also slashed all four tires on his car and left a note on his windshield that said, *Next time this will be your throat, you two-timing bastard!* Interesting choice of words considering what went down, don't you think? I'm told by Jim Conley that she knows the mountain well. Searches for native plant specimens up there. Could be she didn't take too kindly to the way Austin treated her and decided to do something about it. Those voices you thought you heard after Austin dumped you in the root cellar. Could one of them have been a woman's voice?'

I mulled it over. 'It's possible. I really couldn't say for sure.'

He nodded his head slowly before he said, 'OK, now it's your turn.'

'My turn for what, Lieutenant?'

'I'm not sure how you do it, but you and your short friend pick up bits and pieces that I don't. Got anything you care to share?'

'Happy to. Austin claimed to me that one of his brother's ex-Green Berets, Joaquin, kept staring at his pecker after he was captured and thrown in the shower of his personal sanitarium. He also claimed that Joaquin had made sexual advances toward him. There may or may not have been anything to that, but Austin was definitely homophobic. After he escaped from his house all of the bloody mayhem at the Old Lyme Beach Club was triggered, as it were, by Austin witnessing a public display of affection between a pair of young gay guys having lunch out on the deck.'

Tedone nodded. 'Truman Mainwaring, an architect from New York, whose family has a place out here. I've spoken to him at the hospital. He's still pretty doped up. Skip Rimer, his boyfriend or whatever you're supposed to call them this year, was there with him. He's the editor of a men's outdoor magazine. Muscular, macho type. Got real hostile toward me after I discovered from the nursing staff that he left the hospital for several hours while Truman was in surgery. Several hours that happen to coincide with what we're currently figuring is the mid-afternoon time frame when someone was slitting Austin's throat. Rimer refused to tell me where he was. Got real uncooperative.'

'Are you hinting that I, being a fellow New York media type, might have better luck with him when I go back to the hospital to get checked over?'

'Not even maybe,' he said gruffly. 'You are *not* doing this again.'

'Doing what, Lieutenant?'

'Working my case with me.'

'Fine by me. I sensed that you were hinting.'

'I *wasn't* hinting.' He paused, gazing into the fire. 'But Rimer certainly fits the profile. He's in good enough shape to hike seven miles uphill, cut Austin's throat, hurl him into the falls and hike seven miles back.'

'So are the Hardy Boys,' I pointed out. 'They're volunteer firefighters who do a lot of outdoor work. They also grew up here and know that mountain well. Michael Talmadge qualifies as a no. He's too frail. But that doesn't mean he didn't sic one or more of his ex-Green Berets on baby brother to get rid of him once and for all. Did your people find the hunting knife yet?'

Tedone shook his head.

'Did the M.E. provide you with any further details about it?'

'Just that the blade had been recently sharpened. He found traces of mineral oil on the victim's shirt collar. A lot of knife owners use mineral oil when they sharpen a blade on a whetting stone.'

'And what was he able to tell you about the killer?'

'Right-handed. Height's impossible to tell, since the ground's uneven and we don't know whether Austin was standing up, crouching, or on his knees when his throat was cut. He did describe it as a messy kill. A lot of vicious, uneven slashing. Meaning we're probably looking for an amateur, as opposed to a trained killer.'

'Which would rule out one of Michael's guards, such as Joacquin.'

'It might,' Tedone acknowledged. 'Then again, it might not. All of the training in the world can go right out the window if rage takes over.'

'Was the slasher strong?'

'Yes. The cuts are deep. I asked him if a woman could have made them.'

'And . . .?'

'He wouldn't rule it out if she was strong and really pissed off. The victim was a short tub of lard. Easy to overpower.'

'Whoever did it would have been covered with Austin's blood, correct?'

'Undoubtedly.'

'Which means he must have peeled off a layer or two. No way he could risk running into someone on the trail or in the parking lot wearing blood-soaked clothing.'

'Agreed, but the crime scene techies haven't found any bloody clothing so far.'

'He might have buried it.'

'No traces of fresh dug soil anywhere near the crime scene. We have a team of recruits fanned out across the ruins searching. And we're getting warrants to search the residences of the Hardy Boys and Truman Mainwaring. I seriously doubt we'll turn up any bloody clothing, but we might find the hunting knife. Maybe it has sentimental value. I wouldn't bet on it, but we have to cover every single base. That's what police work is,' he said, with a faint bit of reproach in his voice. 'You don't own a hunting knife, do you?'

'What a coincidence. Jim Conley asked me that, too. You guys don't suspect *me* of killing him, do you?'

Tedone mulled it over for a moment. A long moment. 'I don't see how it's possible if you were buried in that root cellar when it happened. Besides, you didn't have any of the victim's blood on you when the rescuers found you.'

'You sound awfully disappointed.'

'Do I?' He glanced down at his notepad. 'It did surprise me to discover that the NYPD has you in their system. Drunk and disorderly, destruction of public property, cocaine possession, assaulting a police officer . . .'

'He poked me in the chest with his big fat finger. I don't like it when people poke me in the chest.'

'It's a pretty impressive list, I gotta say. Yet you always skated. I guess it helps being a famous author.'

'That was a long time ago, Lieutenant,' I said, feeling a sudden tidal wave of fatigue wash over me. 'I'm not that person anymore.'

'Maybe you are, maybe you're not.'

'And in answer to your question, no, I don't own a hunting knife. Haven't got much use for one in the city.'

'Not even for personal protection?'

'I have Lulu for that,' I said, stroking her. 'If anyone tried to lay a hand me they'd be very sorry.'

'If you say so,' he said dubiously.

'I do say so,' I said as I heard footsteps coming from the kitchen.

'Some spackle and paint and it'll be good as new,' Sergeant Bartucca advised Merilee as they joined us. He had the bullet from Austin's revolver tucked in a plastic bag.

'I may just leave it as is,' she responded gaily. 'Makes for a marvelous conversation piece, don't you think?'

'One more question,' Tedone said to me. 'When I was working the Sherbourne Playhouse case you never stopped throwing curve balls at me. You have any other persons of interest who you want to tell me about?'

'He has no one,' Merilee interjected firmly. 'Darling, you're as pale as Casper the Friendly Ghost. I want you to stretch out right this second.'

'OK, you talked me into it.'

'Can you make it to the bedroom on your own?' she asked me.

'I can make it.' I got up slowly and headed off in that direction.

'I guess I tired him out,' I heard Tedone say. 'Sorry.'

'No need to be sorry, Lieutenant,' I heard Merilee say. 'You're just doing your job. Would your wife like some fresh laid eggs?'

Their voices trailed off as I made my way down the hall to the bedroom, feeling the dizziness return. The Hardy Boys had installed the winter storm doors over the French doors in the master bedroom and it was considerably more snug in there. Quiet, too. I made it to the bed and stretched out. Lulu hobbled in, climbed her step stool and parked herself on my hip with her face on my tummy to make sure I didn't go anywhere. I had no immediate plans to. Not the way the room was spinning. A few minutes later Merilee came in, pulled the curtains closed and put a blanket over me. Within ten seconds I was fast asleep.

I awoke with a yelp.

I'd been having a nightmare that I was back down in that black tomb of a root cellar with those heavy stones directly over my head. But no, I was still stretched out on top of Merilee's bed with a blanket over me, Lulu on my hip and the curtains drawn. Safe. I glanced at the bedside clock. I'd been asleep for nearly two hours.

I found Merilee seated at the writing table in the parlor sipping a cup of tea and staring into the fire, lost in thought. She brightened when she looked up and saw me. 'Feel better?'

'Much.'

'How about a cup of tea?'

'I'd love one.' I sat on the sofa. Lulu sprawled out next to me with her tongue hanging out of the side of her mouth. One of her most fetching looks.

Merilee went into the kitchen to put the kettle on as a Volvo station wagon came up the driveway and parked. I heard footsteps on the gravel followed by a discreet tap on the front door. Merilee returned and opened it.

Standing out on the front porch wearing a hooded duffel coat and tight jeans was Dr Annabeth McKenna, who was clutching two large Tupperware containers. 'Merilee, you're back!' she exclaimed in delight.

'Indeed, I am. Mr MacGowan put out a distress call and I got here as fast as I could. It's so good to see you, Annabeth. Come in, come in.'

Annabeth deposited the Tupperware containers on the coffee table before she took off her duffel coat to reveal a tight sweater that did her lean, taut figure no more harm than those jeans did. 'I'm incredibly relieved that you're back. I was so afraid that this helpless man would be fending for himself that I made him a gallon of my chicken noodle soup.'

'From scratch?' I asked as Lulu watched her carefully. Like I said, she's very protective of me when it comes to any attractive female not named Merilee Nash.

'You have to make it from scratch,' Annabeth lectured me. 'Otherwise it has no curative powers.'

'You're a medical doctor. You don't really believe that old wives' tale, do you? Besides, I have a concussion, not croup.'

She shook her rich, chestnut mane at me. 'You're not only helpless, you're hopeless. Old wives' tales are never, ever to be doubted. Sit still, I want to have a look . . .' She came around the sofa to examine my head wound. 'Bandage is nice and clean. That's good.' She fingered it gingerly. 'My God, you must have a dozen staples holding your skull together. That is some laceration. Any dizziness?'

'Yes, but I just took a long nap and feel a lot better.'

'Still, it must ache terribly.'

'Only when I breathe.'

'Are you taking anything for it?'

'Just Tylenol. My doctor wants to examine me again in the morning.'

'Good, good. You're doing everything right. Plus you have the world's best nurse,' she said, smiling at Merilee. 'Mind you, I still think of her as "Our Closer." You should have seen the final speech she delivered at the meeting of the Selden Cove Waterfront Development project. She started in on how it was our sacred duty to preserve this special place that has nurtured countless centuries of wildlife and within thirty seconds she had tears streaming down her face and every developer and lawyer in the room hanging their heads in shame. Some of *them* even started crying. How *did* you do that, Merilee?'

'She can weep on cue. Show her, Merilee.'

My ex-wife glared at me sternly. 'Hoagy, I am not some cheap novelty act. And I didn't fly all of the way here in the middle of the night from Hungary to . . . to perform parlor tricks for . . . for . . .' She broke off as the tears spilled from her eyes and began streaming down her face.

'Remarkable,' Annabeth gasped in amazement.

'That's why they pay her the big bucks. She can also act a little.'

Outside, the Hardy Boys had started hanging the heavy yellow pine storm windows, thudding them into place.

'Join us for a cup of tea, Annabeth,' Merilee said, dabbing at her eyes with a tissue.

'Love to, but I can't stay. I was literally just going to drop this off and . . .' She broke off, suddenly at a loss for words. Or something.

'You must feel totally adrift now that Austin's gone,' I said.

She considered her reply for a moment. 'I do feel a bit disoriented. He's been such a huge part of my life for these past seven years. But mostly I feel racked by guilt.'

'Why do you say that?'

'Because I was responsible for Austin's care once Michael's team delivered him to me at his sanitarium. And I screwed up. I'd been anticipating that he'd be difficult to control, so I'd fully intended to knock him out with a five-milligram intra-muscular injection of Haldol. But after he'd had a shower and shave, put on a pair of pajamas and climbed into bed, he seemed quite calm and composed. Submissive even. So I made the medical decision to opt for a maximum ten-milligram dose of Zolpidem, a powerful, immediate-release sleeping pill they've been using successfully in Europe since 1988. It was just introduced in America this year under the brand name Ambien. My regular nurse, Kate Novak, was visiting her mother in Oregon so I had to use her sub, Eileen Baker. I've used Eileen before with Austin and she's perfectly competent – but not as familiar with how devious he could be. He bamboozled her. Never swallowed the pill. Just spit it out after she'd locked him in his room. When she looked in on him thirty minutes later she reported to me that he was fast asleep, which he wasn't. He was play acting.'

'You say you've used this substitute nurse before?'

'Eileen? Yes. She felt terrible about what happened.'

'Is she a local person?'

'Lives up in East Haddam, I think. Why?'

'Just curious.'

Annabeth let out a sigh of genuine remorse. 'I was responsible for his care, and I blew it. This is my fault. All of it.'

'I think you're being too hard on yourself. If you want to blame anyone, blame the state police for delivering his tricked-out cruiser right to his house, keys in the ignition, instead of impounding it. How stupid was that? And how about that crack team of ex-Green Berets that was stationed in the living room, complete with a guard dog? Heck of a job they did. They let him sneak out of his room, collect his clean clothes and loaded weapon from the laundry room and waltz right out of there. My God, it's almost as if they purposely let him get away.'

Annabeth blinked at me in disbelief. 'They wouldn't actually do that, would they?'

'They do what Michael tells them to do. Maybe Michael *wanted* Austin to escape and wreak havoc. Who knows what goes on in that man's mind?'

'You're very kind, Hoagy, but's no use. I still feel responsible. Yet being totally honest? I also feel a huge sense of relief. Austin was a tremendous burden for seven long years. I've always been on call to rescue him from his latest breakdown and now . . .'

'Now you're not,' Merilee said sympathetically.

'Where were you when he was murdered?'

Annabeth frowned. 'Do they know when it happened?'

'They're guessing some time between three and four o'clock

in the afternoon. Any later than that and the killer would have had to hike down Mount Creepy in the dark.'

Annabeth nodded. 'Makes sense. If that's the case I can tell you exactly where I was – stuck in bumper-to-bumper traffic on the Q Bridge trying to get home from New Haven. I'd been cleaning off the desk in my office at the med school. I don't spend nearly as many hours there as I should.'

'The police didn't want you to stick around here on stand by?'

'Far from it. Jim Conley told me there was nothing I could do. In fact, he gave me the clear impression that I'd just be underfoot. He assured me that when Austin had been corralled they'd contact me.'

'Didn't you find that strange?'

'There's nothing about this that I don't find strange.' She sighed once again. 'It's going to take me a while to adjust to being a normal faculty member. I'll take on some new patients. Devote more time to the Child Guidance Center, not to mention my own unruly brood. And, as a bonus, I'll no longer have to deal with Michael, who I must confess has always given me the willies.'

'Are you still thinking about writing a book about the two of them?'

'I am. Although it's taken quite a different turn.'

'That it has. Might even have a commercial angle now. I'll still be happy to give you any advice I can. Just holler.'

'That would be great, Hoagy. Thank you.'

'And thank *you* for this soup delivery.'

'Yes, thanks so much, Annabeth,' Merilee said.

'It was nothing. The least I could do. And now I'll leave you two.' She smiled at Merilee. 'When do you have to go back?'

'Soon. They can shoot around me for a few days, but if I stay away any longer it'll start costing them money and I'll suddenly develop a reputation for being *difficult*.' Merilee helped Annabeth on with her duffel coat and walked her out to her car, then returned and settled on the sofa next to me. 'Well, well . . . Well, well, well . . .'

'Well, well, well . . . what?'

'Our Dr McKenna has designs on you, mister.'

'Don't be silly. I just met her the other day. We've now had a grand total of two ten-minute conversations.'

'Sometimes that's all it takes.'

'Are you saying this because she made me chicken noodle soup? She was just being neighborly.'

'Neighborly my Aunt Fanny.'

'I've missed your quaint little expressions.'

'She must have stayed up half of the night making that soup. And did you see what she had on? *Everything* good and tight to show off her figure, which is quite excellent, I must admit. She was also wearing blusher, mascara and lipstick. Also a hint of essential lavender oil. A very elegant scent.'

'Well it was wasted on me. All I can smell is eucalyptus.'

'Take it from me, that was not a casual neighborly drop by. That was an attractive, unattached woman trolling for a man.'

'Why, Merilee Gilbert Nash, are you actually jealous?'

'I'm watchful. She's lonely and has, no doubt, encountered a dearth of intelligent, age-appropriate men. Especially tall, good-looking ones who happen to be extraordinarily gifted.'

Lulu coughed.

'Oh, dear, that dampness got into her chest,' Merilee said fretfully.

'No, she's fine. You calling me "extraordinarily gifted" tickled her funny bone, that's all.'

'Dogs have funny bones?'

'Of course.' I took her hand and squeezed it. 'I think maybe you like me a little.'

'What gives you that idea?'

'The way you came rushing home to take care of me. And furnished the office in your apartment for me. Also that wild monkey sex we had the night you left for Budapest.'

She blushed. 'I was a bit tipsy.'

'Does that mean it was an aberration?'

'God, I certainly hope not.'

I reached over and stroked her cheek. 'Good. So do I.'

'Meanwhile, I have to go back to Budapest, then to London, then on to Pamplona for the bullfighting sequences. And who knows what will happen while I'm gone?'

'I can tell you exactly what'll happen. Our short-legged friend and I will go back to the city as soon as Dr Eng gives me the OK and I'll go back to work. That'll never be possible if I stay out here. When I was surrounded by eight million people in the Naked City I was left completely alone. Out here I haven't had a moment's peace,' I said as a convoy of vehicles came speeding up the driveway. 'See what I mean?'

'Who on earth is this?' Merilee asked, gazing out the front window at the three black Chevy Suburbans that had pulled in behind the Hardy Boys' pickup.

'That, my dearest dear, is none other than Michael Talmadge, accompanied by his ex-Green Beret security detail and Pinkie, their extremely scary German Shepherd. Although I still think Pinkie is a wussie name for an attack dog.'

'What do you suppose *he* wants?'

'Only one way to find out,' I said as there was a knock on the front door.

Merilee got up and opened it. One of Michael's bodyguards stood there.

'Good afternoon, Miss Nash. Mr Talmadge was wondering if he could speak with your husband.'

'He's my ex-husband, and he's still not feeling a hundred percent. Please wait, I'll ask him.' She swung the door shut. 'Can you handle another visitor?'

'Let him in. But please ask his guards and Pinkie to wait outside.'

Merilee opened the door and repeated what I'd said. A moment later, car doors opened and closed. And then, a long moment after that, Michael Talmadge stood there by himself in the doorway wearing that same ill-fitting gray flannel suit he'd had on when they'd decided to 'pull the ripcord' – or another one just like it. Also another frayed, yellowing white button-down shirt that was a size too large around his neck and another clip-on tie. Same matching gray hair, complexion and teeth.

Over his shoulder I could see the Hardy Boys gazing at him wide-eyed from their ladders near the front porch.

'You must be Miss Nash,' he said in his thin, reedy voice. 'I'm Michael Talmadge.'

'Please come in, Mr Talmadge. But do try to keep it short. Hoagy's recovering from a concussion.'

'So I understand. I'm terribly sorry.' He came in, moving in that frail, unsteady way of his, and gazed around the parlor. 'The Winthrops were quite wealthy, but didn't go in for grandeur. Still, one could be very comfortable here.'

'We like it,' Merilee said, treating him to a smile.

He looked at Lulu on the sofa with her bandaged paws and, finally, at me. 'I'm probably the last person in the world who you want to see right now.'

'No, not at all, Mr Talmadge,' I assured him, intensely curious to hear what he had to say. 'Please, sit down. Would you like some tea?'

'Nothing, thanks,' he said, his pale tongue flicking at dry lips. He selected the chair Merilee used at her writing table so that his right ear, the functioning one, would be best positioned to hear me, then sat and immediately began to tremble. Austin was in a body bag at the M.E.'s headquarters in Farmington and yet still he trembled. 'I've come to apologize to you for the harrowing ordeal you and your dog were subjected to through absolutely no fault of your own. It didn't sit right with me. Needed to tell you how sorry I am, face to face.'

'That's very kind of you, Mr Talmadge. But it's really not necessary.'

'No, I assure you it is. I've instructed a member of my business staff to contact Dr Jen, the village vet, as well as the billing office at Middlesex Hospital. I'm covering every penny of your expenses.'

'Also not necessary. I'm not a charity case.'

'I'm well aware of that,' he said, glancing over at the world-famous movie star in the room. 'But I need to do it.' He reached a shaky hand into the breast pocket of his suit jacket, removed an envelope and held it out to me. 'I also wanted to give you this.'

Merilee got up off of the sofa, grabbed it and passed it to me. I opened it. Inside I found a check from the Talmadge Investment Group made out to me in the amount of $100,000.

'I can't accept this, sir,' I said.

'Yes, you can. Look at it this way – you'll be doing me and my conscience a huge favor if you do.'

'Sorry, I can't help you. Or your conscience.'

'Will you at least hold on to it? Perhaps you'll change your mind.'

'OK, but I'm not going to change my mind.'

'May I inquire as to how you're doing? You haven't suffered any permanent physical damage, have you?'

'I'll be fine. So will Lulu. But how about you, sir?'

He furrowed his brow. 'Me? Whatever do you mean?'

'You've lived in terror of your brother for your entire life. And yet, even though he's gone, you've still shown up here with four ex-Green Berets and an attack dog. Why?'

'You pose an interesting question.'

'Thank you, I try.'

'Forgive me for smiling.' He wasn't smiling. 'But you no doubt think that this must rank as a joyous day for me. At long last, I'm free of him. I no longer have to hide in my fortress of a home. Can just walk right out my front door, jump in a convertible like that beauty of a Jaguar you have and go zipping around Lyme with the top down like a normal person. But I assure you that nothing could be further from the truth.'

'Why, Mr Talmadge?' Merilee wondered.

'Because I could be next,' he answered darkly.

I tugged at my ear. 'Next?'

'Indeed. What if this wasn't someone getting even with Austin for his deplorable behavior? What if it was actually targeted because of his immense wealth? If so, then his killer is very likely planning to come after me next. Great wealth creates great resentment. There are those who despise people such as me.'

'I see . . .' So the terror lived on, Austin or no Austin. Did Michael have a genuine reason to be afraid, or did he simply know of no other way to exist? I wondered what Annabeth McKenna would have to say about that. 'Mr Talmadge, do you have a woman in your life?'

'I have never had a woman in my life,' he stated flatly. 'I was too afraid of what Austin might do to her.'

'Austin's not around anymore. You're free to take up with anyone you choose, provided she doesn't mind living in a high-security fortress and traveling with an armed security detail. But I suppose that's not so unusual these days among people of great wealth.'

'I know several stars who never go anywhere without a team of bodyguards,' Merilee said. 'Especially if they have children.'

'I have always wanted to find a woman with whom I could share my life,' Michael admitted. 'But how can I be sure that she isn't merely after my money?'

'By choosing someone who has money of her own.'

'You make a wise point, sir.'

'Would you like to have children?' Merilee asked him.

His eyes widened in horror. 'Never. These genes must never be passed along or we could end up with another Austin. No, I'll likely remain a bachelor for the remainder of my days. It's probably for the best. I'm rather set in my ways.'

'Do you have a circle of male friends?' I asked him.

'I have colleagues. I have no friends. In fact, I'm not sure I even know what it means to have a friend. And now I shall leave you nice people in peace,' he said, getting slowly up out of his chair. 'I've taken up enough of your time.'

'It was kind of you to stop by,' Merilee said as she led him toward the door. 'And I'm sorry for your loss.'

He frowned at her. 'My loss?'

'Your brother Austin.'

'Miss Nash, an angry, tormented psychotic was put out of his misery. I don't consider that a loss. Whoever killed Austin did him a favor,' he said as he walked unsteadily out the door toward his waiting convoy.

Merilee watched the Suburbans turn around and speed away before she closed the door. I sat there inspecting Michael's check for a hundred thou.

'What are you going to do with it?' she asked me.

'Hand it to you.'

'And what am I going to do with it?'

'Put it in the fire.'

She narrowed her green eyes at me. 'Are you sure?'

'I've never been more sure of anything.'

She crumpled it up and tossed it in the fire. 'I knew you wouldn't keep it.'

'How?'

'It's blood money. You're very moral, in your own way. It's one of the things I love most about you, you know.'

'Really? I had no . . .' I trailed off. The room had started to spin again.

She studied me with concern. 'Darling, are you fading on me again?'

I didn't nod my head. I'd learned not to do that by now.

'You've had a lot of visitors. Maybe you should lie down.'

'Maybe I should.' I got up, made my way back to the bedroom and stretched out. Lulu hobbled in after me, climbed her stool and curled up on my hip. My dizzy spell soon subsided.

Merilee came in with a glass of water and two Tylenol. After I'd taken them she stretched out next to me, yawning. 'I'm a bit jet-lagged myself. I'm not even sure what day this is anymore.'

We lay there in blessed country silence for a few moments. Right up until the Hardy Boys resumed thudding the storm windows into place.

She let out a weary laugh. 'Shall I send them away?'

'No, never. They're *here*. There's no telling if we'll be able to get them to come back.'

'You don't suppose they killed Austin, do you?'

'Tedone considers them persons of interest. Austin poisoned their dog when they were kids.'

'What an awful thing to do.'

'He was an awful person. Yet I found him strangely pathetic, too.'

She took my hand. 'You and Lulu could come visit me in Budapest, you know.'

'I appreciate the invite, and I'd love to be with you, but I'm a man on a mission. I haven't felt this excited at the typewriter in a long, long time.'

'I'm so happy for you, darling. Can't wait to read it.' She turned on her side, studying my face. 'Do you know yet?'

I lay there getting lost in her green eyes. 'Do I know what?'

'Who Austin's murderer is.'

'I'm the guy who's concussed, remember? It's still a major challenge to figure out how to spell "world" backwards. Besides, that's Lieutenant Tedone's job, not mine.'

'So you're not going to get involved this time?'

'That's correct.'

She reached over and stroked my forehead gently with her fingers. 'That's another one of the things I love best about you.'

'What is?'

'You're such a terrible liar.'

SIX

For dinner we had Annabeth's chicken noodle soup, which I must admit was the best I've ever eaten. The chicken tasted like actual chicken. The vegetables were fresh, noodles firm. Merilee agreed, although she was just a bit more restrained in her enthusiasm, I couldn't help notice. We ate it at the kitchen table with Pilot crackers, a green salad and a bottle of Chianti. I was allowed only one small glass. Merilee was very insistent about that. She also sent me straight to bed while she did the dishes, fed Lulu and closed up the house for the night.

It was nice and warm in the old farmhouse with the storm windows back up. When they left for the day the Hardy Boys promised they'd come back tomorrow to check the new glazing compound they'd applied and put a coat of primer on it. Tony told me that back when they'd first started out doing handyman jobs, glazing compound took two whole weeks to cure before it was dry enough to prime. Now they made this new-fangled stuff that actually cured overnight. I'd never heard anyone talk so excitedly about glazing compound before.

I definitely needed to get back to the city.

I was fast asleep by the time Merilee joined me. I don't even remember her coming to bed. What I do remember is that some time during the night I became aware that she'd snuggled close to me in the darkness, thrown her bare leg over mine and was stroking my face gently. I stroked hers, put my arms around her and held her close, never wanting to let her go. Not ever. Then her mouth found mine and we lay there kissing and kissing until she reached down in search of what had started growing down there, helped it to grow a good deal larger with some deft, artful strokes and slid me deep inside of her.

Home.

We didn't so much as move a muscle for a good, long while. Just savored the bliss of the moment. When we finally did move we took our time, and if arriving at our destination had ever been any sweeter I sure couldn't recall it. I was still inside of her when her breathing got deeper and slower and she drifted off to sleep, purring softly like a big cat. I was awake a few moments longer in a state of profound contentment before I dropped off, too.

I was so sound asleep the next morning that I don't remember Merilee getting up to feed Lulu and put the coffee on. It was the delicious smell of the coffee that woke me. I was still right where she'd left me when she came in carrying a tray laden with two glasses of orange juice, two huge, steaming mugs of rich, strong cappuccino and toasted English muffins with blackberry jam. She was wearing her silk target dart dressing gown, the one that used to be mine until she stole it because it looked better on her than it did on me. Her waist-length golden hair was brushed out. Her cheeks were aglow. She'd never looked lovelier.

She set the tray down on her dresser and threw open the drapes over the French doors to reveal the autumn sun rising over Whalebone Cove. Lulu hobbled in and climbed back on to the bed, her tail thumping.

I sat up, drank my juice, then took a grateful gulp of the hot cappuccino.

'Ready for your English muffin, darling?'

'Not just yet,' I said, gazing at her.

'You look rather pleased with yourself this morning,' she observed, sipping her cappuccino.

'My headache is gone.'

'Is that all?'

'My dizziness is gone.'

'Is that all?'

'I also had the most wonderful dream in the night.'

She set the plate of English muffins on the bed and climbed back in, kissing me lightly on the mouth. 'That, sir, was no dream.'

'Have I told you recently how much I adore you?'

'No, you haven't. Not since November the third, 1982. We

were in a Checker cab riding home from Elaine's. There was a light rain falling. Our driver, Louie, had lived in Canarsie his entire life.'

'You're making all of this up.'

'Am not. I have a photographic memory when it comes to historic moments.'

'In fairness to me, we weren't speaking to each other for several years after that.'

She waved me off. 'Incompetent, irrelevant, immaterial.'

'Well, I do. Adore you, that is.'

'Good.'

'*Good?* That's all you have to say?'

'Why, were you expecting something more – such as "I adore you, too, darling"?'

'Well, kind of.'

'Sorry, you'll have to wait until November of 2004.'

'Suits me.' I bit into an English muffin. 'I can wait.'

'Oh, I see. Playing the lone rider of Santa Fe now, are we?'

'Nope, the romantic. You've just acknowledged aloud, in front of a four-footed witness, that we'll still be together in eleven years.'

Her eyes widened. 'Good gravy. I did, didn't I?'

'Possibly you need more coffee.'

'And you need to shower and dress. Eng.'

'Eng?'

'You have an appointment to see her this morning at eight thirty, remember?'

It was a mild morning. Low forties, no frost. Supposed to top off in the mid-fifties by the afternoon. I carefully removed the bandage from my head and – with the aid of Merilee's adjustable dressing table mirrors – inspected my staples, raw flesh and partially shaved skull. I looked like a character in one of those cheesy old mad scientist movies about brain transplants that I used to love watching when I was a kid. Actually I still love watching them.

After I'd showered, washing and drying my head wound carefully, I put on a fresh bandage. Then I stropped grandfather's razor, shaved and powdered my neck with Floris No.

89 talc powder. I stayed in character in a T-shirt, torn jeans, my Chippewas and leather flight jacket.

After her shower, Merilee dressed a tad more elegantly in a white silk blouse, burgundy cashmere cardigan and pleated gray flannel trousers.

By the time we left for the hospital the Hardy Boys had arrived and Gas was up on a ladder with a paint can and brush putting a coat of primer on the glazing compound.

'Morning!' he called to me. 'How are you feeling today?'

'Much better, thanks. In fact, I'm sure I'll feel well enough to apply the top coat tomorrow if you guys have another job to get to.'

'No, sir,' Tony said firmly. 'When we start a job, we finish it. Besides, I'm under strict orders from Miss Nash to keep you away from ladders.'

'Far, far way,' she chimed in.

I still hadn't been medically cleared to drive so Merilee got behind the wheel of the Jag while I rode shotgun. Lulu hobbled slowly across the gravel on her bandaged paws, settled in my lap and off we went.

'I'll take her to the vet when we get back to have her paws checked,' Merilee said. 'You'll probably be needing a nap.'

'Don't think so. I feel tip top today.'

'Nonetheless, I don't want you to overdo it.'

'Yes, Mommy.'

She stuck her tongue out at me. My real Mommy never did that.

As we zipped by Mr MacGowan's farmhouse, twisting our way past fieldstone walls, meadows, gnarly apple tree orchards and an array of country houses, large and small, my eyes searched for Annabeth McKenna's antique yellow saltbox on the right. Merilee made it easy for me when she slowed up and pulled into her circular driveway. Annabeth hadn't been kidding. I'd driven by it a million times. I'd just never noticed it before because of all of the overgrown privet, forsythia and mountain laurel that shielded it from the road. She also hadn't been kidding about its state of decrepitude. It needed a new roof, a paint job and its wooden foundation sills looked crumbly with dry rot. No one appeared to be home. Her Volvo was gone. Merilee jumped out and left Annabeth's Tupperware soup containers on the front porch with a thank-you note inside. Then she got back in and off we sped.

'Did you know her husband?'

'Not really,' Merilee said, downshifting as she negotiated a steep downhill curve. 'I saw him jogging a few times. He'd wave, I'd wave.'

'Annabeth told me he was a classics scholar. They met when they were Yale undergrads.' On Merilee's silence I added, 'I still can't figure her out.'

'What's to figure out?'

'Why she agreed to treat Austin.'

'I can think of exactly one million reasons.'

'So you really think she just did it for the money?'

'And the sense of security. She has three teenaged kids to put through college and zero chance of finding another husband.'

'What makes you say that?'

'Because Annabeth isn't who men your age are looking for.'

'Who are we . . .?'

'Cindy Crawford, Christy Turlington, Kathy Ireland, Linda Evangelista . . . Need I go on?'

'You need not. And we're not all like that. Take this reporter, for instance. I have zero interest in spending my time with a twenty-something swimsuit model who thinks that a pimple is a global crisis. I'd much rather be with you.'

'Even though I'm over forty?'

'Even though you're over forty. Want to know why?'

'I'm all ears, handsome.'

'Because talent is sexy. Having ideas and opinions is sexy. Having life experience and wisdom and compassion is sexy.'

She glanced over at me expectantly.

I frowned. 'What . . .?'

'Nothing, darling. I was just hoping you had another dozen or so items on your list. But I'll settle for whatever I can get.'

She dropped us at the main entrance to the hospital and kept on going. There was a great family-owned Italian market a few blocks from there, and she wanted to stock up on crusty bread, fresh mozzarella, sausage and whatever other goodies she could find. I encouraged her to take as much time as she wanted.

I had other business to take care of while I was there.

I found a wheelchair inside the front door, plopped Lulu down in it and pushed her down a maze of corridors to the elevator. Middlesex was a big hospital and Dr Eng's office was much too long a walk for her to make on her bandaged paws. I did get my share of odd looks from people as I rolled her along. Clearly, they thought that I was crazy. I wasn't bothered in the least. Authors are expected to be crazy. It's one of the genuine perks of the profession.

Dr Eng examined my head wound and said it was healing nicely so far. She checked my pupil responses with her penlight. Then she ordered me to keep my eyes locked on hers while she held her hands out at arm's length and asked me numerous times how many fingers she was holding up. I passed with flying colors.

'And you say you have no headache this morning?'

'None. And the dizziness is gone. I feel much, much better.'

'That's wonderful. But I still want you to take it easy. Get plenty of rest. Take walks to keep up your stamina, but no strenuous exercise for another week. And be mindful of your balance.'

'When can I start driving?'

'You're an intelligent, self-aware man,' she said, ignoring Lulu's discreet cough. 'You can start making short, local trips today. But I'd stay off of the highway for a while. There's too much happening too fast. Needless to say – but I'm going to say it anyway – if you feel even the slightest trace of dizziness you should pull over, find a pay phone and call your wife.'

'Ex-wife. How long do these staples have to stay in?'

'Another week or so.'

'I intend to be back in New York City by then.'

'In that case your primary care physician can remove them.'

I thanked her for taking such good care of me, wheeled Lulu to the nurses' station and asked where I could find Truman Mainwaring.

Truman was up on the fourth floor in a sunny private room. Not that he knew it. He was deeply sedated, his left shoulder and clavicle heavily bandaged. He was young, in his late twenties, and wore his long blond hair in a ponytail.

Skip Rimer, who was also in his late twenties, was seated in a chair next to him, reading a collection of essays by Edward Abbey. When I wheeled Lulu in, Skip looked up with an expression on his face that was unfriendly, bordering on hostile. He was a clenched fist of a Yushie with curly black hair, a three or four-day growth of beard and power lifter biceps that he was so proud of he'd cut the sleeves off of his *Man's Man* magazine sweatshirt and adorned his bulging muscles with barbed wire tattoos, which was a hot new look among New York City's Young Urban Shitheads, both gay and straight.

'Want something?' he demanded, sticking his stubbly chin out at me.

'I was downstairs having my head wound attended to. Just thought I'd stop by and see how Truman is doing. I'm Stewart Hoag.'

His eyes widened. 'The writer?'

'I'm *a* writer. I don't know if I'm *the* writer.'

Skip's face broke into a grin. 'Damn, you talk exactly like you write,' he said as he stood up and shook my hand. He was a short stack, no more than five feet six, but he had one hell of a handshake. 'I'm a huge admirer of *Our Family Enterprise.* I keep hoping you'll write another novel.'

'You and me both.'

'You found that nut job's body, didn't you? Had been trapped in some kind of root cellar all night.' He glanced down at the wheelchair. 'Wow, this must be the famous Lulu.' He reached down and patted her head. She sat up, sniffed his fingers with intense interest for a moment before she settled back down, totally calm. Evidently, it wasn't Skip who'd followed us to the top of the mountain that day. Then again, it was possible that she was playing it cool, which she's been known to do. Crafty. She's crafty.

'That homicide lieutenant, Tedone, told me her paws got messed up really bad tunneling you out of there. Is she going to be OK?'

'The vet thinks so.' I glanced over at Truman. 'How about him?'

Skip grimaced, his eyes moistening. 'The bullet shattered Tru's clavicle. A surgeon had to piece it back together with all sorts of pins and screws. It'll be a while before we know if he'll regain full mobility and strength in his shoulder. Are the doctors out here any good?'

'They know what they're doing. I wouldn't worry about that.'

'Let me tell you, bro,' he said. 'You have no idea how lucky you are.'

'Not feeling very lucky right now.'

'No, you are. Total strangers don't hate you on sight.'

'That's true. They usually wait until they get to know me better.'

'Gay people don't *choose* to be gay. We just are who we are.'

'And Austin Talmadge was who he was – a highly unstable delusional psychotic.'

'As if I give a damn,' Skip shot back furiously. He gazed over at Truman, who remained fast asleep, before he turned back to me, softening. 'Hey, listen, if you ever feel like writing an article for my magazine, I'd love to publish it. Your name on the cover of *Man's Man* would give our marketing and sales people a major thrill. We're mostly about extreme fitness. But we also do front-of-the-book stories on clothing, wristwatches, hair and skin care – anything and everything that goes into being the properly outfitted man. Which, I mean, you're famous for. I am loving your antique motorcycle jacket.'

'Flight jacket. It's a 1933 Werber's. Bought it in a junk store up in Provincetown one summer when I was in college.'

'And you're still wearing it? Damn, that's a thousand-word story right there. Our readers would eat it up, I'm telling you. See, I'm all about trying to help guys find their own individual style as opposed to just fitting in with everyone else's. That's my guiding philosophy. And I can't believe I'm standing here talking to *Stewart Hoag* about it. I also can't believe I neglected to ask how *you* are feeling.'

'I have a concussion and a head laceration that's held

together with a set of staples that make me feel like Boris Karloff on a bad hair day. But the doctor thinks I'm doing well, thanks. Just figured I'd stop by and pay my respects while I was here. I heard about Truman yesterday when Lieutenant Tedone descended on me at my ex-wife's farm in Lyme.'

'I didn't care for that bastard's attitude at all. He clearly can't stand gays. I suggested he take his homophobic ass and get the hell out of here. What Tru needs right now is positive energy, you know?'

'I do. I came in contact with Tedone on another case over the summer that involved theater people. Noticed right away that he didn't care for gay men. But the guy's been real unpleasant toward me, too. He's a homicide detective. They don't get paid to be cuddly.'

'I hear you,' Skip said with a grudging nod. 'So he questioned you?'

'He did. Seemed real annoyed that he couldn't get a word out of me. But I was buried in that root cellar, unconscious, so how could I possibly be able to . . .?' I broke off, shuddering. 'Sorry, that damned cellar still freaks me out.'

'I can imagine,' Skip said sympathetically.

'He told me he couldn't get a word out of you either.'

Skip narrowed his gaze. 'A word about what?'

'Where you were when Austin was getting his throat slit. He claims the nurses told him you weren't here.'

'He doesn't think *I* did it, does he?'

'You certainly qualify as a suspect. You must be aware of that.'

'Tru was being prepped for surgery. I was climbing the walls. His surgeon told me it would be a lengthy procedure but that Tru wasn't in any danger and that there was no reason for me to stick around. So I went back to his folks' place on Cove Road. They have an apartment in the city, too. His father's a Wall Street guy. He put up the seed money for my magazine, in fact. Their house has a full gym in the basement, so I blew off some steam. Pumped iron and used the treadmill for a couple of hours. Then I came back here.'

'Did any of the neighbors see you?'

'No disrespect, but why does it feel like you're interrogating me?'

'Actually, I'm trying to give you a heads-up. I've had to tangle with the law myself more than a few times.'

'That's for damned sure. I've been reading about the insane messes you're always getting yourself into ever since I was a little kid.'

'Thank you large for mentioning it, Skippy.'

He reddened. 'No offense intended. I just meant . . .'

'I know how their so-called minds work, OK? When we were hiking up the mountain Lulu got a whiff of someone tailing us. This would have been maybe a couple of hours before the killing. Since you weren't here, they're going to wonder whether you could have driven to Mount Creepy in time to catch up with us on that trail. It's, what, a thirty-minute drive from here to the mountain? And I stalled Austin at Merilee's farm for as long as I could when he showed up after the shooting. The little tubbo put away an entire half-gallon of rocky road. So time is not on your side. You're in play, except for the how.'

Skip shook his head. 'The how?'

'How would you have known where Austin had taken us? Unless, that is, did you speak to the resident trooper?'

Skip stood there in uncomfortable silence, his jaw muscles clenching and unclenching. 'I did phone the resident trooper,' he admitted.

'From here?'

'That's right. He told me that a neighbor had heard gunfire at Merilee Nash's farm and that your car was there but you weren't. The resident trooper was convinced that Austin had snatched you and Lulu and was heading for Mount Creepy to hide out.'

'Did you jump in your car and head there yourself?'

'No!' he insisted angrily, his biceps bulging. 'I *told* you, I went to Tru's folks' house and worked out in the basement.'

'Weren't you tempted to go there?'

'You mean like Rambo or something? I'm a magazine editor, not a Sly Stallone character. I worked out and came straight back here from the house. Didn't stop for gas or a meal along

the way. Didn't see a soul. Tru was still in the recovery room.
I hung around until they sent me home. Came back in the
morning.' Skip stuck his stubbly chin out at me again. 'I'm
telling you the truth. You believe me, don't you?'

'I have no reason not to.'

He glanced fondly over at his lover. 'Tru's going to be super
sorry he missed meeting you. You're one of his idols.'

'Please give him my best regards for a speedy recovery.'

'I will.' Skip dug his business card out of his wallet and
handed it to me. 'And I wasn't kidding. I'd love to publish
that article about your vintage motorcycle jacket.'

'Flight jacket.'

'Or anything else you feel like writing.'

'I'll be sure to keep it in mind,' I said as I wheeled Lulu
out the door to the elevator and rode it down to the ground
floor.

We were making our way toward the hospital's main
entrance when Merilee flung open the door to one of the
telephone booths there and waved to me. 'Please hang on a
sec, Jeff . . .' She put her hand over the mouthpiece. 'I'm
talking to my agent. What did Dr Eng say?'

'I'm doing great. She cleared me to start driving.'

'That's wonderful news, darling . . . Jeff? He just got a
clean bill of health, so tell them I'm on my way.' Then she
said goodbye, hung up and joined us with an extremely glum
expression on her face. 'The doo-doo has hit the fan in
Budapest. They've run out of scenes to film without me. I
have to be on a six o'clock flight tonight out of JFK. The
studio is sending a car and driver out to pick me up at two
o'clock.'

I felt an ache in my chest. 'I was hoping you could stay a
bit longer.'

'So was I, believe me. But I'm under contract. I have to go
back.'

'Of course you do. And you'll never know how much
it meant to see you sitting there by my hospital bed when I
woke up.'

She gazed at me with those green eyes of hers. 'You're my
man. Wild white horses couldn't keep me away.' She glanced

at the clock on the wall. It was not yet ten a.m. 'I got us all kinds of goodies for lunch. We still have plenty of time left. I'll take Lulu to see Dr Jen while you get some rest.'

'I can take her after you leave.'

'No, I want to do my part. I insist. Wait right here, OK? I'll go get the car and pull up outside. Make straight for the car with the wheelchair and ignore the noise.'

'What noise?'

'The media horde is back, I'm afraid. Times ten.'

I waited for her to pull up outside the door in the Jag, then pushed Lulu out the handicapped access door and made straight for it, paying no mind to the microphones that were being shoved in my face by the multitude of TV reporters. Although I did notice that *Entertainment Tonight* and *Inside Edition* were in on the action now.

'*How does the head feel, Hoagy?*'

'*Hey, Merilee, is it true they fired you for walking off the production?*'

'*Hey, Hoagy, did Austin Talmadge torture you?*'

'*What did he do to your dog?*'

'*Merilee, we hear Sigourney Weaver's replacing you. Any comment?*'

'*What did he do to your dog?*'

I opened the car door, hoisted Lulu out of the wheelchair and into the passenger seat. Sent the wheelchair rolling toward the front entrance, climbed in, wrestled Lulu into my lap, slammed the door and off we sped, leaving them in our wake as I sat there inhaling the wonderful fragrance of the Italian groceries that were stowed behind the front seats.

Merilee steered us on to Route 9 and headed for home. 'Here's what I'm thinking, darling. After I take Lulu to the vet we'll treat ourselves to a stroll down to Whalebone Cove followed by the world's greatest lunch.'

'Don't you have to pack?'

She let out a snort. 'I'm an old trouper. I can be ready to go in less than ten minutes.'

When we arrived back at the farm a half-dozen more TV news crew vans were lining Joshua Town Road and a different state trooper with a somewhat less blocky head was parked in front of the gate. He waved and backed up so that we could pass on through. The Hardy Boys had finished with their priming and had taken off. We had the place to ourselves. Sort of. Merilee and Lulu stayed put in the car while I got out and gathered up the grocery bags filled with two loaves of fresh baked bread, fresh mozzarella, sausage and other goodies. Then I kicked the door shut and off they sped to visit Dr Jen.

I headed for the kitchen by way of the mudroom door. Was busy depositing containers of olives, roasted peppers and marinated artichokes in the refrigerator when Merilee's unlisted business line rang. I answered it.

'How are you feeling, dear boy?' It was my agent, the Silver Fox. She'd finished reading the hundred new pages I'd sent her. I could tell from the tone in her voice. Right away, I felt a nervous uptick in my pulse.

'I'll be fine. Lulu got the worst of it, actually.'

'But your head's clear?'

'Absolutely.'

'Listen, I've read these pages of yours . . .'

'Do they seem OK to you?'

'That's a bit of an understatement, dear boy. I'm still tingling with excitement. It's a masterpiece in progress. You *have* to finish it.'

'I intend to,' I said, maintaining a calm, steady voice even though I felt like dancing a jig around the kitchen. And I don't even know how to dance a jig.

'How far along do you think you are?'

'Maybe halfway. Can't tell for sure. I'm still peeling the onion.'

'Well, keep peeling. Hold nothing back. Publishers are begging for big books this season, nothing but big books, so if you end up with more than 400 pages it won't be a deterrent, understand?'

'I understand. Thank you for taking the time to read it, Alberta.'

'It was a privilege. I'm so thrilled that you've found your voice again, and that it's bursting with so much confidence, maturity and brilliance.'

'Stop it, will you? You know how easily my head swells.'

She let out a laugh. 'Goodbye, dear boy. Feel better.'

I hung up the phone and finished putting the groceries away, beaming. The Silver Fox was famous for her blunt honesty. She didn't toss praise around lightly. I went in the bedroom and stretched out, feeling elated, not fatigued, but Dr Eng wanted me to take it easy and I was raring to hit the ground running when I went back to work. Motivated beyond belief now.

Merilee wasn't at the vet with Lulu for long. I got up to greet them when I heard the Jag's throaty roar come up the driveway. Lulu hopped out, moving much more nimbly.

'Dr Jen's very pleased,' Merilee reported. 'She gave her smaller bandages that have little cushions to make walking more comfortable. Her New York vet can remove them in about a week.'

'Or maybe my doctor can do it after he takes my staples out.'

She gazed at me, smiling. 'You, sir, just got some good news.'

'How can you tell?'

'Because your eyes are sparkling.'

'Alberta loved the pages I sent her. The words "masterpiece in progress" were even bandied about.'

Merilee rushed to me and hugged me tightly. 'Darling, I'm *so* proud of you.'

'Mind you, I still have a long, long way to go.'

'But I know how much her feedback means. Do you feel like taking a short walk before lunch?'

'I do. I want to keep up my stamina.'

'Good. Dr Jen wants Lulu up and walking, too. Said she'll turn into a sub-compact automobile if she doesn't.'

We three started our way down to the cove.

'Feeling OK, darling? Not tired out or dizzy?'

'I'm fine,' I said as Lulu walked gamely along with us. 'It feels good to be out and about, doesn't it, girl?'

Lulu let out a low whoop of assent.

Merilee had grabbed a pair of baskets from the barn. When we reached the orchards she paused to pick some apples and pears for me to take back to New York, filling them to the brim. We shared a crisp, juicy Macoun, my favorite variety of apple, as we resumed our stroll.

'I spoke to Kate on the phone while you were napping yesterday,' she informed me off-handedly. 'Kate' would be Katherine Hepburn, who lived in a shorefront mansion in the Fenwick enclave across the Connecticut River in Old Saybrook. The two of them had become friends. Kate was a fan of Merilee's work. And Merilee worshipped her, as did every actress on the planet. 'I told her that Brett doesn't seem real to me.'

'What did she say?'

Merilee went into her drop-dead impersonation of Kate, trembly voice and all. 'Then *make* her real, by golly. If you're not happy, take charge. Fight for her. They'll call you a bitch behind your back. Let 'em! It's *your* face that's up there on that fifty-foot screen!'

'I like that woman.'

For all of my bold talk I got tired a lot sooner than I expected and we started back to the house. I sat at the kitchen table while Merilee sliced the bread, salami and cheese and laid out our antipasti feast. Lulu stretched out under the table with her head on my foot. She was pooped, too.

As soon as Merilee sat down I dove in, sampling this and that. All of it was amazingly good.

'If you want to work on your book here, please don't hesitate to come back,' she said as she devoured some fresh mozzarella on a slice of bread. 'I want you to think of this as your home. The apartment, too.'

I studied her curiously. 'What are you saying exactly?'

She lowered her gaze. 'That I guess I don't understand anymore why we're not together. You're *that* man, again.'

'What man?'

'The man I fell in love with. The only man I want to be with. I enjoyed every minute that we spent together over the summer. I missed you as soon as you went back to New York. I've missed you every day in Budapest. I think about you all of the time.'

I put my hand over hers and gazed deeply into her green

eyes. 'Are you sure you're not just saying this because I have staples in my head?'

She let out a laugh, her eyes welling with tears. 'Positive. When I'm done with this movie, maybe we should sit down and have The Talk.'

'About getting back together for real, you mean?'

'Unless, that is, you'd be averse to the idea.'

'Merilee, you know how I feel.'

'No, I don't know. And it would be helpful if you said some words out loud about it right now.'

'You're the only woman I want to be with, but . . .'

'But what?'

'I can't promise you who I'll be from one year to the next.'

'Neither can I, darling. We're both artists, not to mention totally wifty. But we're also ten years older and wiser, and that has to mean something.'

'It does.' I leaned across the table and kissed her softly, stroking her cheek as I got lost in her green eyes. I let out a contented sigh before I glanced at Grandfather's Benrus. 'Damn, your car and driver are going to be here in a few minutes. You'd better finish packing. And, by the way, that was a yes.'

'To what, darling?'

'When you get back, maybe we should have The Talk. Except you can drop the word "maybe."'

Glowing, she darted off to the bedroom to finish packing while I wrapped up the remains of our lunch. By the time her Il Bisonte bags were ready and waiting by the front door a black Lincoln Town Car was easing its way up the gravel driveway. A driver in a black suit got out.

I carried her bags out to the car. He deposited them in the trunk, Lulu watching him with keen suspicion.

Merilee joined us a moment later, her shearling winter coat thrown over her arm. She tossed it in the back seat and we hugged each other tightly before she said, 'There's a murderer on the loose. Promise me you won't do anything dangerous or foolhardy.'

'I promise.'

'Promise me and mean it.'

'I mean it.'

She knelt to give Lulu a goodbye hug as Lulu gazed at her forlornly. 'Sweetness, I'm counting on you to look after him. He means well but you and I both know that he can be a total bozo.' Then she got in the back seat and rolled down her window. 'Goodbye, darling.'

'You'll do what Kate suggested?'

'It was more of an order. And I will. Mind you, they might fire me.'

'They can't. Without you the studio will pull the plug. You're Merilee Nash, remember?'

We kissed through the open window, then she rolled it up and off they went down the driveway. Lulu and I stood there and watched them drive away. Lulu started whimpering. I asked her to shut up. She didn't. I told her to shut up. She didn't. I gave up trying after that.

I couldn't blame her. I felt like whimpering, too. But I'm a semi-mature adult male and we're not supposed to whimper, so instead I got busy. Went back in the house. Fished my address book out of my briefcase. Sat down at Merilee's writing table in the parlor and phoned an old friend.

SEVEN

Megan Marshack.

That's who Donna Willis reminded me of.

I don't blame you if the name doesn't ring a bell. For you to remember Megan Marshack you'd have to be someone who lived in New York City on January 26, 1979 and the possessor of a voracious appetite for tabloid gossip. If you're neither of the above then please, please allow me to jog your memory. It was Megan Marshack, a twenty-seven-year-old aide to former US Vice President and New York Governor Nelson Rockefeller, who had the misfortune of finding herself stark naked directly underneath a similarly stark naked Rockefeller in the townhouse he'd bought her at 13 W. 54th Street when Rocky suffered a massive heart attack and died while in the saddle. The New York tabloid press was intensely eager to portray the much younger mistress of the married Rockefeller as a slinky sexpot. Unfortunately, the file photos of her standing in the background behind Rocky at press conferences were those of a big-boned, plain-faced young woman wearing thick glasses and unflattering office attire. The tabloids couldn't bear to describe Megan as homely, because it took all of the sizzle out of the story. So the word they eventually settled on, no doubt after spending a tortuous hour at the copy desk poring over Roget's Thesaurus, was 'sturdy.' It was such an odd choice of words that it made readers snicker. And it stuck.

It certainly stuck with me.

The Donna Willis who opened the door to her parents' handsome white center chimney colonial on Sill Lane – one of the choicest historic lanes in Old Lyme – was sturdy indeed. About five feet eight, big-boned and the possessor of thighs like beer kegs. Plain-faced as well. Too much jaw, not enough forehead. Her dark brown hair was cropped in a short, unflattering style that looked as if she'd cut it herself in the bathroom mirror.

'May I help you?' she asked, noticing Lulu's bandaged paws as we stood there on her front porch. 'My goodness, what happened to your dog's . . .?' Then she noticed the bandage atop my partially shaved head. 'You're Stewart Hoag, aren't you? The man who that lunatic took hostage.'

'I am. I was hoping we could talk for a few minutes.'

Donna's gaze drifted to the Jag in the driveway, puzzled. 'About what?'

'I understand from the resident trooper that you were victimized by Austin Talmadge, too. That he pulled you over one night, pawed you and said all sorts of awful things to you. I guess I just need to talk to someone else who understands what it feels like.'

'Oh, I understand, believe me,' she said angrily. 'I filed a complaint against him, and I was incredibly pissed when the state police refused to follow up on it. Especially because it wasn't the first time that psycho had accosted me. Last month, he chased me away from the moss I was studying on Mount Creepy. Threw rocks at me like an eight-year-old boy, bruised my shoulder and screamed obscenities at me until I finally left because he was making it impossible for me to do my field research. The state police did nothing that time either. I won't speak to them again. *Ever*.' She paused, softening a bit. 'But of course I'll speak to you. Come in, please.'

As with many of the antique houses in the area, the inside and outside were centuries apart. It was circa-revolutionary war on the outside and circa-1962 inside, as in shag carpeting, Danish-style furniture and walls filled with an eclectic array of abstract art. Or some people would call it art.

'Lovely house,' I said as Donna led us into a book-lined study off of the living room. She offered me a seat on the sofa, which faced windows that looked out over the Lieutenant River.

'It's been in my dad's family for generations. Mom and Dad have taken off for their condo in Vero Beach. They leave in late October and stay there for precisely six months and a day so that they can declare themselves Florida residents and avoid paying the governor's new Connecticut state income tax, thereby starving our public schools, transit system and highways of much needed revenue. It's a perfectly legal loophole, but it makes me sick. Mind you, they think I'm a socialist. Do you think I'm a socialist?'

'No, I think you're ethical.'

'Thank you,' she said, noticing that Lulu was delicately sniffing the cuffs of her jeans. 'Why is she doing that?'

'I don't know. She doesn't always tell me everything.'

'I'll bet she smells my Deet. I spray it all over myself by the gallon when I go into the woods because I hate deer ticks. Lyme disease is one of the occupational hazards of being a botanist. I've had it twice and it's not a lot of fun, believe me. Right now's one of their peak seasons. They're looking for a warm body to latch on to.'

After Lulu decided she was done sniffing at Donna's jeans she moved away, stretched out on the floor and yawned. Evidently it wasn't Donna's Deet that she'd gotten a whiff of when Austin was marching us up that mountain.

'Did you hike up there today?' I asked her.

'No, I just took a quick three-mile jaunt in the Champlain Farms preserve at the end of Library Lane. I needed to clear my head of *this*,' she said, waving a meaty hand over the messy heap of books, notepads, and printed-out manuscript pages that were on the desk as she sat down there. 'My thesis. I'm a grad student at Cornell. I came down here to focus since I have the whole place to myself. It didn't exactly turn out the way I planned. First, that crazy toad pulled me over for no reason, pawed me and asked me if I was having my period, can you imagine? Then he shot some poor guy at the beach club, kidnapped you and got his throat cut. What a sick bastard,' she said coldly. 'Not like his brother, Michael. He's a real gentleman.'

'You've met?'

'Not in person, but we've corresponded. I wrote him to ask for his permission to study the moss near the ruins of Talmadge Farm.'

'It's a state forest now. You don't need his permission, do you?'

'Technically, no. But that's still his family's heritage up there and it seemed like the right thing to do. He responded with such a nice letter telling me how considerate it was of me to ask. I still have it in my apartment in Ithica. It's not every day you exchange mail with a billionaire.'

'I'm curious. When Austin pulled you over that night, did he know you were the same person he'd thrown rocks at a few weeks earlier?'

'I doubt it. He never got close enough to me on the mountain to get a good look at my face. And when he pulled me over it was dark out.' She sat up a bit straighter in her chair, narrowing her gaze at me. 'You said you heard about my encounter with him from the resident trooper. Did he say anything else about me?'

'The resident trooper? No. But the homicide detective, Lieutenant Tedone, did. He told me that your ex-boyfriend has filed a restraining order against you. Claims that you have an anger management problem.'

'Why on earth did *that* come up?'

'You'd have to ask Lieutenant Tedone. I was just sitting there listening.'

'That whole business was blown *completely* out of proportion. Stephen, my ex, was averse to confrontation. I'm not a shrinking violet, OK? Whenever I'd raise my voice he'd flee in terror.'

'He's alleging you physically assaulted him.'

'I slapped him to get his attention. Is that an assault?'

I had no answer for that so I left it alone.

'It was because he was a billionaire, you know. The reason why they didn't follow up on my complaints against Austin. It's obscene. It's an outrage.'

'You're not wrong about that, but the world isn't a fair place.'

'Don't patronize me!'

Lulu let out a low, warning growl.

Donna peered at her. 'Why is she doing that?'

'She doesn't like it when people yell at me. I was agreeing with you, as it happens. I'm quite certain the only reason that they reeled him in, or "pulled the ripcord" as they called it, was that he showed up at my ex-wife's farm.'

She nodded. 'Merilee Nash is a famous movie star. They had to cover their booties in case anything happened to her.'

'Exactly. Except it didn't happen to her. It happened to me.'

'I'm sorry that it did. Do you get nightmares?'

'Yes.'

'You'll be OK. You just need to get away from this place.' She gazed down at the pile of research work on her desk. 'We both do. I've sure had enough.'

'Were you doing research up on the mountain the afternoon when it happened?'

'No, I was right here trying to make sense of this gibberish.'

'Did you see anyone? Talk to anyone?'

'No one. Why?'

'I've been through this sort of thing before. I know how the police think, using the term loosely. The first thing they do is cast a wide net. Anyone who has crossed paths with the victim gets caught up in it. It so happens that you crossed paths with Austin more than once.'

'So?'

'So that means they'll try to place you at the murder scene.'

'How?' she demanded. 'How would I have known what had happened to that poor man at the beach club? Or to you and your dog? I didn't find out about any of it until I saw it on the news that evening.'

'No offense, Donna, but I'm not as dumb as you seem to think I am.'

'No offense, but I have no idea what you mean by that.' She glared at my bandaged head. 'Are you sure you're thinking straight?'

'Quite straight. I'm seeing straight, too. Looking directly at that bookshelf right behind you.'

'What about it?'

'It's filled with emergency band radios. The one on the left is a police scanner. Next to that is a volunteer fire department radio. John, the village barber, is assistant chief and has one just like it in his shop. It was always on whenever I went in to get a haircut this summer. He's famous for dashing off to respond to a fire in the middle of a haircut, which explains why so many men around here have such oddly styled cuts.

And the radio next to that is . . . hmm, I've never seen one of those. What is it?'

'Coast Guard,' she said tightly. 'They're my dad's. He likes to listen in on the emergency channels. A lot of the men out here do. It's what they do instead of watching *Roseanne*. Dad sails, so he's always interested in what the Coast Guard has to say about weather warnings. And he was a member of the volunteer fire department himself until three years ago. Not that he went out on the trucks or anything. He handled their purchasing orders and kept the books. But he still thinks of himself as a member and he still listens in. Habit of a lifetime.'

'A habit that you picked up from him.'

'No, I didn't. I never turn those things on.'

'And I believe you, if you say so.'

'I *do* say so!'

'But the police can say otherwise. They can say you had the police scanner on while you were here working on your thesis and heard all about Truman Mainwaring's shooting and my abduction. That you put two and two together, jumped in your car and headed straight for Mount Creepy, where Austin had shouted obscenities and hurled rocks at you.'

'What are you telling me – that I need a lawyer?'

'No, I'm telling you that you're a person of interest.'

'What does that mean?'

'It means you're someone who has a motive and no alibi.'

'OK, now you're just being lame. I didn't kill Austin Talmadge. Why on earth would I do that?'

'Because he was making your life miserable.'

Donna Willis let out a humorless laugh. 'Trust me, if I killed everyone who was making my life miserable, the world would be a very empty place.'

It was dusk by the time I steered the Jag up Route 156 toward the farm. As I turned off at Hamburg Cove for Joshua Town Road I felt a wave of fatigue wash over me. Dr Eng had been right. I still needed to take it easy. Spending an hour in the combustible presence of Donna Willis definitely didn't qualify as taking it easy.

I found myself glancing at Annabeth McKenna's ramshackle saltbox as I drove by. Her Volvo wagon was parked out front. There were at least a dozen lights on in the windows, upstairs and down, and she was no doubt in there coping with what a woman with three teenagers had to cope with each and every day. Warning Max, her seventeen-year-old son, as tactfully as possible that if he brought home another D on an English exam he'd regret it deeply later in life. Tussling with her fifteen-year-old daughter, Sarah, over whether she could or could not get a nose piercing. Informing Gloria, age thirteen, that she could NOT go to the U2 concert at the Hartford Civic Center on Saturday night without adult supervision – and that her friend Heather's eighteen-year-old brother, Axel, and Axel's girlfriend didn't qualify as adult supervision. Truly, I couldn't imagine being a parent and having to put out such brush fires every minute of every day of the year. Lulu, who was dozing on her blanket in the passenger seat, was plenty for me.

Happily, the news vans had taken off as soon as Merilee had, as had the state trooper. All was quiet as I drove up the farm's gravel driveway and the motion detector lights came on. Don't misunderstand me, Merilee was awfully easy to get used to having around. But now that she was gone I welcomed the solitude of her empty farmhouse. I didn't want to talk to anyone. Didn't want to see anyone. All I wanted to do was make a fire in the parlor fireplace, stretch out on the sofa with a Bass ale, and not move or think.

Unfortunately, that wasn't to be. I did get the fire started and opened a Bass after I'd put down some 9Lives mackerel for my favorite nose bowl champ. But before I could stretch out on the sofa, a silver Crown Vic came up the driveway and parked. Lieutenant Carmine Tedone got out and plodded his way slowly toward the front door. He was by himself. No sign of Sergeant Bartucca.

I opened the front door and forced a smile on to my face. 'Greetings, Lieutenant. I just built a fire and opened a Bass ale. Care to join me?'

'Wouldn't say no,' he answered wearily.

I fetched him one. He parked himself in the wing-backed chair next to the fireplace. I settled on the sofa, put my legs up on the coffee table and took a long, grateful gulp of my Bass. I swear that neither one of us spoke for five minutes. Just sat there staring into the fire and drinking our beers. Lulu finished her dinner, wandered in and greeted Tedone by conking his knee with her head. After he patted her absently she made her way over to the sofa and climbed up next to me.

'I stopped by an hour ago,' Tedone said finally. 'No one was around.'

'Merilee's on a six o'clock flight back to Budapest, and I was visiting Donna Willis.'

He glared at me. 'You're doing it again, aren't you?'

'Doing what, Lieutenant?'

'Sticking your big, fat nose in my case.'

'I prefer to think of my nose as a well-proportioned blade. And I wasn't interfering in your case.'

'Is that so? Then what were you doing there?'

'Sharing my Austin Talmadge victimization syndrome with her.'

'I'm from Waterbury. Smaller words, will you?'

'Each of us suffered at his hand. I've got staples in my head and recurring nightmares that I'm still down in that tomb of a root cellar. Donna got pulled over and sexually harassed when he was playing cop. He also chased her away from the moss specimens she was collecting on Mount Creepy by throwing rocks at her. Bruised her shoulder with one. That qualifies as assault. She notified the Connecticut State Police twice and got ignored twice – because he was Austin Talmadge. She swore to me she won't ever speak to you guys again, which means I can get information out of her that you can't.'

'And did you?' he asked.

'She's a mass of contradictions. Not a happy person.'

'Do you actually know any happy people?'

'On the one hand, she was considerate enough to write Michael Talmadge a personal letter asking for his permission to do her botanical research on his family's ancestral farm – even though it's now a state park and she didn't need to ask.'

'Did he write her back?'

'He did. She said he sent her a very kind and appreciative response. She was quite moved by it.' I got up, put another log on the fire and poked at it before I flopped back down. 'On the other hand, she sure does have a short fuse.'

Tedone puffed out his cheeks. 'One more time – did you get any information out of her?'

'I did, as a matter of fact. She has no alibi for the approximate time of Austin's murder. Said she was alone in her parents' house working on her thesis.'

'OK, but how would she have known where Austin was?'

'Interesting you should ask. Her father has a wide array of emergency response radios. It's his hobby. She was listening in. Mind you, she insisted to me that she wasn't. But I didn't believe her. She was just a touch too vehement. This is an individual who knows the mountain well, is plenty strong – or sturdy if you prefer, which I do – and despised Austin. That spells definite suspect to me. Same goes for Skip Rimer.'

'Truman Mainwaring's boyfriend? What about him?'

'I spoke to him when I was at the hospital getting checked over this morning.'

'Why?'

'Dr Eng wanted to see how I was progressing.'

'No, I mean why did you speak to Rimer?'

'I got the impression you wanted me to. Now you're about to tell me that, no, I was mistaken. Please don't bother. It's beneath you and you'll be insulting my intelligence.'

Tedone let out an exasperated sigh. 'What did you get out of him?'

'For starters, the reason he gave you such a hostile attitude was because you gave him the impression you were anti-gay and that Truman deserved to get his clavicle blown to bits.'

'That's not true!' Tedone objected heatedly. 'I've got nothing against the gays. The little bastard just went out of his way to piss me off, that's all.'

'How did he manage to do that?'

'With that chippy attitude of his. Plus he kept flexing his biceps with those stupid barbed wire tattoos.' He sipped his Bass. 'So are you going to tell me what you got out of him or make me beg you?'

'Haven't decided yet.' I drained my own Bass. 'Care for another?'

He glowered at me. 'I swear, Hoagy, if you don't start . . .'

'He's in the same boat as Donna. Can't account for his whereabouts at the time of Austin's murder. The surgeon had sent him home because he told him the procedure would take hours. Skip said he went back to the Mainwarings' house on Cove Road, pumped iron and ran the treadmill in their basement gym. And the answer to your next question is no, he didn't see any neighbors. Nobody can vouch for him.'

'OK, but how would *he* have known where Austin was?'

'He phoned Jim Conley, who filled him in.'

Tedone shoved his lower lip in and out. 'Gotta say, I like him for it.'

'I do, too. Austin shot his lover. Plus he's an outdoorsman who hikes, rock climbs and thinks he's a tough guy, although I should point out that Lulu got nothing off of him.'

'Meaning . . .?'

'Meaning if he was the person who was tailing us up the mountain, she didn't recognize his scent. Which isn't necessarily conclusive. He could have been wearing Deet. Donna Willis was. She's had Lyme disease twice and is afraid of deer ticks. Lulu got nothing off of her either.'

Tedone considered this before he said, 'Yeah, I would, now that you mention it.'

'You would what?'

'Care for another Bass.'

'Fine idea.' I fetched two more bottles from the refrigerator, popped them open and returned with them. 'So that's a pair of very solid suspects right there.'

He took a gulp of his Bass. 'I can give you two more – the Hardy Boys.'

'Frank and Joe?'

He frowned. 'Frank and *who*?'

'Don't mind me, I'm still concussed. Their alibi's no good?'

'Let's say it is but it isn't. They told Ang Bartucca they were spreading gravel on a driveway at a house on Griswold Avenue at the time of Austin's murder. Ang confirmed they were doing the gravel job like they said. Trouble is, the homeowner is their cousin, Gail, who's real tight with Tony and Gas. In fact, she was at that beach party Austin broke up a couple of weeks ago when he was playing cop. And it so happens that she's hated Austin ever since they were in the third grade – a good two years before he poisoned the Hardy Boys' dog.'

'Why, what did he . . .?'

'Cut off all of her beautiful long blond hair with a pair of scissors during a classroom crafts project. The teacher was standing right there. Dragged him straight to the principal's office and he was suspended. Ang says there's no way Gail can be considered a reliable alibi. He has zero doubt she'd lie to cover for Tony and Gas.'

'Could be a two-way street.'

'Meaning?'

'The Hardy Boys are *her* alibi. Revenge can taste pretty sweet after forty years, or so I've been told.'

Tedone shook his head. 'No chance. She has rheumatoid arthritis. Can barely get around, let alone climb Mount Creepy.'

'OK, so much for that idea. What about Joaquin, that ex-Green Beret bodyguard of Michael's? Austin told me he kept staring at his pecker when they threw him in the shower, and that he was always giving him yearning looks. Any chance he's in play?'

'I had a conversation with Joaquin Sandoval. He has a wife and two kids in Houston, with a third one on the way.'

'That doesn't necessarily mean he's not interested in men, too.'

'True, except he claims that it was Austin who was always giving him the yearning looks. Dr Annabeth McKenna would know a whole lot more about this than I would, but if you ask me Austin had so many issues with gays because he was gay himself and couldn't deal with it.'

'That thought has occurred to me, too,' I said.

'But in answer to your question, no, he's not in play. All four members of Michael's security team were guarding Michael in his fortress after Austin escaped and shot Truman at the beach club, the reason being that Michael was totally convinced that Austin was coming for him next. Joaquin told me his assignment was to patrol the grounds with that attack dog of theirs.'

'I still think Pinkie's a wussie name.'

'Plus the other three members of the team vouch for Joaquin a hundred percent. He never left Michael's house.'

'Could they be lying to cover for him?'

'Possibly, except for something that the M.E. told me. Austin's throat was slashed with what he described as crude aggression. It was the work of a crazed amateur, not a trained soldier. If Joaquin had been the one who slit Austin's throat, it would have been quick and clean.' Tedone drained his Bass and set it on the end table next to his chair, rubbing his tired eyes. 'I feel like I'm nowhere. It'll crack open eventually. They always do. But I don't have the luxury of "eventually" with this one, not with Colin Fielding, the governor's personal hatchet man, breathing down Deputy Superintendent Mitry's neck, which translates to Mitry breathing down *my* neck.' He glanced at his watch. 'Guess I'd better hit the road. The wife will be expecting me for dinner.'

'Sure. I'll walk you out to your car.' Lulu was fast asleep and didn't join us. I couldn't make out any stars overhead. The sky had clouded over. 'Lieutenant, I was wondering about something . . .'

He gave me a wary sidelong glance in the motion detector lights. 'Oh, yeah, what's that?'

'Have you obtained Austin Talmadge's medical file from McLean Psychiatric Hospital?'

'Ang's put in an official request. We don't have it yet, and they won't go out of their way to make it easy for us. There are patient confidentiality concerns. People have a right to protect their privacy, even after they're dead. But with a case like this we might turn up something valuable.'

'Such as . . .?'

'Such as someone who came in contact with Austin while he was there who now happens to be a person of interest in his murder.'

'A fellow patient, you mean?'

'Could be. Could also be someone who was employed there. A nurse, security guard, custodian, groundskeeper . . .' He peered at me in the motion detector lights. 'Why are you asking?'

'Just curious.'

'And why is it that whenever you get curious, my stomach starts to hurt?'

'I wouldn't know. Perhaps you should have your doctor check you over.'

'Yeah, I'll get right on that.' He climbed into his Crown Vic, peering at me. 'You look all in. You're still not a hundred percent, you know. Ought to make an early night of it.'

'I intend to. Goodnight, Lieutenant.'

He rolled up his window, started up his engine and sped down the driveway for home. I went back inside. I was too tired to cook anything so I raided the bread, sausage, cheese and other goodies that Merilee had scored at the Italian market in Middletown. Then I turned out the lights, made a fire in the bedroom fireplace, brushed my teeth, didn't floss, undressed and climbed into the cozy flannel sheets, barely able to keep my eyes open. Lulu sprawled out next to me, somehow managing to take up her usual three-quarters of the bed. I turned out the bedside lamp and lay there in the firelight, exhausted. But I couldn't fall asleep. I'd gotten accustomed to sleeping alone after Merilee dumped me – if you can consider sharing a bed with Lulu sleeping alone – but now that Merilee had come and gone like a whirlwind, the bed felt empty and I ached with loneliness.

So my mind went back to work on who'd killed Austin Talmadge. And why so savagely? I lay there for an hour or more with my wheels spinning before I finally gave in, turned my lamp back on and read Mrs Parker for a while until my eyes absolutely, positively would not stay open. I flicked the lamp off and fell fast asleep – only to awaken with a yelp because I thought I was buried in that damned root cellar tomb again. Eventually, my heart stopped racing and I managed to fall back to sleep. But it was a restless, fitful sleep. And I'd been lying there awake for at least an hour in the country darkness before Quasimodo started crowing.

I was thinking about getting up to make the coffee when the unlisted line rang. I reached for the bedside phone eagerly, hoping it was Merilee calling to tell me she'd arrived safely in Budapest and missed me as much as I missed her.

It wasn't Merilee.

It was Tedone. And he wasn't calling to tell me how much he missed me. He was calling to tell me that Michael Talmadge had been murdered.

EIGHT

Michael Talmadge's cold, dead body had been found at six o'clock that morning in the entry hall of his high-security mansion high atop Mitchell Hill Road by his long-time housekeeper, an elderly Lyme widow named Connie Pike, who arrived at six every morning to prepare the richest man in Connecticut his breakfast of grapefruit juice, two soft boiled eggs, wholewheat toast and black coffee. Michael had no live-in help.

'The man liked his privacy,' Tedone informed me as we sped to Michael's house in his Crown Vic. He'd stopped at Merilee's to pick me up thirty minutes after he'd phoned me, which gave me just enough time to feed Lulu, down two cups of coffee, shave and dress. It was a clear, frosty autumn morning. A beautiful morning, actually. Lulu rode between us, her tail thumping eagerly as Tedone filled me in.

'Connie found the front gate open, which she said didn't surprise her. Michael informed her last evening when she served him his dinner of meat loaf, mashed potatoes and string beans that he would no longer be keeping it locked now that Austin was dead. He'd already dismissed his four-man security team and sent them to New Orleans for an all-expenses-paid blow out. He also told her that from now on he intended to live his life as he pleased.'

'Didn't get to live it for very long, did he?'

'No, he did not.'

'I find this very strange, Lieutenant. He stopped by the farm when I got home from the hospital to express his condolences for what Austin had put Lulu and me through. Told me he intended to pay all of our medical and veterinary bills. He also gave me a check for a hundred thou for my pain and suffering.'

'Did you accept it?'

'Sure did. And then it went straight into the fireplace.'

He shook his head. 'You are one stubborn guy.'

'Are you telling me you would have accepted it?'

'Sworn personnel aren't allowed to accept gratuities. And I'm still waiting for the strange part.'

'He hadn't stopped trembling. He was terrified that Austin's slasher wasn't someone who had a nasty personal history with the toxic little bastard but someone who killed him strictly out of bitter resentment over his immense wealth. Meaning that he, Michael, would be the killer's next victim. Does that sound to you like a man who was raring to cut his security detail loose and leave his front gate unlocked?'

'Far from it.' He frowned. 'Something must have changed his mind.'

'Or someone. You were telling me about Connie Pike.'

'Correct. She parked her Nissan Sentra in the circular drive, unlocked the front door and—'

'Not the kitchen door?'

'I wondered about that, too. She said Michael permitted her to come and go by the front door because the kitchen door is all the way around in back, it's still dark out at that hour and she's afraid of being attacked by a wild animal. There are coyotes around here, bobcats . . . I guess I don't have to tell you that.'

'No, you don't,' I said as Lulu made sour, unhappy noises.

'She found him right there on the floor in the entry hall under the chandelier, in his flannel pajamas and old, threadbare flannel robe. He was lying on his back in a pool of congealed blood. A whole lot of blood. He was covered with it. His throat had been cut from ear to ear, just like his brother's. Connie kept her wits about her and called nine-one-one. Jim Conley was there in ten minutes along with two state troopers from Troop F to cordon off the street.'

'Was the chandelier on or off when Connie arrived?'

'On. Why are you asking?'

'Just trying to get a complete picture. Does Annabeth McKenna know about this yet?'

Tedone nodded. 'Phoned her right after I phoned you.'

'Did she have anything to say?'

'She got quiet for a very long time, actually.'

'And then . . .?'

'And then she said, "After all of those years of being tormented by Austin he was only allowed to experience one day of peace. How sad."'

'It is sad,' I said as we climbed Mitchell Hill Road, which was in a very steep, remote section of Lyme where not many people lived. We arrived at the state police roadblock and passed through it, Michael's house looming there before us. It was a huge brick manor house built on at least ten acres of land and surrounded by a high wall topped with razor wire. As we went through the gate I noticed that the lush green lawn was uncommonly free of fallen leaves for late October. A leaf-blowing crew must have been there yesterday afternoon.

Sergeant Ang Bartucca was there when we pulled in, as was the M.E. and two crime scene vans. Also a silver Crown Vic cruiser with a uniformed trooper seated behind the wheel. Behind him, in the back seat, were Deputy Superintendent Buck Mitry and Colin Fielding, the governor's special envoy. I was curious what they were doing there. Almost as curious as I was to know why Tedone wanted me there with him. Had he come to enjoy my company? That seemed plausible, all except for the *no way* part. Did he find my keen insights helpful? Again, *no way*. So what was I doing there?

Tedone rolled down his window as Sergeant Bartucca approached us. 'Morning, Loo. Hey, Mr Hoag. The M.E. thinks the victim's been there at least ten hours, based on his body temperature and the extent of rigor.'

'Any sign of a break-in?'

'None that we can find. And the place hasn't been ransacked. We asked Connie, the housekeeper, to walk us through it, room by room. She doesn't think anything's been so much as touched. There's a safe in his office, but it wasn't opened and Connie doesn't know the combination. We'll have to get one of our people out here to open it.'

'Something tells me that robbery's not what this was about,' Tedone said.

'I'm with you, Loo, especially because Connie said he didn't keep any valuables in the house. Didn't collect rare stamps or coins. There are no paintings missing from the walls. The man wore a Timex watch. His wallet was on his bedroom dresser. Had twenty-three dollars in cash and a couple of credit cards in it. Kind of weird, you ask me. The man owned a castle but you walk inside and . . .'

'And what, Ang?'

'He lived like a school teacher.'

'Have you spoken to his ex-Green Berets?'

'Just got off of the phone with Joaquin. He told me Michael gave each of them a limp handshake, a five-thousand-dollar bonus and a toot in New Orleans, which is where they've been since yesterday morning. Michael booked first-class airline tickets and hotel suites for each of them. I don't see any way they're involved in this, Loo. Besides, Joaquin told me they all liked the guy. They thought he was very polite. Didn't treat them like chumps.'

'Who employs them?'

'A private security outfit in Bethesda. They'll return there in a few days and await their next assignment. They protect politicians, international business titans, Arab sheiks. Work overseas a lot.'

'Do they usually work together?'

'No. Joaquin said this was the first time they'd teamed up.'

'What about Pinkie?' I asked.

'His trainer flew up from Baltimore to Hartford, rented a van and is driving him home,' Sergeant Bartucca answered me.

'He doesn't like his dogs to fly?'

'No, he has a girlfriend in Allentown.'

'The trainer or Pinkie?'

Tedone glared at me. 'Do you mind? Trying to work here.' Again, I wondered why he'd wanted me to come along. 'Anything else, Ang?'

'I'm supposed to tell you that Deputy Superintendent Mitry and the governor's man want to see you when it's convenient. Both of you.'

'Both of us?' I said.

'That's what I was told.'

'How did they know I'd be coming?'

'Because I was ordered to bring you,' Tedone answered irritably.

'Oh. And here I thought we were male bonding.'

'Guess again. Thanks, Ang.'

'You got it, Loo.' He went loping back toward the house.

We remained in Tedone's cruiser. 'So whoever killed him must have visited him late last night,' he mused aloud. 'The killer knew he'd be alone. We can check to see if Michael got any phone calls. My guess is the killer just showed up unannounced and rang the bell.'

'Why do you say that?'

'Because Michael wouldn't have been in his PJs and bathrobe if he was expecting company.'

'Fair point. He also knew his killer. Otherwise, he wouldn't have let him in, right?'

'Right. It's not as if a frightened soul like Michael Talmadge would open the door to the Fuller Brush man at that time of night.'

'Do they still have Fuller Brush men?'

'It was a figure of speech,' he growled at me.

'So who *would* he let in? Couldn't have been a friend. He told Merilee and me he had no friends. Just colleagues.'

Tedone mulled this over. 'Maybe there's someone he was close to who we still don't know about. I'll have Ang search his desk for an address book, letters . . . Come on, let's go have a look.'

We got out of the car and went up the steps toward the open front door.

'Please stay outside for now,' a crime scene tech wearing protective booties said to us from the doorway. 'We're dusting the floor for shoe prints.'

They were also taking Polaroids of Michael's body, the congealed blood under his body, the blood spattered on the entry hall walls, even on the chandelier. When you sever someone's carotid artery, the heart is still pumping and shoots blood everywhere. The M.E., a large, fleshy man in his fifties, was bent over Michael examining the slashes in his throat. I couldn't take my eyes off of Michael's dead face. Unlike Austin, who'd died angry, Michael looked serene and peaceful, as if he was relieved to be gone.

'They didn't exactly have a brandy in front of the fire, did they?' I said. 'He got less than six feet inside the door before he let Michael have it.'

'Any signs of a struggle?' Tedone asked the M.E. from the doorway.

'There appear to be traces of skin and blood under his nails,' he replied. 'You'll find some scratch marks on his killer. Hands, face, somewhere.'

'And are you going to make my morning by telling me it's the same knife that was used on his brother?'

'No can do, Lieutenant. I'll need a microscope. Does appear to be the same type of weapon, a short-bladed hunting knife. And the slasher *is* right-handed and the wounds *are* similarly deep and savage. The victim's Adam's apple is barely even recognizable as such.'

I looked past the entry hall through the wide doorway into the mansion's living room, which was conspicuously lacking in the human touch department. There were no models of the sailboats Michael had owned because he hadn't sailed. No gun case or duck decoys because he hadn't hunted. No antique pool table with leather pockets because he hadn't shot pool. He'd been a man without hobbies or interests. He worked and he slept. The furniture was functional but not luxurious. It looked as if he'd hired the same decorating firm that did Courtyard by Marriott.

As we stood there I noticed Lulu was nosing her way toward us from a spot in the driveway about ten feet away from the front steps, moving very slowly and carefully, large black nose to the ground, snuffling and snorting as she climbed up the front steps, then crossed the porch to the doorway, where she came to a halt, parked her tush and let out a low moan.

'Why's she doing that?' Tedone asked me.

'She recognizes the scent of his killer.'

'Recognizes as in . . .?'

'It's someone with whom she's come in contact.'

'Do you mean when Austin was dragging you up that mountain or somewhere else?'

'Lieutenant, at times like this I really do wish she was a short-legged Mr Ed, I was Wilbur Post and I could simply ask her. But this is so-called real life. All I can tell you is that she's a scent hound, and that she recognizes the scent, meaning the odds are extremely good it's the same killer – which you'd already surmised since both brothers died the same exact way.'

'The M.E. will have to confirm that.'

'Why, Lieutenant?'

'Because that's his job, and he's been doing it for twenty-three years.'

'No, I mean why kill Michael? Did someone have a personal grudge against him? I highly doubt it. He was so private that hardly anyone even knew him. If he was killed for the very reason that he feared – sheer resentment over his wealth – then we're right back to why he suddenly felt safe enough to let his security team go.'

'You make a good point,' he allowed, thumbing his jaw.

'This turns your entire case on its ear, doesn't it?'

'How so?'

'You've been assuming that Austin's murder was a violent payback of some sort. Now the scenario changes.'

'Again, how so?'

'It's entirely possible that this was never about Austin at all. That he was killed simply so that his fortune would pass to big brother Michael so that big brother Michael could be eliminated and then . . .' I trailed off, my wheels turning.

Tedone stared at me. 'And then *what*?'

'Riddle me this, Lieutenant. Where do their combined billions and billions go now that they're both dead? Do you know who Michael's lawyer is?'

'Didn't have one, I'm told. Handled all of his own legal affairs himself.'

'Still, there has to be an executor of his estate. *Someone* knows what will happen to all of those billions.' I glanced over at the cruiser where Deputy Superintendent Mitry and Colin Fielding sat waiting to speak with us. 'And I have a pretty good idea who that *someone* is.'

'Mitry did say they wanted to talk to us when it was convenient,' Tedone allowed.

'It's convenient right now, wouldn't you say?'

We strolled over to their car. Deputy Superintendent Mitry rolled down his window as we approached and nodded to us coolly, which I gathered passed for a greeting.

'Morning, sir,' Tedone said to him. 'Ugly way to die.'

'They're all ugly, Lieutenant.'

Fielding said nothing. Just watched us with those same piercing eyes of his. Or I should say watched me. His eyes never left me. He wore a navy-blue pin-stripe suit with a light blue shirt and burgundy knit tie.

Mitry wore a charcoal-gray suit much like the one he'd worn the other day, a white shirt and muted tie. 'How does that nasty bump on your head feel?' he asked me, not unkindly.

'Better, thanks. No more dizzy spells.'

'Glad to hear it.' He turned back to Tedone. 'What have you got?'

'We have to re-think why Austin Talmadge's throat was slashed.'

'Explain.'

'Our working theory was personal revenge. He'd pissed off a lot of people in his time. But Michael, who inherited Austin's billions, didn't have an enemy in the world – except for Austin, that is. Now that Michael's throat has been slashed, too, we have to face the likelihood that this is entirely about the Talmadge fortune. Who stands to inherit it?'

Colin Fielding cleared his throat. 'There were cousins by the carload,' he said in his slightly nasal voice. 'But none of them come into a penny of it.'

'So who does?'

Mitry leaned forward and tapped his driver on the shoulder. 'Mind stepping out for a few minutes, Sergeant?'

The driver got out and we got in – Tedone behind the wheel, me in the passenger seat with Lulu between us. Tedone and I both turned sideways, the better to look back at the tall, imposing deputy superintendent and the governor's small, slightly built personal envoy.

Mitry glanced over at him. 'Have something more you want to say?'

Fielding cleared his throat again. 'There's a reason the governor was involved in "pulling the ripcord" on Austin the other day.'

'Damn, I was really hoping I'd never have to hear that expression again,' I said.

'And there's a reason why I'm here this morning on the governor's behalf,' he continued, ignoring me. 'He and Michael Talmadge had a very special relationship. Went to prep school and Princeton together, which not many people know because they seldom spent time together in public. But, in private, they shared a common interest.'

I studied him across the seat. 'Which was . . .?'

'Something they've been working on together, with my assistance, for quite a while. Michael was fifty-two years old. What very, very few people know is that on the day he turned fifty-five, he intended to divest himself of most of his vast fortune – which amounted to approximately twenty-eight billion dollars depending upon the ups and down of the world markets – sell this house and live the remainder of his life on a much more modest scale. He told the governor that all he wanted to do was sit and read the books that he'd never had time for. He kept a list of authors in a little leather notebook in his desk. Your people will find it. There was Anthony Trollope. There was Henry James, Somerset Maugham, Ford Maddox Ford, Joseph Conrad and more than a dozen others. He intended to read a novel per week for the rest of his life, seated in a comfortable chair drinking hot cocoa. He also wanted to travel. He'd never been to London, Dublin or Edinburgh. Those were the three destinations at the top of his list. He was afraid to fly. So he intended to go by boat. Or tramp steamer, as he liked to call it.'

'And what about all of his money?' Tedone asked with a slight edge of impatience in his voice.

'It so happens that the governor is the executor of Michael's estate. Michael's last will and testament is tucked away in the safe in the study of the governor's mansion. It was Michael's wish to leave his fortune, which I'd estimate now exceeds forty billion dollars with Austin's passing, to the state of

Connecticut for the betterment of its public school system –
elementary through high school – so as to make it the gold
standard of the nation. Michael Talmadge was an interesting
man. Politically conservative by nature. But it bothered him
greatly when President Reagan's tax cuts began to starve our
public schools to the point where teachers had to buy their
own classroom supplies. He also thought that Connecticut's
state university system should not only be greatly expanded
but tuition free for all in-state high-school students who
wished to attend and had graduated with a B-average. Students
who'd only managed to graduate with a C-average would be
able to attend one of a dozen or more newly built community
colleges, tuition free, and if they maintained a B-average for
a full academic year they'd be eligible to move up to a state
university. And there was more. He wanted better-funded
state institutions for the elderly and the mentally ill, so that
they could live with dignity. He also wanted to build a network
of low-cost walk-in clinics throughout the state where the
working poor could get access to affordable health and dental
care. He was, in his own quiet way, quite a forward-thinking
man. He and the governor had already roughed-out an agency
to administer the programs he had in mind. Absolutely no one
knew a thing about it. Michael wanted it that way.' Fielding
paused. 'But there's no reason not to keep it under wraps now.
It'll be made public soon enough.'

'Is there any reason to believe that there's a connection
between Michael's plans and these murders?' Tedone asked
him.

'I don't see how. He hadn't told a soul besides the governor
and me.'

'What about Austin?'

'Austin didn't know a thing about it,' Fielding replied. 'No,
I don't see any connection. I think someone out there had a
personal reason for wanting Austin dead and then was put in
the position of having to kill Michael because Michael could
identify him. But that's just my personal opinion.'

'Not a shabby one at that,' conceded Tedone, studying the
governor's man with newfound interest.

'What about resentment?' Deputy Superintendent Mitry

wondered aloud. 'An angry relative who hated Michael and Austin for not sharing the family fortune?'

'A ton of people in Lyme were related to them,' I said. 'But it was Michael and Austin's father, a relentless business titan, who made most of those billions. And he didn't share them with anybody. He left them to his two sons, period. My sense from talking to Merilee's neighbor, an old-timer, is that their relatives seemed to accept the way things were – which was that Austin was obscenely rich and crazy and that Michael was obscenely rich and private.'

Colin Fielding glanced at me and said, 'Feel like stretching your legs?'

Lulu and I got out and joined him on a tidy pea gravel footpath that circled around behind the brick manor house before it led us to a scenic lookout with a panoramic view of Hamburg Cove and most of Lyme. We were way high up. So high we could actually look down and see a red-tailed hawk slowly wafting below us on the morning breeze before it suddenly plunged downward and snatched up its prey – an unsuspecting rabbit – which, somehow, was still alive, its paws flailing helplessly as it was carried off to its doom. Nature, I reflected, is utterly ruthless. As we resumed walking, not a word spoken yet, I thought about what a boost it would be for the governor to unveil Michael Talmadge's grand multi-billion-dollar public education and health scheme three years ahead of schedule. The governor's popularity had plummeted ever since he'd imposed the state income tax. Most political observers believed he had zero chance of being re-elected. I couldn't help wondering if he was behind these murders.

Politicians, after all, are even more ruthless than hawks.

As we continued to walk, Lulu keeping pace with us on her healing front paws, I found myself looking over at Fielding and noticing that he wasn't as slightly built as he'd initially appeared. He wasn't tall, maybe five feet nine, but he was wiry and fit. Stomach flat. Shoulders straight. Big hands that looked strong and capable.

'Spend much time in the great outdoors?' I asked him, breaking the silence.

'Why, yes, I do. I love to kayak. Love the water.'

'How about the woods?'

He ran a hand over his thinning sandy-colored hair. 'Not so much. Not unless there's snow on the ground. I enjoy cross-country skiing, but I'm not much of a hiker. Reminds me too much of basic training.'

'You were in the military?'

He nodded. 'Army.'

'Did you serve in 'Nam?'

'If you consider pushing papers around at the Pentagon serving then, yes, I served.'

'What kind of papers?

He glanced at me sidelong. 'I was in Army Intelligence.'

'So you were a spook?

He let out a laugh. 'Hardly. I collated information and prepared briefing papers for the Joint Chiefs. Then they started sending me over to Capitol Hill as a military liaison, which is how I first met the governor. He was a congressman in those days. Before long I was his go-to advisor on military affairs. Now I'm his chief of staff, political consultant, campaign coordinator, all of the above.'

'Meaning you do whatever needs doing?'

'That's right.'

As we walked, me with my hands buried in the pockets of my flight jacket, I wondered just how broad his job description was. Could *he* have been the one who was tailing us up Mount Creepy that day after Austin's rampage at the beach club? Had *he* slashed Austin's throat at the waterfall and shoved his body over the safety railing down into the gorge below? And what about Michael? He wouldn't have opened his door to just anyone last night. His killer had to be someone he knew. Could that someone have been Fielding? The M.E. had said he'd found blood and skin under Michael's fingernails. I glanced over at Fielding. Didn't see any scratch marks on his face or hands – but that didn't mean he didn't have any on his neck or forearms.

'I'm also a marathon runner,' he said. 'I try to do New York City and Boston every year. Running keeps me sane.' He looked at me. 'I suppose your writing is what keeps you sane.'

'When it's going well. When it's not it keeps me insane.'

'You didn't serve in 'Nam.' It was a statement, not a question.

'No, I was still in school when we pulled out.'

'Chucked spears at Harvard, didn't you?'

'You checked up on me?'

'Of course I checked up on you. Hypothetical question . . . Say we'd stayed in 'Nam long enough for you to lose your 2-S deferment and get drafted. Would you have served?'

'I was opposed to the war, if that's what you're wondering. I thought we had no idea what we were doing there and that our government was lying to us.'

'You weren't wrong.'

'Now is it my turn?'

'Your turn to what?'

'Ask you a personal question that's none of my damned business.'

He frowned at me. 'Is that what I was doing?'

'Kind of.'

'Just trying to get a read on you. Fair enough. Ask away.'

'Where were you last evening?'

He took a deep breath, letting it out slowly. 'Oh, I see. Sure. I was with the governor and his wife at a political symposium at Trinity College. Dragged on forever. We didn't get out of there until after eleven. Got home just before midnight.'

'Where do you live?'

'Farmington.'

'Are you married?'

'Divorced. You don't actually think *I* killed Michael, do you?'

'And let's not forget about Austin.'

He shook his head in disbelief. 'That's lunacy.'

'Lunacy happens to be my middle name.' Actually, it's Stafford, but he no doubt already knew that.

'I'll admit I've done some pretty awful things in my time. I've double-crossed good friends. Lied. Cheated. Ruined perfectly decent men's lives. Politics isn't beanbag, as the old saying goes. But I have absolutely nothing to do with these deaths. I give you my word on that. And I'd also like to give you some advice. Pull over, turn off your engine and throw away the keys.'

'That sounds more like a threat than advice.'

'Then let me put it to you this way: I can be a good man to have as a friend, but you don't want me for an enemy. Plus it's always wise to stay out of things you don't understand. I'm truly sorry you got mixed up in all of this. You came out here to enjoy the fall foliage. Next thing you know you're in the middle of a major shit storm.'

'Actually, this happens to me a lot. I'm not sure why, but it seems to have something to do with my personality. Besides, it hasn't been a total bust. My ex-wife flew home from Budapest to take care of me for two whole days.'

'I admire Merilee Nash's work. She seems authentic. Down to earth.'

'She is. Loves nothing better than to put on her overalls and muck out the chicken coop.'

'Is she interested in Connecticut politics?'

'She doesn't get involved in partisan politics, if that's what you're wondering. But she does champion women's causes. Reproductive rights, equal pay for equal work . . .'

'The governor has a long record of being pro-choice. I'd love to get the two of them in a room together some time. If she's ever interested, that is.' He left it there as we made our way back out front. He'd planted his seed. Mission accomplished.

Tedone was waiting by his car with his arms crossed impatiently.

Fielding stuck out his hand, gave me a firm handshake and said, 'I'm glad we had this talk. I hope we get to know each other better some day.' Then he got back in Deputy Superintendent Mitry's car.

I made my way over to Tedone's cruiser, Lulu ambling along beside me.

Tedone checked me out, tilting his head slightly from left to right. 'What was that?'

'That, Lieutenant, was my idea of one slippery customer.'

'Fielding? He barely opened his mouth in your kitchen the other day.'

'He had plenty to say today, most of it in code.' I scratched at my staples, which were starting to itch under their bandage, and gazed at Michael Talmadge's brick manor house with its lush green leaf-free lawn. The crime scene and M.E.'s vans were still there along with a half-dozen cruisers. Mitry's driver got back in his cruiser and the deputy superintendent and Colin Fielding drove off, neither of them so much as looking at us as they drove by. 'I don't like this place,' I said. 'Can we get the hell out of here?'

'Actually, it would be a pleasure.'

NINE

The savage murder of Michael Talmadge, Connecticut's richest man, was soon all over the local airwaves. The state's TV news crews were already doing their stand-ups as Tedone and I drove out the front gate. The story would spread quickly to New York and go national by that evening. No way it wouldn't, considering that it had happened so soon after the identical slashing of Michael's younger brother, Austin, aka Connecticut's second-richest man. All that was missing to make it into a perfect tabloid trifecta was a link, any link, to a sleazy porn star with giant breasts. Based on my extensive experience, the tabloids would just go ahead and invent one.

But that would take a little while. It was still early, not yet nine a.m., when Tedone dropped Lulu and me off at the foot of Merilee's driveway.

'I'll be in touch,' he said, his dark eyes studying me. 'That works both ways. If you hear anything I want you to let me know right away, got it?'

'Absolutely, Lieutenant.'

'Are you jerking me off or do you really mean that?'

'Of course I mean it. Why wouldn't I?'

'Because you did your share of freelancing on the Sherbourne Playhouse case. My stomach can't deal with that kind of aggravation again.'

'If I hear anything I'll let you and your stomach both know, promise.'

When Lulu and I made our way up the gravel driveway we encountered two pickup trucks parked in the courtyard. One belonged to Mr MacGowan, the other to the Hardy Boys, who'd come to apply the top coat of paint to the storm windows – although at that very minute the hulking brothers were seated at the picnic table on the deck with Mr MacGowan eating donuts and drinking mugs of hot coffee from a Thermos.

'Well, you sure were up and out early this morning, young fellow,' Mr MacGowan said to me. 'What with the Jag being here I figured you were still sacked out in the feathers.'

'Not even maybe,' I said as Lulu ambled over to Gas Hardy to get thoroughly fussed over.

'Here, have one of my sister's cider doughnuts,' Mr MacGowan said. 'Fresh made. Best in Lyme.' They were in a basket with a dishtowel over them, still warm. I took one and bit into it. Practically melted in my mouth.

'Lulu's getting around real good now,' Gas said, pleased.

'She is. And so am I, thanks to you guys. I don't know what would have happened if you hadn't found us.'

'Don't think about it, son,' Mr MacGowan said, slurping his coffee.

'It's kind of hard not to after what I just saw.'

He peered at me. 'You saw Michael's body?'

'His throat was hacked from ear to ear just like Austin's was. He was lying in a pool of blood in his entry hall in his pajamas and a ratty old robe. It wasn't a pretty sight, let me tell you.' I reached for another donut. Murder makes me hungry. Always has. I have no idea why. 'The word's out about it?'

'Resident trooper called me. He always calls me when he has news.'

'Who'd want to kill Michael?' Tony wondered, munching on his donut. 'I mean, *nobody* could stand Austin, but people hardly even knew Michael. He was a whatcha call it, recluse.'

'What do you know about his gardener?'

'Earle Drake? I went to high school with him,' Mr MacGowan said. 'He's been working for the Talmadges his whole life. Lives alone in a little cottage by Uncas Pond. Nice enough fellow. Kept his mouth shut about Michael, same as Connie did. Never gossiped. If they had, Michael would have cut 'em loose.' He helped himself to another donut. 'Does that homicide detective have any idea what's going on?'

'Not really.'

'I guess that means you and Lulu will have to figure it out.'

'What makes you say that, Mr MacGowan?'

'The man dragged you out of bed at dawn and drove you to the crime scene. Face it, he needs you and he knows it.' He slurped some more coffee. 'I have me a theory.'

'OK, let's hear it.'

'Michael figured out who Austin's killer was, so the killer had to put him down, too, to save his own hide.' He paused, his brow furrowing. 'Except if Michael *did* figure out who killed his kid brother, he would have been so grateful he wouldn't have said a word to anyone. Then again, the killer wouldn't necessarily have known that, would he?' The old man scratched his tufty white head, befuddled. 'OK, now I understand it.'

'Understand what, Mr MacGowan?'

'Why that homicide detective needs your help.'

The Hardy Boys finished their donuts and coffee, wiping their mouths with the backs of their hands.

'We better get back to work,' Gas said.

'Thanks for the donuts, Mr MacGowan,' Tony said.

'Any time, fellows.' He sat there watching them as they went back to painting the storm windows, in no hurry to move himself.

I helped myself to another donut, gazing at a hawk that was circling overhead in search of its breakfast. I immediately flashed on standing with Colin Fielding at Michael Talmadge's mountain-top lookout watching that other hawk swoop down, pick up that rabbit and fly away with it, the rabbit's paws flailing helplessly. I was certain I would never forget that moment for the rest of my life.

'Planning to stick around?' Mr MacGowan asked me.

'The doctor wants me to stay off of the highway for a few more days. Figured I'd head back Sunday so I can get back to work bright and early Monday morning.'

'Will you be OK here by yourself?'

'I'll be fine, thanks. That doesn't mean I won't miss Merilee.'

Lulu let out a low grumble.

'*We* won't miss Merilee.'

'Well, sure you will. Heck, I miss her myself when she's not here. She's like a ray of sunshine.' He ran a hand over his jowly face. 'But what if nothing has happened?'

'Sorry?'

'Will you still go back to New York on Sunday even if they haven't caught the killer yet?'

'Not to worry. This case will be cracked wide open by then.'

'You sound awful confident for a man who has staples in his head.'

'I do, don't I?' I watched Gas pass one of the heavy storm windows to Tony up on the ladder. Tony took it from him, hung it from its latches and tapped it gently but firmly into place. 'The Hardy Boys are doing a nice job.'

'They're solid workmen, and they've got that good, hard yellow pine to work with. You've got to have good material. Doesn't matter how much skill you have if you're working with crap.' He gazed admiringly at the farmhouse. 'They don't build 'em like this anymore. Why, it's been standing here more than two hundred and fifty years. You think those vinyl-sided Lego toys they're putting up now will still be here in two hundred and fifty years? I think not.' He turned and peered at me. 'You already know who it is, don't you?'

'What makes you say that?'

'I may look dumb, but I'm not.'

'Mr MacGowan . . .?'

'Yeah, young fellow?'

'You don't look dumb.'

The tiny Lyme Library was located next to Lyme's tiny elementary school on Route 156. I'd paid many visits there over the summer to check out books and fell deeply in love with the place because it smelled exactly like the tiny library of my own small-town Connecticut childhood. The first time I walked in there I immediately wanted to head straight for the children's section, locate *Journey to the Center of the Earth* by Jules Verne, plop down on the rug and start reading it, sorry I hadn't thought to sneak a Snickers bar in with me. None of this is unusual when it comes to writers. Most of us grew up in public libraries and get a special glow on our faces whenever we sit around talking about the unique smell of an old library book.

Theresa, the Lyme Library's soft-spoken head librarian, was

actually the library's only librarian. The rest of her 'staff' consisted of elderly volunteers and high-school kids. She'd been thrilled all summer long to have me stop by, and was happy now when I came strolling in with Lulu. Bustled over to greet us and fuss over my bandaged head and Lulu's bandaged paws.

Theresa did have a microfilm reader but, as I'd feared, the Lyme Library was too small to have enough space to store the material I needed. She directed me to the bigger library in Old Lyme, so I steered the Jag down Route 156 to Old Lyme, Lulu riding with her front paws on the armrest and her large black nose stuck out of the window. She was definitely starting to feel like her old self. I turned off of Route 156 at Ferry Road and found myself in Old Lyme's Historic District, with its steepled white picture-postcard Congregational Church and immaculate center chimney colonial mansions. The Historic District was a place where time had stopped. The town hall, elementary school and grange hall were all from out of another century. The barbershop with its vintage Wildroot sign and barber pole was from out of a Norman Rockwell painting.

The library, which sat up on a rise, was an imposing two-story red-brick Victorian with dormer windows and a slate roof. A fire was going in the fireplace in the main reading room. A snowy-haired geezer was tending it while he read the *Wall Street Journal* in an overstuffed chair that was parked before it. They had two microfilm readers there. Kept them in the Genealogy Room, which had shelves of books devoted to local history. Also a solid oak door that could be shut so that the whirring noise of those microfilm readers wouldn't annoy the library's patrons.

An assistant librarian led me upstairs to the attic where microfilm rolls of the *New London Day*, *Hartford Courant* and *New Haven Register* dating back ten years were stored in boxes. I wasn't sure of the date I was looking for, beyond the fact that it would be a Monday, or possibly Tuesday, sometime in what I believed to be 1988. I figured that I could probably eliminate the coldest winter months when there would be snow and ice on the ground. But beyond that I definitely had some serious hunting ahead of me. I started with an armload of boxes of the *New London Day*, carried them down to the Genealogy Room and shut the door. Loaded the month of March into the microfilm reader, settled myself in front of it and started reading. Lulu circled three times at my feet before she curled up there with her head on my foot.

Most of the front-page news was about the 1988 Democratic Party primary campaign to decide who would be going up against President Reagan's two-term vice president, George Bush, in November. For those of you whose memories have dimmed, the Democrats' clear front runner early on had been Gary Hart, the extremely charismatic, extremely married Colorado senator who had to withdraw from the race after the *Miami Herald* reported he'd taken an overnight cruise to Bimini with a sexy young model named Donna Rice on a yacht aptly named *Monkey Business*. Once Hart dropped out, all that was left was the usual cast of uninspiring characters – Dick Gephardt, Al Gore, Joe Biden. Somehow, the nomination eventually landed in the lap of Massachusetts Governor Michael Dukakis, a height-challenged man who seemed to have the word *schnook* tattooed across his forehead. He was slaughtered in November, leaving us with George Bush and his young, exceedingly dim vice president, Indiana Senator Dan Quayle, who became best known for getting into a raging battle with a fictional TV sitcom character named Murphy Brown and for his inability to spell the plural of the word potato.

But as absorbing as I found the campaign coverage it was the local police news that was my reason for being there. And the story I was searching for eluded me, week after week, month after month. After two hours of watching the microfilm pages go whizzing by, I'd arrived at June and had nothing, aside from a slight case of dizziness – which had nothing to do with my concussion. Those damned machines always make me dizzy if I stare at them for too long. I got up and went outside, Lulu following along. Sat on the library's front steps with my hands in the pockets of my flight jacket and soaked up some fresh, cool air and autumn sunshine.

One of the librarians followed us out there. She was a slender woman in her fifties with a blunt, chin-length haircut who was wearing a navy-blue wool dress, tights and woolen clogs that looked vaguely Scandinavian. 'I don't mean to be forward, but are you Stewart Hoag?'

'I'm afraid so.'

'I thought I recognized you from your book jacket photo. I'm Judy, the head librarian. It's such an honor to have you here with us. I loved your novel.'

'Thank you. I hope you'll have reason to love my next one.'

'So you're at work on another?' she asked with keen interest.

'I am.'

'Is our microfilm part of your research?'

'As a matter of fact it is,' I said, knowing it would make her day.

'Well, I won't interrupt your creative process any further. I just wanted to say hello. If you need any help at all, please holler.'

'Thank you, I shall.'

She went back inside. I stayed out there a few more minutes, long enough to smoke a Chesterfield, then led Lulu back inside to the Genealogy Room and that microfilm machine. It took me another hour of staring at those whirring pages of the *New London Day* before I finally found the story that I was looking for. It was dated Monday, July 16, 1988. I carefully jotted down the particulars, then unspooled the microfilm, packed it up in its box and returned the boxes to the attic. Paused to thank Judy for her help. Went back outside and steered the Jag up Route 156 back to the farm, bleary-eyed and starving for lunch.

The Hardy Boys were still there, working away. I waved hello as I headed straight for the kitchen, where I fed Lulu a half-can of 9Lives mackerel and myself a fat sandwich of crusty bread filled with sliced sausage, fresh mozzarella and roasted peppers. Then I went into the master bedroom, took off my Chippewas and stretched out on the bed with a blanket over me. My intention was simply to rest my tired eyes for a few minutes. I woke up more than an hour later with Lulu curled up next to me, snoring softly.

I still wasn't a hundred percent, much as I hated to admit to myself.

By then, it was two thirty. I splashed some cold water on my face and put my Chippewas and flight jacket back on. Lulu stirred and followed me as I headed out to the Jag, waved goodbye to the Hardy Boys and drove to the Old Lyme A&P, which, sad to say, was the one place in town where Lulu was forbidden to join me. She had to wait glumly in the car.

I spotted Joanie at her usual post at the courtesy desk. She was in her late forties and built like a refrigerator with frizzy blond hair. She'd been working at the A&P ever since high school along with her best friend, Sandy, a cashier who was built like a refrigerator with frizzy black hair. Both were grandmothers who'd married their high-school sweethearts and started having kids before they were twenty. I'd shopped regularly at the A&P over the summer and discovered that they were major founts of gossip, not to mention smart. Not book smart. People smart. Plus they were fun to flirt with, although Joanie was a swatter. If I spent more than five minutes with her I came away with a welt on my shoulder.

'Hoagy!' She lit right up when she spotted me. Came out from behind the courtesy desk and put me in a bear hug. 'You poor, poor man. That lunatic almost split your head in half.'

'He tried. Fortunately, it's a hard one.'

'It's so good to see you again, hon. How long are you in town for?'

'A few more days. Merilee was here but she's left, so now's your chance.'

That earned me my first swat. 'You are *still* such a flirt.'

'Where's Sandy? I didn't spot her at any of the registers.'

'They moved her to produce, which she is *not* happy about. She misses chatting with her regulars. But will she ever be thrilled to see you.' Joanie grabbed the store intercom, flicked it on and said, 'Sandy to the courtesy desk, please. Sandy to the courtesy desk.'

Sandy let out a squeal of delight from halfway across the store when she spotted me. Once again I got put in a bear hug. 'I've missed you, you tall drink of water. But, my God, your head . . .'

'I'll be happy to get these staples out, believe me. What time do you girls get off?'

'Four o'clock,' Joanie said.

'Can I buy you a beer up at the Rustic?'

Sandy considered this gravely. 'Gee, I don't know. I'll have to think about it . . .' Then she let out a shriek of laughter that turned heads. 'What are you, kidding? We're there!'

Joanie peered at me suspiciously. 'Wait, you're not getting any funny ideas, are you? Because I got to warn you – Sandy may be fast and loose, but I'm not into threesomes.'

'Really? That's not what I hear around town.' *Swat.* 'I've missed you girls.'

'Do we get to see Lulu?' Sandy asked.

'Of course you do. She's out in the car.'

'How's she doing?'

'Her paws were in really rough shape, but she's doing much, much better. We have Gas Hardy to thank for that. If he hadn't rushed her to Dr Jen, well, I don't even want to think about it.'

'Believe me, some things you're better off not thinking about,' Sandy said.

Joanie said, 'We'll see you at the Rustic a little after four. I sure do hope you brought plenty of cash because we are thirsty girls.'

The Rustic was a tiny burger and beer shack up the Boston Post Road a few miles past Rogers Lake. During the balmy summer months an outdoor deck doubled its seating capacity. Once it started getting frosty, the door out to the deck was sealed up tight and there were only ten tables and half a dozen stools to be had at the bar. There was a TV that was off. There was a sound system that I wished was off. It was playing a truly manic mix that segued from Fontella Bass to the Monkees and then to Lynyrd Skynyrd before it veered sharply to the Kingston Trio. I tried my best to tune it out. The last thing I needed crowded into my concussed skull right now was 'Where Have All the Flowers Gone?'

The Rustic had great onion rings and Guinness on tap. Who could ask for anything more? I had no trouble grabbing us a table because we had the place to ourselves. I ordered us three baskets of onion rings and a Guinness for myself. Joanie and

Sandy, who'd changed out of their A&P smocks into sweat-shirts and jeans, ordered Miller Lites. We clinked mugs when our beers arrived and took healthy slugs. The onion rings followed a moment later and were as crisp and flavorful as I remembered them. Karen, our slender young barmaid, was notable for her effort to single-headedly bring back the mullet hairdo. But she doted over Lulu and brought her two anchovies on a little plate.

Sandy, who used to follow me out to the parking lot to visit Lulu over the summer, made an even bigger fuss over her. 'You are *such* a little cutie,' she cooed, petting her. 'If Hoagy ever, I mean *ever*, doesn't treat you right, you can move in with me any time.'

Lulu whimpered and licked her hand in response. Never forget that Lulu's mother is a great actress. I don't.

'Is the poor thing in a lot of pain?' Sandy asked me.

'She was, no question. But she's doing much better. Her bandages come off in a few days.'

'I could have sworn you went back to New York City for good after the summer.'

'I did. Just came back for a few days to clear my head.'

'You got it cleared, all right!' Joanie roared. *Swat.*

I was already getting a welt and we hadn't even finished our first round. 'Let me tell you, seeing Michael's body this morning with his throat cut open was a real head clearer, too.'

Joanie turned serious. 'What were *you* doing there?'

'The homicide detective who's working the case wanted me along for the ride.'

'Does he have the slightest idea what's going on?'

'Not really.'

'But it must be the same killer, right?' Sandy nibbled on an onion ring. 'I mean, both brothers getting their throats cut the same way and all, am I right?'

'It sure seems that way,' I agreed. 'Who's ready for another round?'

Before I had a chance to catch Karen's eye, Joanie called out, 'Yo, Karen! Hit us again!'

Karen laughed merrily and got busy obliging us.

'So I heard a weird story the other day,' I said. 'Is it true that Austin actually used to work with you at the A&P back when he was taking his meds and hadn't gone totally around the bend?'

The two of them exchanged a rather sorrowful look.

'It's true,' Joanie said. 'Up until a couple of years ago.'

'Might have been three,' Sandy said.

'Might have,' Joanie acknowledged, polishing off her last onion ring. She sat back in her chair, lit a Merit with a disposable Bic lighter and took a deep drag on it. 'He wasn't up to cashiering. You never knew when he might lose it and go cuckoo-bird on a customer. But he was fine at re-stocking shelves. He'd show up on time every day in his green A&P shirt and trousers. Do his job. Keep to himself. If out-of-towners asked him where to find the tuna or what have you, he'd politely tell them and off they'd go, having no idea whatsoever that the chubby little guy they'd just spoken to was a multi-*billionaire*.'

'Did you get to know him?'

Sandy bit down on her lower lip, her eyes moistening. 'We did. We felt sorry for him, which I guess must sound pretty weird for a Swamp Yankee like me to say. But he had a mental illness. It wasn't his fault.'

'He was super shy around women,' Joanie said. 'Especially the young ones. But we'd kid around a little with him and he got so he'd kid us back. Or at least try. He was so lonely. He didn't have anyone to talk to except for *her* – Dr McKenna, his high-class personal shrink. She'd stop by regularly to buy groceries and look in on him.'

'Boss him around is more like it,' Sandy sniffed.

'I'm getting the impression you two don't care for her.'

'Let's just say she's got a real high opinion of herself,' Joanie responded. 'And never has a friendly word for any of the cashiers. Doesn't bother to remember anybody's name. Doesn't even say hello.'

'She's rude,' Sandy said, sipping her Miller Lite.

'Really? She's been super nice to me. Even brought me a vat of homemade chicken noodle soup.'

Sandy let out a laugh. 'Well, she would, wouldn't she? She's a widow with a houseful of kids and you're a famous, handsome author who used to be married to a movie star. You're a catch, hon, as you know perfectly well. But when she's around regular folks like us she acts like she's special just because she's a Yale professor who can still fit into a pair of tight jeans.'

'Take it from me,' Joanie said. 'A woman in her forties who still wears jeans that tight has something wrong with her. I'm no Yale shrink like she is, but I know women.'

'Did you know her husband?'

'Paul?' Sandy nodded. 'Sure, we did. He was a sweet man. And he loved those kids. He'd always bring them to the store with him. Of course, they were a lot younger then. Now they're teenagers. If *she* brings them with her she gets testy with them. She's coiled real tight, that one.'

'She has a lot on her plate,' I said.

'She did get handed a rough deal,' Joanie admitted grudgingly. 'What with being widowed so young.'

'You said she would come in to check up on Austin?'

Joanie nodded. 'Wanted to make sure he wasn't causing any problems. Our manager, Frank, strictly gave him the job as a favor to Michael. We all figured that Michael slipped him a little something under the table.'

'And did Austin cause any problems?'

'Nothing major,' Joanie recalled. 'Though she chewed him out a couple of times right there in the store, remember?'

'I do,' Sandy said. 'Once because he was a half-hour late for work.'

'And another time because he called the assistant manager, Ron, a dickhead right to his face.'

'Which would have gotten anyone else fired on the spot,' Sandy said. 'But she made Austin apologize and shake Ron's hand, and all was forgiven.'

'And then she chewed *us* out when she caught us chatting with Austin,' Joanie said. 'Didn't care for it at all. We said we were just trying to make him feel welcome. She told us to "let him find his own path." Those were the exact words she used. I said to her, "If he makes friends that's a good thing, isn't it?" She said to me, "Excuse me, what school of

psychiatry did you graduate from?" That skinny bitch is lucky
I didn't smack her.'

Sandy went to work on her last onion ring. 'She's nothing
like Merilee, who lord knows has plenty to brag about. But
you'd never know it because she's just plain folks. Treats
everyone like an equal. That's why we all love her.'

'That's why we put up with you, too,' Joanie said teasingly.
'Although you don't have nearly enough meat on your bones
for my taste. I'm never comfortable being with a man whose
butt's smaller than mine.' *Swat.*

I'd definitely have to ice my shoulder when I got home. 'So
you'd say Austin generally got along OK with people?'

'No one was afraid of him or anything, if that's what you
mean,' Sandy said. 'Mind you, we didn't see him when he
wasn't doing well. He'd be hospitalized for months at a stretch,
poor thing. Then he'd be back for a while, doing fine. And
then, poof, he'd be gone again.'

'I keep hearing that Austin made a lot of enemies for himself
when he was growing up.'

'He shot his own brother in the head with a pellet gun,'
Joanie recalled. 'Poisoned the Hardy Boys' dog. Cut off all
of Gail's hair. Tormented Jim Conley's sister, Deirdre, so
mercilessly that she took her own life.'

'That was just awful,' Sandy recalled sadly. 'Of course, you
have to remember that Deirdre had the cuckoo-bird gene
herself. Not that I mean to speak ill of the dead, but there's
no getting around the bloodline.'

'Bloodline?'

'Jim and Deirdre's mother was Austin and Michael's aunt.
She was their father's youngest sister. Passed away from cancer
when she was young.'

'You ask me,' Joanie said, 'Jim's got it, too. The Talmadge
cuckoo-bird gene, I mean.'

'Really? He seems so under control.'

Sandy shook her head. 'That's strictly his resident trooper
personality. Trust me, you don't want to be around him at a
Sunday barbeque after he's had a couple of Pabst Blue Ribbons.
He starts saying *the* strangest things about the upcoming race
war.'

'There's an upcoming race war?'

'He thinks so. Believes the black and brown people in this country are going to unite, wipe out the whites and take over.'

'And he for sure wasn't under control when we were growing up,' Joanie said. 'Always getting in fights. Always getting sent to the principal's office. He knocked up Linda Angelico, who had to move in with her grandmother up in Glastonbury. He even stole some money from a couple of widowed sisters whose lawn he mowed. Just walked right in the house and cleaned out their purses. They called the state police on him. The judge told him he could either go to jail or to Vietnam. He enlisted in the Army and came back from Vietnam such a serious law and order type that he became a state trooper, just like his daddy was. But he's still got the Talmadge cuckoo-bird gene. Trust me, you do not want to be around him after he's had a couple.'

'Thanks for the warning. I'll remember that.'

I didn't have to remember it for long.

The resident trooper showed up at the farm not ten minutes after I got home from the Rustic. I was busy poking around in the freezer for something to heat up for dinner. Found a container of caldo verde, a Portuguese potato and kale soup with spicy sliced linguica sausage that Merilee had made a giant vat of over the summer when she'd grown enough kale to feed the entire city of Cleveland. It wasn't quite dark out when his cruiser came up the gravel drive and Jim Conley get out of his cruiser, put his hat on his head, squared his shoulders and strode toward the mudroom door.

I opened it before he had to knock. 'Greetings, Trooper. I sincerely hope you're not here to arrest me.'

'No, nothing like that.' Conley removed his hat as he came inside, smiling faintly. 'Lieutenant Tedone asked me to stop by. He was hoping to swing by himself but he had to report to his captain up at Major Crime Squad headquarters in Meriden.'

'Can I offer you a beer?' I asked him, wondering if Merilee had any Pabst stashed in the old fridge down in the basement.

'I'm all set, thanks,' he said politely as Lulu sniffed carefully at his brogans and trouser cuffs, snuffling and snorting. He watched her, his jaw muscles flexing. 'Why is she doing that?'

'She's a scent hound. It's how she gets to know people. If she's bothering you . . .'

'No, no. It's fine.'

'Would you care to move into the parlor? I'll build us a fire.'

'I don't want to keep you, thanks,' he said, sitting down at the kitchen table. 'I know you're still recovering from that concussion. The lieutenant just asked me to fill you in on what we know about Michael Talmadge that we didn't know this morning.'

I sat down at the table with him. 'OK . . .'

'They opened the safe in his office. Found some deeds and legal documents. No money or valuables of any kind. Also, a thorough room-by-room search of the house was conducted by Connie Pike. I accompanied her. I've known Connie forever and she made it clear to me that she'd feel a lot less qualmish if I was with her.'

'And . . .?'

'She said nothing seems to be missing. It was . . .' Conley trailed off, rubbing the back of his head. 'A curious experience, I must say.'

'Curious how, Trooper?'

'For a man of his immense wealth, Michael had very few possessions. His bedroom closet, for instance, was nearly empty. He had four identical gray suits and a topcoat hanging in there. And a rack with a half-dozen of those clip-on ties he wore. On the floor he had two pairs of identical wing-tip shoes. That was it. Nothing else. In his dresser there were maybe ten white dress shirts, underwear, socks – all of it of modest quality. I'm talking J.C. Penney's, Sears. He had two V-neck sweater vests. No other sweaters. No sport shirts, sweatshirts, jeans – nothing like the sort of thing you or I might wear when we're unwinding.'

'Evidently he never unwound.'

'There are six bedrooms upstairs, each with a private bath

and a view of Hamburg Cove – with the exception of his. He preferred the only upstairs bedroom that *doesn't* have a view of the cove. It's also considerably smaller than the others. He insisted that his security team stay in the nicer rooms when they were there. Each man had his own room. Nice, considerate fellows, Connie said. Did their own laundry. Cooked their own meals and did the dishes themselves. Really went out of their way to make no extra work for her.'

'What about Pinkie?'

'Connie said the dog was well trained and no bother at all. He had free run of the grounds but one of the guys always made sure to pick up after him so that Earle, the gardener, wouldn't have to.' Conley scratched the back of his head again. 'Downstairs, there's a formal dining room that would seat two dozen people easily, and a huge, paneled den with a wet bar. Connie said that Michael never so much as set foot in either room. He preferred the pocket-sized den off of the kitchen where he'd have his dinner on a fold-up tray so that he could watch TV while he ate.'

'What did he watch?'

His lean face creased into a faint smile. 'I asked her that, too, because I couldn't imagine. You'll never guess in a million years.'

'*The MacNeil-Lehrer Report*?'

'No.'

'*Jeopardy*?'

'No.'

'*Family Feud*?'

'No again. Believe it or not, he liked to watch a situation comedy from the seventies called *The Odd Couple* with Tony Randall and Jack Klugman.'

'Based on the Neil Simon play. Sure.'

'I wouldn't know about that. Don't get to the theater much. What I do know is that he owned a boxed set of all five seasons on cassette, which I suppose qualified as his only personal indulgence, and that Connie swore to me he must have seen every episode fifty times.'

'Did she ever hear him laugh?'

'Uproariously.'

'How odd. He didn't strike me as someone who had even a nodding acquaintance with a sense of humor.'

'I'm with you there. And get this – he was such a huge fan, he mentioned to Connie a few days ago that it was time for her to start thinking about planning his special menu for Happy Felix Unger Day.'

'Sorry, it must be my head wound. You lost me back there somewhere.'

'No, that one threw me, too. Apparently, if you watch the show, a narrator says at the beginning of each episode that Felix Unger's wife threw him out on November the thirteenth. So Michael considered November the thirteenth to be a kind of holiday. Connie told me he ordinarily ate very plain fare. The meat loaf like he had last night. Roast chicken. Tuna casserole. Absolutely nothing elaborate. But on November the thirteenth she always made him a porterhouse steak from Walt's Market, cooked medium rare, a baked potato with sour cream and chives, and creamed spinach. He would even pop the cork on a bottle of Dom Perignon like it was New Year's Eve.'

'Did Connie find this a tiny bit odd?'

'She found everything about Mr Michael, as she called him, a tiny bit odd. If you ask me – not that you did – I find it kind of pathetic.'

'Did you know him well?'

'Can't say that I did.'

'Even though your mother was his father's youngest sister?'

'She was one of eight brothers and sisters,' he responded, tensing slightly. 'It was a large family.'

'Still, it seems strange to me that this didn't come up before.'

Now he tensed more than slightly. '*What* didn't come up before?'

'That you, Michael and Austin were first cousins.'

'You're an outsider here, so I can understand how it might seem that way to you. But pretty much everyone in Lyme is related to everyone else. This was a remote area founded more than three hundred years ago by a very small group of families.'

'Yet none of the other founding families had quite the same reputation for standoffish behavior that the Talmadges did.'

'I'm the product of my forebears, same as you are. That doesn't mean I belong to a weird religious cult, worship Satan, countenance incest, rape or any of the other crazy things that the people around here think.'

'Still, I understand that you were a pretty wild kid,' I said as I searched his face and hands for any traces of fingernail scratches. I saw none.

He narrowed his gaze at me. 'Who have you been talking to?'

'Nobody in particular. I just pick up gossip here and there.'

'There's too damned much of it in this place,' he fumed. 'And whenever something happens it all comes bubbling back up. Since you'll no doubt end up hearing the sordid details third-hand from one of the village hens, I'll tell them to you myself. Better you hear it directly from me. Back when I was twelve years old, I was a powder keg. Partly because of what Austin had done to my sister, Deirdre. Partly it was just plain old raging hormones. But I was angry at everyone. Got in fights. Got suspended from school more times than I care to remember. My father took a strap to me, but it didn't settle me down one bit. And when I discovered motorcycles and girls I got into even more trouble.'

'I hear you got a girl pregnant.'

'Yes, I did,' he said, his nostrils flaring. 'I also wrecked two bikes. When I needed the money to buy a third one, I lifted it from the handbags of a couple of sweet old ladies who I did chores for. They called my father and he hauled me in. It was made real plain to me – either enlist or get locked up. So I ended up in 'Nam. Let me tell you something. Having your best friend bleed to death in your arms with his intestines hanging out all over you has a way of knocking some sense into you. It sure knocked some into me. When I came home I settled down and decided to serve the public, same as my father did. Married Millie. We have two beautiful girls.' He broke off, breathing in and out. 'Now, do you want to tell me why this is any of your damned business?'

'I'm just trying to get a sense of things.'

'No, that's not what you're doing,' he argued.

'OK, what am I doing?'

'You're suggesting that *I* followed you up that mountain and paid Austin back for Deirdre after all of these years. That's total bull. Never happened. I was down in the parking lot coordinating the response team.'

'There's no chance you could have slipped away for an hour or two? Austin was also making your life miserable by trying to do your job for you. That had to be incredibly humiliating.'

'So what if it was? It doesn't mean that I slit his throat.' He shook his head at me in total disgust. 'Can I give you some advice?'

'Please, do.'

'You should get that head of yours checked.'

'I just did.'

'Then you should get it checked again. You're nuts.'

'There are those who would agree with you.'

'I have a good life here. I would never do anything to jeopardize it. I wouldn't kill Austin. And I for damned sure wouldn't kill Michael. I mean, why would I do that?'

'I don't know. Why would you?'

He stood up, squaring his big Smokey hat on his head and glowered at me menacingly. 'Are we done here?'

'We are as far as I'm concerned. Thanks for stopping by with the news.'

Resident Trooper Jim Conley said nothing in response to that. He was already out the door and gone.

I made a fire in the parlor, opened a bottle of Chianti Classico and put the caldo verde in a pot on the stove on low heat to thaw. Decided some Italian parsley would liven it up, so I moseyed out to the herb garden with a pair of kitchen pruners to see if there was still some growing. There was. It's very hardy. I snipped off a handful and was starting back to the kitchen when a silver Crown Vic came up the driveway, setting off the motion detector floodlights.

It was Lieutenant Carmine Tedone. He climbed out of his cruiser slowly and wearily. It had been a long day that had started at dawn and was seemingly not over yet. Lulu ambled over to greet him. He knelt down and patted her.

'Good evening, Lieutenant. I thought you were up in Meriden.'

'I was. Thought I'd stop by on my way home.'

'You live in Waterbury. That's in the opposite direction.'

'You're right, it is. I lied. There are some things I wanted to talk over with you. I take it Jim Conley stopped by.'

'He did, and I'm fairly certain that I pissed him off.'

'I can't imagine how that could happen. You're always so tactful.'

'He has quite a temper. He keeps it carefully under wraps, but it's there. Did you know that?'

Tedone didn't bother to reply. Just sniffed at the air and said, 'Smells like rain.'

'I just made a fire, Lieutenant. Come on in, have a seat and I'll pour you some Chianti Classico.'

'Thanks, I will – except for the Chianti part.'

I deposited my parsley on the kitchen counter and joined him in the parlor. He took the wing-backed chair and gazed into the fire. I took the sofa. Lulu curled up next to me, watching him.

'This sure is a nice place,' he said. 'Cozy.'

'Yes, it is. Merilee has exceptional taste, along with her many other attributes.'

'Did Conley fill you in on what we know? Or should I say don't know?'

'Do you mean before he almost bit my head off? Yes, he did. And I have a question for you. Wouldn't Michael's killer have been covered in his blood?'

'You'd certainly think so. But they've found no bloody handprints or footprints at the scene. No trail of droplets out to the driveway. Nothing.'

'What does that suggest to you?'

'Someone who was careful. Brought a change of clothes and shoes.'

'Which means the bloody clothes and shoes have to be somewhere.'

'Yes, they do. But we'll never find them. This is no dummy we're dealing with.'

'So you're sure it's the same killer.'

'The odds of it being two different people are so slim as to be nonexistent. The M.O. in both cases is exactly the same – throat cut from ear to ear. And the M.E. said both brothers were slashed by someone who is right-handed, strong, used the same type of knife – possibly even the same exact knife, although we can't prove that yet – and attacked them with a tremendous degree of ferocity. Trust me, it's the same killer.' He turned from the fire, raising his chin at me. 'Why did you harass Jim Conley?'

'I didn't harass him. Or at least I wouldn't characterize it that way.'

'Well, he sure did. Called me up and said you practically accused him of killing Austin.'

'I did no such thing. I merely laid out a plausible scenario.'

'He was furious.'

'Then he's awfully thin-skinned, which I wouldn't think of as an asset in your trade. We had a constructive conversation. We talked about Felix Unger Day . . .'

'Felix Unger *what*?'

'I did tell him I thought it was strange that he'd never mentioned that he, Austin and Michael were first cousins. Also that I'd heard he had a pretty wild youth. Got in lots of fights, stole some money. Almost ended up in jail, in fact.'

'I take it he didn't like you bringing it up.'

'That's putting it mildly.'

Tedone gazed back at the fire. 'He's under a lot of pressure. We all are. Me, I feel like my head's on a chopping block. We've just lost the two richest men in the state, one of them a close confidante of the governor. You know what they call cases like these? Career killers.'

'Are you any closer to cracking it than you were this morning?'

'Can I change my mind?'

'About . . .?'

'That glass of Chianti.'

'Absolutely.' I fetched the bottle and a glass. Filled his and handed it to him, then topped mine off before I sat back down.

He took a sip, smacking his laps. 'This is the good stuff. Warms you right down to your toes.' He took another sip, looking at me, then at Lulu dozing next to me. 'Something sure smells good in the kitchen.'

'I'm thawing a Portuguese potato and kale soup with linguica that Merilee makes. Care to stay? There's plenty.'

'Sounds terrific, but my wife will be expecting me.' He ran a hand over his layered Travoltage pompadour. 'I just realized something about you that I didn't quite grasp when we worked that case last summer.'

'Which is what, Lieutenant?'

'You're one very lucky guy.'

'You wouldn't have said so if you ran into me ten years ago. But I kept battling until I turned my luck back around. It wasn't easy. I needed someone who believed in me. Someone who gave me a reason to get my act back together.'

'That would be Merilee?'

'That would be Merilee.'

'I suppose being genuinely talented helps, too.'

'Doesn't hurt.'

He let out a laugh. 'You've got yourself an ego, haven't you?'

'All writers do. We wouldn't set pen to paper if we didn't.'

'I'll have to read that great American novel of yours some time.'

'I sincerely hope you do,' I said, wondering why Tedone was suddenly being so nice to me. Was he caving to the pressure? Seeing his career crash and burn right before his eyes? Or did three sips of wine just make him into a big teddy bear? 'Would you mind putting another log on the fire, Lieutenant?'

'Sure thing.' He laid an applewood log atop the blaze, poked at it and sat back down, gazing down into his wine glass for a long moment before he said, 'I know I'm going to regret saying this, but I can't seem to stop myself . . .'

'What is it, Lieutenant?'

'I don't suppose *you* have any ideas, do you?'

'I do, actually.'

'Somehow I thought you would. Or I should say *hoped* you would. Hoagy, you're looking at a desperate man.'

'No need to worry. Twenty-four hours from now you'll be a hero.'

'Is that right? What are they? Your ideas, I mean.'

'I need for you to find out something that I can't, since I don't have the legal authority. A date.'

'A date? What kind of a date?'

'It may prove to be totally insignificant. Then again, it may steer you exactly where you want to go.'

'OK . . .' He took another sip of his wine. 'Tell me what it is.'

So I told him.

TEN

Tedone was right. The rain arrived in the night. It was about three a.m. when it started falling. Lulu was fast asleep with her head on my left shoulder, snoring softly. Me, I was lying there in bed wide awake. Couldn't stop thinking about the Talmadge brothers, about who had wanted them dead and why.

I did doze off for a bit as the rain pattered outside, but I was wide awake again when Quasimodo announced the dawn. Got up, put on my silk target dressing gown, fed the fire in the bedroom fireplace and went into the kitchen to make a pot of coffee, rubbing my bleary eyes. Lulu followed me in there and nudged my leg with her head. I put down her 9Lives mackerel. Toasted a thick slice of Italian bread and slathered it with blackberry jam. Took a tray with my coffee and toast back to bed and dove under the covers as the fire warmed up the room and a chilly rain fell over Whalebone Cove.

I wondered where Merilee was right now. I wondered if she was deeply immersed in Brett. I wondered when I'd be able to disappear back into my own work. I did think about pulling the manuscript out of my briefcase and glancing through it, but there was no point. I was no longer back in the '70s, living my sweet season of madness. I was living right here, right now with the Talmadge brothers. My mind couldn't stop dwelling on their cousin, Jim Conley, the not-so-cool and collected resident trooper, and on sly, cagy Colin Fielding, and on the Hardy Boys, Tony and Gas. It was on Skip Rimer, Truman Mainwaring's infuriated lover. It was on Donna Willis, the sturdy botanist who'd clashed repeatedly with Austin, and on Joanie and Sandy at the A&P and how they'd been fond of Austin, but not Annabeth McKenna.

Let me tell you, real life can be a genuine pain in the ass

when all you want to do is get lost in your own alternative reality.

When I'd finished my coffee and toast I went into the bathroom and removed the bandage on my head. The wound looked clean and was healing nicely, although my shaved scalp was getting itchy and the staples were starting to feel annoyingly *there*, which I took as a sign that they were getting ready to come out. I showered and washed the wound carefully, patting it dry before I applied a fresh bandage. Then I stropped Grandfather's razor, shaved and put on my six-ply shawl-collared cashmere cardigan over a viyella shirt and jeans. It was damp in the old farmhouse that morning. I couldn't seem to get warm.

The bedside phone rang. The unlisted number. Yet again, I raced to pick it up, hoping it was Merilee calling from Budapest to tell me how much she missed me.

Yet again, it was Carmine Tedone. 'Morning, Hoagy. Hope I didn't wake you.'

'Not a chance, Lieutenant. I've been up for hours.'

'So have I. My wife elbowed me awake at two o'clock to tell me I was grinding my teeth in my sleep so loud that I was keeping her awake. I ended up spending half the night pacing the living-room carpet.'

'They do have bite guards for that sort of thing.'

'Yeah, I'll be sure to put that right at the top of my list of priorities. So, listen, I got hold of that date you asked me for.'

'That was fast. Did he give you any trouble?'

'Not a bit. He was happy to help. Are you ready?'

'Hang on just a sec. Let me get my notes.' I fetched my notepad from the parlor and returned to the bedroom, leafing through it. 'OK . . .'

'*Now* are you ready?'

'Good to go.'

We traded dates. And immediately fell silent after that.

'You still there, Hoagy?' Tedone said finally.

'Still here,' I said, my pulse quickening

'I thought maybe you blacked out or something.'

'No, I'm fine. Well, I'm not fine, but I'm fine. Tell me, do you have any free time today?'

'You kidding? Aside from working the Talmadge double homicide and having the governor and the entire hierarchy of the state police breathing down my neck, I've got nothing but free time. In fact, I was thinking of scarfing up a Denny's Grand Slam breakfast and then taking in a noon showing of *Jurassic Park*. Want to join me?'

'Actually, I wanted to ask you for another small favor.'

He let out a pained sigh. 'Can I tell you how much I'm already hating this? I feel like any moment now Deputy Superintendent Mitry's going to lower the boom on me and I'll be back in uniform working the Sunday-morning speed trap on I-395 in Killingly.'

'Lieutenant . . .?'

'What a crap detail that was. Standing out in the freezing cold, ticketing every poor slob for the crime of going sixty-six miles an hour when they came around a blind curve after a long, steep downhill stretch of highway. I swear, there's not a living soul who could stay under sixty-five on that particular—'

'Lieutenant . . .?'

'If they try to send me back there, I'll turn in my shield and go private with my cousin Pete. He's been after me for years to partner up. No bosses. No red tape. No one breathing down your—'

'Lieutenant . . .?'

'WHAT?'

'You don't even know what I'm about to say.'

'Like hell I don't. You're about to propose some whacka-doodle end-around play and try to drag me into it.'

'You want to catch your killer, don't you?'

'Of course, but on the off-chance that no one's ever told you, there's such a thing known as proper police procedure. If I don't follow it to the letter then the case will never hold up in court.'

'This will hold up. Not to worry. About that small favor . . .?'

'My stomach is starting to hurt again.'

'You need to chew on a couple of Gaviscons.'

'I need for you to go back to New York City and stay there.'

'Lieutenant, it's very simple. You're either in or you're out. Which is it?'

'In, in. I'm in,' he said hurriedly. 'What do you want me to do?'

I built a big fire in the parlor fireplace as the chilly rain continued to fall. I even closed off the hallway door to the master bedroom suite to make the parlor more toasty.

She arrived a socially correct ten minutes after her midday invitation, although I doubt that Miss Manners was much on her mind at that particular moment. She came in by way of the mudroom and took off her wet raincoat and hat, which I hung up in there for her.

'I'd better take off my rain boots, too. They're all muddy.' They were rubber wellingtons – the only thing that did the job out there. 'It was awfully nice of you to call,' she added brightly.

'And I made sure I picked a perfect day, didn't I?'

She declined my offer of a sandwich but did say yes to tea.

I already had the kettle going and made us a pot of Earl Grey. 'I'm afraid I don't have any cookies to offer you.'

'That's quite all right. I'm not much for sweets. If I eat them I puff up like a blowfish.'

'I find that very hard to believe'

'You, sir, are one smooth talker,' Annabeth McKenna said as she sat on the sofa in the parlor and put her feet up on the coffee table, the better to warm her toes in her black stockings. Her feet were small and slender. She had lean, muscled calves – a runner's calves. There was absolutely nothing casual about her appearance, I noticed. She'd brushed out her lush mane of chestnut hair until it gleamed. Wore lipstick, eyeliner and eye shadow. Her charcoal-gray wool skirt and contrasting pale-gray cable-stitched sweater were extremely becoming. She'd even dabbed on some of that subtly intoxicating essential lavender oil. Her scent of choice.

I fetched the teapot and put it on a tray with mugs, spoons, a small pitcher of milk and jar of local honey. I set it on the coffee table and filled our mugs. She sat up and stirred milk and honey into hers, then sat back, put her feet back up on the coffee table and crossed her ankles, her stockings rustling.

There's something about the rustle of stockings that makes a man's blood boil. Maybe that's why women wear them. Maybe there's no maybe about it.

I stirred milk and honey into my own tea and sat down next to her.

Lulu was curled up in the wing-backed chair next to the fireplace, the better to eye us guardedly.

'I don't think Lulu likes me,' Annabeth observed, sipping her tea.

'Why would you say that?'

'Something about the way she keeps watching me.'

'She regards you as a potential threat to her happy home, that's all.'

Annabeth tilted her head at me curiously. 'Am I?'

'Are you what?'

'A potential threat to your happy home.'

'You certainly could be. You're extremely attractive. My ex-wife is in Budapest. And we had a terrible fight before she left. Major ten-round bout.'

'You and Merilee? May I ask what it was . . .?' She stopped right there. 'Please forgive me. It's really none of my business.'

'No, it's OK, I don't mind. It's the same old fight that anyone who's involved with a movie star always has. Kind of pathetic really, but there you have it.'

Annabeth frowned. 'I'm not following you, I'm afraid.'

'When a leading lady and leading man go away on location for months and their characters are supposed to be involved, then *they* get involved.'

She shook her head. 'Sorry, I still don't . . .'

'She's having an affair with Mel Gibson, OK?'

Annabeth's penetrating brown eyes widened. 'She's not. I don't believe it.'

'Believe it. Hell, if I rattled off the list of leading men with whom she's had affairs since I first met her, it would make your jaw drop. Why do you think I crash landed?'

'Are you telling me *that's* why you got into drugs and the two of you split up? Because she was sleeping around on you?'

'I'm afraid so. We've managed to make it work again these past few months because she swore to me that it would never, ever happen again. But it was a big, fat lie. She hasn't changed a bit. And I refuse to put myself through this humiliation all over again. So when she left for Budapest I told her that we're history. It's over.'

Annabeth studied me with concern. 'This is such awful news – especially because you two seemed so happy together. I thought you might even be on the verge of a return trip to the altar.'

'So did I,' I said bitterly.

'I'm sorry, Hoagy. Truly, truly sorry.'

'No need to be. I'm a lot stronger now than I was ten years ago. I'll go home to my crappy old fifth-floor walk-up on West 93rd Street, bolt the door and dive head-first back into my book. I'll be fine.'

'That sounds like a good plan. And if you don't mind some professional advice, I'd stay away from self-medicating. If you start to feel overwhelmed by anger or despair, go to the gym. Or call someone. Call *me*.'

'Thank you. That's very kind of you. But there's no need to worry. My self-medicating days are behind me.'

'I'm glad to hear that.' She sipped her tea, wiggling her toes inside her black stockings. 'Sometimes I wish I weren't such a goodie-goodie.'

'Meaning . . .?

'Meaning if I were a shameless slut bomb I'd try to steal you. I have the world's hugest crush on you,' she confessed, coloring slightly. 'Surely you've sensed it. You're very perceptive, not to mention kind, funny, talented and *so* handsome. You even smell good.'

'It's Floris No. 89 talc. You do, too. Smell good, I mean.'

'Thank you, it's—'

'Essential lavender oil.'

'How did you know that?'

'Because you smell subtly of lavender yet you're not making Lulu sneeze. She's allergic to most alcohol-based scents.'

'If I knew for certain that you were genuinely available I'd be all over you in a second. But I have this stubborn moral streak. I would never try to steal another woman's man.'

'Even if he wanted to be stolen?'

Those penetrating brown eyes of hers narrowed at me. 'Deep down inside, I don't think you do.'

'Deep down inside, you happen to be wrong. I find you incredibly attractive, not to mention fascinating.'

A vein in her forehead started to throb faintly. 'I . . . have to keep reminding myself that you're still recovering from a concussion. How is your head wound anyhow?'

'Fine. Or at least I think it is. I didn't go to medical school.'

'Well, I did. Here, let me have a look.'

'You really don't have to do that.'

'Don't be absurd. It's no bother. Duck your head a little.' She put her mug on the tea tray, sat up on her knees and raised an edge of the bandage. 'The wound shows no sign of infection.' She prodded the staples gently. 'It's healing nicely. They did a good job at Middlesex.' She carefully tamped the bandage back down, stroking my hair – where I had hair –with the fingers of her right hand. Her left hand was resting on my thigh. She snuggled closer, curling up next to me with her feet underneath her and rested her head on my shoulder. I put my arm around her, inhaling her scent while Lulu watched us from the chair on full alert.

'This is nice,' I said softly, gazing into the fire. 'I could sit here like this all day.'

'I feel the same way.' Her voice was almost a whisper. 'I like being with you. You make me feel so at ease.'

'Good, I'm glad.'

'I'm glad that you're glad.'

'That's what makes this so hard.'

She raised her head from my shoulder, frowning. 'Makes what so hard?'

'That stubborn moral streak of yours . . .?'

'What about it?'

'You didn't bat a thousand.'

'I'm afraid I'm not particularly well versed in sports terminology. I don't know what that means.'

'It means that you lied to me the other day. Just a little lie in the grand scheme of things, but now that both Talmadge brothers are dead, it turns out it was actually pretty huge.'

Annabeth swallowed, her eyes probing mine. 'What on earth are you talking about?'

'You told me that Austin was checked into McLean Psychiatric Hospital in Massachusetts five years ago when your husband, Paul, was killed while he was jogging early one Sunday morning by a hit-and-run driver. That was a lie. I spent a couple of hours at the library yesterday and found the police report of his death in the Monday, July eighteenth, 1988 edition of the *New London Day*. Paul was killed on Sunday, July seventeenth.'

'You *don't* have to remind me of the date.'

'Actually, it seems that I do.'

Annabeth shook her head at me. 'I still don't understand where you're going with this.'

'According to Austin's employment records with the Great Atlantic & Pacific Tea Company, better known as the A&P, Austin was actually on the job in Old Lyme on the seventeenth of July, stocking shelves. He punched in at noon, according to the manager's employee records. Frank had to dig pretty deep to find them, but those places never throw anything away. In fact, the records show that Austin kept showing up for work there until three days *after* Paul was killed.'

Her face tightened. 'Meaning what exactly?'

'Meaning Austin murdered Paul. What's more, you knew he murdered him or you wouldn't have lied to me that he was hospitalized at the time. Why did you lie to me?'

Annabeth didn't answer me for a long moment. Just stared into the fire with a faraway look on her face. 'Because I–I was ashamed,' she finally stammered. '*Am* ashamed. I got Paul killed. It was my fault. I said something incredibly stupid to Austin during one of our sessions and I got Paul killed. I wake up every morning knowing that deep down in my soul.'

'What was it that you said? Something that made Austin angry?'

'Austin had admitted to me in our Friday therapy

session that he'd stopped taking his Thorazine again. I warned him that he would have to go back to McLean if he didn't resume taking it immediately. He became enraged with me because he actually enjoyed working at that store. He'd even made a couple of lady friends there.'

'Joanie and Sandy, sure.'

She looked at me in surprise. 'You know them?'

'Absolutely. We're pals. They told me they felt sorry for him.'

'Me they hated. They thought I was a shrew because I'd come into the market and bawl him out for being rude. They thought he was a lonely sad sack. Had no idea that he was a seriously ill individual. Austin hated the Thorazine. Hated that it made him into such a fatso, as he put it. But he needed to be on it in order to function. In one of our sessions a few weeks earlier I'd suggested he try embarking on an exercise regimen. I mentioned, for example, that Paul liked to run the country roads near our house, especially early on Sunday mornings when very few cars were out. People in my profession are trained to be very careful about revealing any details about our personal lives. I should never, ever have said what I said.'

'Sounds like a pretty harmless remark to me.'

'It wasn't. It was a fatally stupid mistake. Lyme's a small village. Austin knew where we lived. And I knew that I was dealing with a patient who had a history of exhibiting violent behavior.'

'Did Austin admit to you that he was responsible for Paul's death?'

'Never.'

'There's no chance that it was someone else, is there?'

'No chance. Frank phoned me from the A&P not long after they took Paul's body away to tell me that Austin had shown up late for work and was acting peculiar.'

'Peculiar as in . . .?'

'Agitated. Muttering to himself. Frank had to send him home for the day because he was disturbing the customers.'

'The police report in the *New London Day* was pretty scant on details. Apparently no one saw it happen. The state police were hoping a witness might come forward. I take it that no one did. I also take it that you didn't report Austin.'

She breathed in and out slowly. 'I should have called Jim Conley and told him. It would have been the right thing to do. But I didn't do the right thing. Instead, I called Michael.'

'Why Michael? We're talking vehicular homicide here, Annabeth. Austin *murdered* the father of your children.'

'Do you honestly think I don't realize that?' Her eyes welled up with tears. 'I called Michael because that's what I'd been ordered to do when I took Austin on as a patient. That was the deal. If there was any kind of trouble, I was to call Michael. No one else. So I called him. I–I was a shattered wreck when I did. I'd just lost the great love of my life. Paul was . . . He was so kind, funny and sweet. You remind me of him sometimes.'

'Please don't say anything like that again.'

'But it's true,'

'I don't care. Please don't say it.'

'OK.' She lowered her head back on to my shoulder, nestling close to me. 'I did tell Michael we should inform the state police immediately that Austin was responsible for Paul's death. He said, "We will do no such thing." Furthermore, he said that if I did so on my own he'd see to it that I lost my position at Yale as well as my license to practice. Put yourself in my position, Hoagy. I was a grief-stricken thirty-seven-year-old woman who'd just lost her husband and had three small kids to support. What choice did I have? So I did what Michael told me to do. Continued to treat Austin and collect my million dollars a year.'

'Annabeth, there's something I really don't understand.'

'What is it?'

'Michael was so utterly terrified of Austin that he couldn't even be in the same room with him unless there were armed guards present. Wouldn't he have welcomed the opportunity to have Austin arrested and put away for life? Wouldn't he have wanted to be free of him?'

'Austin was his kid brother. Family. And it was Michael's responsibility to look after him, even if he was terrified of him. It sounds crazy, I know. But the Talmadges have never been like other people. Besides, they're above the law. Austin would never have been charged with a crime or seen the inside of a jail. So I kept my mouth shut and sent him off to McLean.'

'Did he go willingly?'

'Far from it. Two of Michael's bodyguards had to hold him down so I could shoot him up with Haldol. He was transported there by private ambulance.'

'How often did it come up in your subsequent therapy sessions with Austin over the years?'

'How often did what come up? What are we talking about now?'

'The fact that he killed your husband. What do you think we're talking about?

She let out a sigh. 'I guess I was just hoping you'd changed the subject. I don't find this a very pleasant one to talk about. Austin always pretended he had nothing to do with it. Told me he hoped I found out who was responsible for Paul's death so that law and order would be served. He was very big into law and order, as you know.'

'Why did he kill Paul?'

'I already told you. He'd stopped taking his Thorazine. When I threatened him with a return trip to McLean he became enraged.'

'I'm not buying it. You must have had that very same conversation dozens of times before. Why did he really do it?'

She snuggled there against me in silence for a long moment. 'To show me that *he* was in charge.'

'OK, that I can believe.'

'Part of me died inside after that, I swear. I became like a zombie. Just kept on treating him and putting one foot in front of the other. He'd stay at McLean for weeks or months at a stretch, return home, stay on his meds, show up for work at the A&P and our therapy sessions. Then, inevitably, he'd stop taking his meds, stop showing up, grow increasingly erratic and have to be hospitalized. The pattern repeated itself over and over and over again until two years ago, when Frank told Michael that Austin was simply too disruptive and that he couldn't allow him to work at the A&P anymore. Michael was dismayed, but it came as no surprise to me. Austin's condition, despite my best efforts, was steadily deteriorating.'

'Were you ever concerned that he would attack you?'

'Never. He was too dependent on me.'

'What about one of your children?'

'I never, ever mentioned a single morsel of personal information about them. And I made sure they were never on their own after school. If I had to be in New Haven then my mother would pick them up and stay with them until I got home. Mind you, these past two years were less of an issue because he was away at McLean most of the time. Practically all of last year and most of this year, until just a few weeks ago.'

'Which explains why I never saw him on patrol this summer when I was working on my novel in Merilee's guest house. When I came out here last week he showed up almost instantly in his tricked-out police car, incredibly anxious to meet her. I just figured he was a goofball celebrity stalker with a serious personal hygiene problem, but Mr MacGowan warned me he was much more dangerous than that and told me to report the encounter. Next thing I knew the kitchen was full of Very Important People who were talking about "pulling the ripcord."'

'The matter was taken quite seriously,' she acknowledged. 'Merilee is a huge star and Austin, he wasn't doing well. I don't need to tell you that.'

'No, you don't.'

'After Michael's security team had reeled him in and brought him home to his private sanitarium, I had the substitute nurse, Eileen, knock him out with a heavy dose of Ambien, as I told you. Except he'd become incredibly adept over the years at pretending to swallow pills. Also at sneaking around. He managed to get out of a locked room without attracting the attention of Michael's guards, their dog or me. Grabbed his clothes and took off.'

'Are you sure you didn't let him slip out?'

She raised her face to mine, puzzled. 'Whatever do you mean?'

'He had an awfully easy time getting away. It was almost as if you wanted him to escape.'

'Not true, Hoagy. I had no idea that Austin had a copy of the key to his room. And I certainly had no idea that Captain Rundle of Troop F, who must have sawdust between his ears, would actually return Austin's patrol car to the house and leave the keys in the ignition. Seriously, how stupid is that?'

'Seriously? Very stupid. But, on the other hand, it did provide you with a golden opportunity to do what you'd been wanting to do for years – avenge Paul's death.'

She blinked at me in utter shock. 'You think *I'm* the person who slashed Austin's throat?'

'No, I don't think it. I know it. When I was ghosting Hollywood memoirs I learned quite a few things about the dark side of human nature. The single most important one I learned was that if a person lied to me from the get-go, that it was no fluke. It was who they really were, and that they would lie to me again and again. Lie to me whenever it furthered their personal agenda – which, in your particular case, happens to be covering up the fact that it was *you* who followed us up that mountain, cut Austin's throat from ear to ear and shoved him over the safety railing into the gorge below. You lied to me from the get-go, Annabeth. You told me that Austin was hospitalized at McLean when Paul was killed. He wasn't. That lie? That told me who you really are.'

She lowered her gaze, her face reddening. 'Here I thought we were having a friendly conversation, maybe even a bit more than friendly, and it turns out that you invited me over to accuse me of murder. I truly don't have the slightest idea what you're talking about.'

'See? You're lying again right now. You do know what I'm talking about. Don't bother to deny it, because that will just be another lie and we'll keep going around and around in circles. When you were nice enough to drop off that delicious chicken noodle soup, you mentioned you'd been stuck in traffic on the Q Bridge in New Haven at the time of Austin's murder. You said you'd been clearing off your desk at the med school that day.'

'So?'

'So I phoned my old Cambridge pal T.J. That would be Dr Thomas Joshua to you, whose office is right down the hall from yours. He told me he was in his office the entire day working on a book review that some scholarly journal had asked him to write. I said to him, hey, the writing thing is *mine*. Get off of my cloud. And he—'

'Is there a point to this?' she asked with a slight edge in her voice.

'He swore to me he didn't catch so much as a glimpse of you that day. In fact, he told me he hardly sees you at all anymore, and when he does you seem very somber. He's been wondering if you're doing OK, which it so happens you're not. T.J. could tell. He has a razor-sharp mind, I understand.'

'Is there a point to this?' she repeated, this time with a much harder edge.

'As a favor for a rowdy old friend – that would be me – he called Dr Prakesh, the psychiatrist who has the office directly across the hall from yours. Then he called me back five minutes later. Guess what? She didn't see you in your office that day either, the reason being that you were never there. That was a lie. Yet another lie.'

I paused, waiting for Annabeth to contradict me. She didn't. She didn't so much as say a word. Just sat there, breathing in and out.

So I plowed ahead. 'You do have my sympathy, you know. Austin murdered your soul mate. But you and I both know that you weren't stuck in traffic on the Q Bridge in New Haven at the time of Austin's death. You were high atop Mount Creepy with a hunting knife in your hand and Austin Talmadge's steaming-hot blood all over you. So why don't you just come clean? I can help you. The governor's fixer, Colin Fielding, likes me for some reason. He told me if I ever needed a favor to give him a call. He's a former spook.

I guarantee he can make all of this disappear. But if you keep lying to me, I can't help you. And I want to help you. You see, it so happens that I've grown rather fond of you.' Her eyes searched mine. There was hope in them. Desperate hope. 'More than fond, actually. The truth is that I'm absolutely crazy about you,' I confessed as Lulu grumbled at me unhappily from the wing-backed chair.

Annabeth studied me curiously. 'You're a strange one. First you accuse me of being a pathological liar and murderer, then you tell me you've fallen for me.'

'No one's ever accused me of being normal. Go ahead, ask around.'

'I don't have to,' Annabeth said softly. 'Because I've fallen for you, too.' She raised her face to mine and kissed me lightly on the lips. Her mouth tasted sour despite the honey she'd been drinking in her tea. She took my hand and held it, squeezing it tightly. Hers was ice cold. 'Jim Conley phoned me at the sanitarium to tell me that Austin had just shot Truman Mainwaring at the beach club and then had gone roaring out of there. I knew immediately he'd flee to his mountain to hide. It was his safe place. So I drove straight home – the kids were still at school – changed into hiking boots, jeans and an old wool mackinaw shirt of Paul's and drove to Talmadge State Park. I parked my Volvo around the bend a good distance from the parking lot and was hiding in the brush near the entrance, waiting, until he showed up just like I knew he would – although I sure wasn't expecting to see *you* with him.'

'He didn't exactly give me a choice.'

'I had no idea what to do about you. I certainly didn't want to kill you. Fortunately, Austin took care of that for me when he knocked you out and buried you in that root cellar, which I considered a genuine blessing.'

'That makes one of us,' I said, as Lulu grunted sourly. 'Make that two.'

'I followed you up there to the ruins, making sure I kept a good, safe distance behind you.'

'It was *you* who Lulu smelled. It's a good thing for you that you weren't wearing any of your essential lavender oil that day. If you had been she would have recognized your scent when you stopped by here with that chicken noodle soup and started barking her head off.' I glanced over at her in her chair. She had an extremely alert, watchful expression on her face. 'Everything went blank for me once Austin conked me over the head and entombed us in that root cellar. Tell me, what happened after that?'

'He kept hiking his way up through the ruins of the old farm. I caught up with him and called out his name. He was utterly horrified to see me. "Go away! I don't want you here!" he screamed at me. "I'm your doctor, Austin," I said. "You're sick. You have to come back with me." He refused. Kept right on hiking, panting for breath, sweat pouring down his face. He was toting some kind of duffel bag. I stayed with him, stride for stride. "I'm never coming back and don't try to make me!" he warned me. Then he pulled his gun on me and said, "I don't want to kill you but I will." I said, "Like you killed Paul, you mean?" We'd reached the railing next to the falls by then. "Sure, I killed Paul," he confessed. "He was asking for it. He had a beautiful wife, three healthy kids. He was happy. He was smart. He deserved to die. Every person on the planet who's happy and smart deserves to die. I hate them all. I hate *you*." He kept on ranting. I let him rant. Just walked slowly toward him, staying calm and non-threatening. Whenever I hike in the woods I always carry a folding hunting knife in the back pocket of my jeans. Paul gave it to me in case I ever encountered a coyote or rabid raccoon in the woods. I keep it razor sharp. "It's going to be OK, Austin," I said gently. "I promise you it'll be OK." He'd exhausted himself enough by then that he let me approach him and put my hands on his shoulders.'

'And then?'

Annabeth stared into the fire. 'And then I spun him around, whipped out my knife and slit his throat from ear to ear,' she said in a voice utterly devoid of emotion. 'He wasn't hard to kill. Didn't even put up a fight. Besides, I'm strong. I do an hour of weights every day, don't forget. He bled out fast once I'd severed his carotid artery. Then I leaned him up against the railing, picked up his legs and shoved him over the side.

He was already dead by the time he landed in the stone gully at the base of the falls.'

'How did it feel? Any regrets?'

'None. It was payback, Hoagy. It was justice. In fact, a feeling of incredible calm came over me as I started back down the mountain trail the way I came. And it's stayed with me ever since. I've never slept better.'

'Still, you must have gotten Austin's blood all over you.'

'I did get some on my hands and face, which I washed off in a stream along with my knife. Also on Paul's mackinaw shirt, which I wadded up just in case I ran into someone on the trail. The rest of my clothes were fine. When I got back down to the base of the mountain I heard voices and realized that Jim Conley had already set up a command post in the parking lot and recruited the volunteer fire department's search and rescue team. They'd found Austin's car, I gathered. I was glad I'd parked a good distance away. I got off the trail at once and made my way as quietly as I could through the brush in the direction of my car. When I finally managed to reach the paved road, I found it parked on the shoulder less than a hundred yards away. I got in and sped away, unnoticed. I made it home well before my mom brought the kids home from their after-school team sports. I buried Paul's mackinaw shirt in the woods out behind the house. Then I took a shower and washed my hair thoroughly just to make sure there was no trace of Austin's blood on me. I put on clean clothes, threw the ones I'd been wearing in the washing machine and started a load of laundry. By the time my mom brought the kids home I was seated at my desk, calmly working away in my home office.' She stroked my leg, gazing at me with warm affection. 'You want to know something? It feels incredibly cathartic to be telling you all of this. It's almost as if it's bringing us closer together. We're sharing something that no one else knows. I *want* you to know. It matters to me, dear. You don't mind if I call you that, do you?'

'You can call me anything you want,' I said, gently caressing her cheek with the back of my hand.

She took my hand, kissed it, and held it against her cheek.

'When Austin's body was found the next morning with you and Lulu right near him, not in great shape, but alive, my heart soared with relief.' She swallowed. '*Until* two days later, that is.'

'Why, what happened then?'

'I got a phone call from Michael. He knew that I'd killed Austin, of course.'

'How?'

'Because he was Michael. The man knew everything, I swear.'

'How do you know he wasn't just bluffing?'

'Because he told me he was in possession of a bloody mackinaw shirt. I asked him to hold on for a moment and ran out the back door. Sure enough, someone had dug up Paul's mackinaw and taken it.'

'Who?'

'Hoagy, I truly don't know.'

I mulled it over. 'It wouldn't surprise me a bit if Colin Fielding keeps an old spook buddy on retainer to do his dirty work for him. Fielding has forty billion reasons to keep Michael happy. As long as Michael's happy, the governor's happy. Whoever the guy was, he must have tailed you home from Mount Creepy. What did Michael say to you when you got back on the phone? Did he intend to turn you in to the police?'

'Oh, heavens, no. He had something much more insidious in mind. He intended to hold it over me.'

'Hold it over you how?'

'He wanted me to marry him.'

'You're kidding me.'

'Trust me, I'm not. He said he'd been drawn to me for a long, long time. He thought I was lovely, spirited and warm-hearted. Someone he felt comfortable with. He told me that he would enjoy nothing more than to help me raise my children and to make them happy. Make all of us happy. And that if I accepted his proposal he'd never breathe a word to anyone about what I'd done to Austin.'

'Unreal.'

'No, absolutely, totally, one hundred percent real.'

'So what was your response?'

'Total shock, at first. Then I wanted to laugh. The idea of me marrying that pale, trembling scarecrow was utterly preposterous. Just the thought of seeing him naked made me shudder. But it would not have been wise to insult him, and I knew it, so I said, "This is much too important to talk about on the phone." He agreed and suggested I drop by later that night. We could talk candidly because we'd be all alone. Connie Pike always went home after she'd finished his dinner dishes and he'd dismissed his security detail and sent them on their way.'

'OK, now this part starts to make some sense.'

'What part?'

'He stopped by here when I came home from the hospital to apologize on behalf of his family for what had happened to Lulu and me. I figured he'd be relieved that his life-long nemesis of a kid brother was dead. Far from it. He was still utterly terrified. Trembling same as ever. When I asked him why, he told me he was convinced that Austin's killer would come after him next. But then he turned right around the next day and dismissed his security detail. He even treated the guys to a trip to New Orleans. Which made no sense, but now it does. Because when he came to see me he didn't know it was *you* who'd killed Austin. Fielding's spook hadn't dug up Paul's bloody mackinaw from your yard yet. Perhaps you'd been sticking around the house a lot and didn't give him the opportunity.'

'I did stay close to home, now that you mention it.'

'It's also possible that Fielding and the governor had to strategize about whether or not Michael would be better off knowing or not knowing – strictly as it related to the governor's own political health and well-being. Once they decided to tell him, Michael promptly dismissed his security detail. He felt he no longer had any reason to be afraid. He certainly had no reason to fear you. After all, he intended to marry you, right?'

'That's right. I said I could come over after the kids went to bed, at perhaps ten o'clock, unless that was too late. He said no, it would be fine. He usually retired early but for me he would wait up, and leave the front gate open.'

'You drove over there last night after the kids went to bed?'

'I did.'

'They didn't hear you leave?'

'My oldest, Max, did. I told him I was restless and felt like taking a drive down to the beach to look at the moon over the water the way his dad and I used to. Max thought nothing of it. They're so self-absorbed at that age. When I arrived at Michael's, the front gate was open and there were no more ex-Green Berets around, just as he'd said. I rang the doorbell. He opened the front door dressed in an old flannel bathrobe, pajamas and slippers, which I found profoundly weird but . . .'

'He was a Talmadge.'

'Indeed. If he chose to greet me in his jammies, so be it. He said, "Welcome, my dear. This is a momentous day for both of us, is it not?" I agreed that it was. I was wearing an old dress that I'd been meaning to get rid of. It's very low cut, not that I have a lot to show off.'

'You've got plenty to show off.'

She kissed my cheek. 'You're so sweet. I made sure I unbuttoned my coat before I rang the doorbell so he'd get a good look. I also made sure I dabbed on a great deal of essential lavender oil so that he'd think I was in a romantic mood.'

'Which was a huge mistake on your part.'

She furrowed her brow at me curiously. 'How so?'

'Lulu picked up the scent out on the driveway, followed it up the front steps to the door and raised quite a ruckus.'

'But I'm wearing it right now. Why didn't she start barking her head off the second I walked in the door?'

I glanced over at her again in her chair. She had that same alert, watchful expression on her face. 'Because she knows I invited you here. She's being cagy. Very cagy.'

'Not possible. Dogs aren't capable of that level of cognition.'

'We're going to pretend we didn't hear you say that,' I responded. 'Mind you, when I was standing there on Michael's front porch, it did occur to me that the scent she'd picked up was the Deet that Donna Willis was wearing when we paid a call on her. Donna practically drowns herself in it when she goes into the woods. She's had Lyme disease twice and is afraid of getting it again. Plus she has serious anger-management issues and detested Austin. Only, Donna had no reason to kill Michael. In fact, she even liked the guy.'

'They'd met?'

'Corresponded. She thought he was very nice. A gentleman.'

'He was a mean bastard,' Annabeth said coldly.

'OK, so you were standing there in the mean bastard's doorway wearing your sexy low-cut dress with your coat unbuttoned, smelling as if you were in the mood for romance. What happened next?'

'He ushered me inside and helped me off with my coat. My knife was in my coat pocket. Since we didn't actually have anything to talk about, I didn't bother to waste any time. Slit his throat from ear to ear right there in the entry hall. Once I'd severed his carotid artery he was gone very fast.'

'Where are they?'

'Where are what, dear?'

'The fingernail scratches. The M.E. said he found skin and blood under Michael's nails.'

She glanced down at her chest. 'He did claw at me a bit, but it was more of a reflex than anything else. He didn't actually put up a fight. He was exactly like Austin in that regard. He didn't want to be alive either. After he fell to his knees and flopped over on to his back on the hallway floor I grabbed a handkerchief from my coat pocket and wiped the blood off of the knife and my hands. I stepped my way carefully back out the door, making sure I left no bloody footprints, then I used a clean second handkerchief to open and close it. Before I got in the car I took off my bloody coat and dress and changed into the old sweater and jeans I'd brought with me. Then I wadded up the coat, dress and handkerchiefs and wrapped them in a newspaper.'

'What did you do with them?'

'A mile or so down the hill from Michael's place I pulled off on to the shoulder of the road and got out. There's a very deep ravine in the woods there. I hurled them down there. The leaves are falling so fast now that I'm certain they're already covered over. No one will ever find them.'

'Fielding's spook will, if Fielding asks him to search for them.' I tugged at my ear. 'But I'm guessing he won't. No, I feel certain that Fielding and the governor will keep their mouths shut. These are ruthless men. Politics isn't bean bag.'

'Politics isn't *what*?'

'The governor will pridefully collect Michael's billions on behalf of the state and Michael's dreams for public education and health care will come true. Should you attempt to implicate him in any way, shape or form the governor will simply shrug and say he has no idea what you're talking about. Who do you think the state police will believe – a woman who has just savagely murdered Connecticut's two wealthiest citizens, or the esteemed governor of the state?'

Annabeth didn't respond. Just stared into the fire in taut silence.

'Were there many cars out on the road at that time of night?'

She took a deep breath, letting it out slowly. 'I didn't encounter a single car on my way home. When I got there the kids were fast asleep. All was quiet and peaceful. I took a long, hot shower, climbed into bed and lay there, feeling the most profound sense of accomplishment. I'd done what I had to do to protect my family. If I'd refused Michael's proposal he would have destroyed me for killing Austin. Made sure that I was locked away for life and that my kids were taken away from me. There was no way I could allow that to happen. If I'd accepted his proposal – well, it was utterly inconceivable that I'd accept his proposal. He'd left me with no choice, really.' She held my hand to her soft cheek for a moment before she kissed it and said, 'But now I have to decide what to do with you, dear. You present me with a much different dilemma. I'm madly in love with you, yet you know everything there is to know. Can pick up the phone today, tomorrow or two years from now and tell the police that I confessed to murdering the Talmadge brothers.

I'm so incredibly torn. I truly can't decide whether to kill you or get naked with you.'

'I vote for getting naked. We'd have a huge amount of fun and I'd end up alive afterward. I can offer you flannel sheets, a wood-burning fireplace and an unparalleled view of Whalebone Cove out of the master suite's French doors, not that I'm trying to sound like a realtor.'

Annabeth gazed at me, her eyes glittering. She was not only beautiful but incredibly desirable at that moment. I can't explain why. She'd just shared the details of how she'd killed two people. Was talking out loud about killing a third person – me. Yet I wanted her more at that moment than I'd wanted any woman other than Merilee in a long time. 'They're not panty hose,' she informed me. 'My stockings, that is to say.'

'And you're telling me this because . . .?'

'In case your tongue might be feeling adventuresome, which it is. I've aroused you. Would you like to know how I can tell?'

'Desperately.'

'Because I'm aroused, too. In fact, I've never been so aroused in my entire life.' She turned sideways on the sofa and raised her wool skirt, the better to show me that her black stockings were indeed thigh highs. Then she lay back, opened her legs wide and raised her heels up off of the sofa.

'Just out of curiosity, are you wearing panties?'

'It so happens that I'm not.'

'I've always noticed that about you Yalies. When you want something you're very direct about it. Don't beat around the bush, as it were.'

'Well, are you just going to sit there or what?'

I didn't bother to answer her. Not out loud, anyhow. I turned and knelt before her. Reached my palms underneath her and cupped her bare, firm butt cheeks in my hands. Her skin was incredibly smooth. She reached for me, put her hands gently behind my bandaged head and lowered it slowly between her legs. Ever so slowly . . . slowly . . . until . . .

Until I felt the point of a knife against the exposed skin of my neck. Her damned folding knife. She must have tucked it inside of her sweater's thick wristband.

I raised my head up, exceedingly carefully, and said, 'What are you doing?'

'I'm sorry, Hoagy.' She sat back up, holding the open blade against my throat as I knelt there before her. 'You have no idea how sorry. I want you so badly right now I'm soaking wet, I swear.'

'Thanks for sharing that little detail but—'

'I'm afraid that you have to die, too, dear. There's no other way. I simply can't trust you. I feel terrible about this, especially because you'll never get to finish your novel. I know how much that means to you.' She kissed me softly again. It was a goodbye kiss. Her lips still tasted sour. And then, with savage quickness, she grabbed my head and spun it halfway around as she went for my left ear with the knife's razor-sharp blade.

That was when Lulu dove across the coffee table and sank her teeth deeply into Dr Annabeth McKenna's right wrist. Annabeth let out a shriek as the knife fell to the floor and screamed in pain as Lulu clamped her wrist between her powerful jaws, growling ferociously.

That was also when the hallway door swung open and Lieutenant Carmine Tedone, who'd been standing behind the door missing none of this, rushed in with his weapon drawn. He kicked the knife farther away. 'All good, pal?'

'All good, Lieutenant. It's OK, Lulu, you can let go now. Good girl.' I patted her head. 'Good girl. Let go.'

Lulu released her hold on Annabeth's wrist and backed off, still growling, her eyes never leaving Annabeth.

'Your dog *bit* me!' she howled, gaping at me in shock and pain.

'You didn't really think she was just going to sit idly by and watch you do me bodily harm, did you?'

'Besides, if she hadn't bit you I would have put a bullet in your brain,' Tedone said. 'So consider yourself lucky.'

'I know I sure do,' I said. 'There aren't many things I can count on in this life but one of them is my fierce protector.' I patted her again and told her she could relax now – the danger had passed. She let out a low whoop, her tail thumping. 'She's up to date on her shots, by the way, so there's no need to worry, Annabeth. You won't get any more rabid than you already are.'

'But it *hurts!*' Annabeth cried out, her face contorting in pain.

'Yeah, those deep puncture wounds can be a real bitch,' Tedone said sympathetically. 'Just hang on. I'll have an ambulance here in five minutes and the EMT can give you a shot of something.'

He reached for the phone on Merilee's writing table to phone it in while I fetched some ice cubes from the freezer and wrapped them in a dishtowel. I also stopped off in the mudroom to fetch Annabeth's panties from the pocket of her raincoat. They were black silk, in case you were wondering. I know I was.

'Here you go,' I said, pressing the ice pack against her wrist. 'Do you need help with your panties?'

She looked at me blankly. 'Do I *what*?'

'Your panties. Can you put them on with one hand?'

'I'm *fine*,' she said indignantly, her cheeks mottling as she tucked her stocking feet into them and slid them up her legs one-handed, raising her butt up off of the sofa so she could wriggle into them.

Tedone finished his call and hung up the phone, watching her. 'You're a distinguished psychiatric professional,' he said, shaking his head at her. 'Where is your dignity?'

'My *dignity*?' She let out a mocking laugh. 'I lost my dignity the day I met the Talmadges.'

'The ambulance will be here right away, along with two state troopers.' He pulled a latex glove and plastic evidence bag from the back pocket of his trousers and bagged and tagged the knife.

'Did you hear everything?' I asked him.

He nodded. 'Every word.'

'I'll deny it,' she said as she held the ice pack against her wrist.

'You can try, but it won't do you any good.' I retrieved my microcassette recorder from the kindling basket where I'd hidden it. It has a lot of mileage on it from my ghosting days, but is still top grade and amazingly powerful.

'I'm not exactly a stranger to a courtroom, you know,' Annabeth said, climbing up on her high horse. 'I've been asked countless times to provide expert testimony about a criminal defendant's mental fitness to stand trial. You've just recorded me without my knowledge or consent. That makes it inadmissible in court.'

'Who do you think you're fooling, lady?' Tedone said brusquely. 'Your case will never go to court. It'll be handled very discreetly in a judge's chambers, where you'll plead guilty by reason of insanity and be remanded to the psychiatric wing of York Correctional, our illustrious state's maximum-security women's prison, for the next twenty or thirty years. Your mother will have to raise your kids from now on. Maybe they'll come visit you. Then again, maybe they won't want to when they find out what a monstrous lunatic you are. Hell, you're almost crazy enough to be a Talmadge.'

'You're one cold-hearted bastard,' she said, raising her voice at him.

Which was enough to prompt Lulu to start growling at her again from the foot of the sofa.

Annabeth drew in her breath. 'Keep her away from me,' she pleaded.

I led her into the kitchen for her reward. 'You saved my life, Lulu,' I said as I fed her one, two, three anchovies. 'You're a genuine heroine. Why, they make movies about dogs like you. Just wait until Mommy hears about this. She'll be so proud of what a brave girl you are. Tell you what, first thing we'll do when we get back to the city is head to the Oyster Bar in Grand Central for a pan roast.' The pan roast in Grand Central's Oyster Bar was her favorite food in the whole world. 'How does that sound?'

She didn't respond, which wasn't her style at all. I bent down to give her a belly rub, but she didn't want a belly rub, which wasn't her style either. Instead, she sat up and raised her bandaged paw the way a dog does when it shakes hands. But that wasn't what she wanted either. She wanted me to sit down on the kitchen floor with her so that she could climb into my lap and lick my face. I put my arms around her and hugged her as she whimpered softly. 'Hey, we're OK, girl. We're both OK. Yes, we are.'

I was saying a few more things to her that I won't bother to repeat here when the ambulance came speeding up the gravel driveway trailed by two silver Crown Vics. I got up and let them in through the front door. The EMT gave Annabeth a shot of novocaine and put a temporary bandage around her wrist. Also wrote down Lulu's rabies vaccination number from her tag and the name of her veterinarian in New York City. The two huge state troopers stood there in their rain slickers with Tedone, watching.

'Would you mind getting my raincoat and boots, please?' Annabeth asked me.

'Sure, no problem.'

'Search the pockets,' Tedone ordered one of the troopers. 'And cuff her. I want you riding to the hospital with her the whole way.'

After the trooper had searched the pockets of her coat – and found nothing but her wallet and keys – he helped her to her feet, draped it around her shoulders and held her steady while she stepped into her rubber Wellingtons. Then he cuffed her left wrist, the one that Lulu hadn't sunk her teeth into, to his own right wrist.

'You'll be fine,' I said to her as they started for the door together. 'You just got mixed up with a family that was a good, solid three hundred years' worth of deranged. Take care of yourself, OK?'

Annabeth McKenna said nothing in response. Didn't even look at me as the trooper escorted her outside into the rain with the EMT leading the way. While they got settled in the back of the van, the other trooper hustled out to his cruiser to serve as escort to the Shoreline Clinic. And then off they went, sirens blaring.

Tedone and I stood there in silence for a moment, emotionally spent, before I said, 'Thanks for backing my play, by the way.'

'No problem. It wasn't what I'd call a conventional play, but it got the job done.'

'Seriously, what'll happen to her?'

'Seriously? Exactly what I said. No way she'll put her kids through the ordeal of a trial. She'll quietly cop to an insanity plea and take up residence in York's criminal psych ward. Kind of a strange place for a Yale School of Medicine professor of psychiatry to find herself living, but it's been my experience that the world's getting stranger and stranger lately.'

'I've noticed that, too.'

'You've had yourself quite a week. You OK?'

'Who, me? I'm fine.'

'C'mon, I'll drive you up to Meriden and take your formal statement. Why don't you wait here while I fetch my cruiser? No sense in both of us getting wet.' He'd stashed it in the barn before Annabeth got there. He started for the door, then stopped. 'I've got to say, you showed some real nerve taking her on in that way.'

'I felt sorry for her more than anything else.'

'Don't kid a kidder, Hoagy. She murdered two people and was more than ready to murder you, too. You telling me you weren't scared shitless?'

'Little bit.'

'Oh, hey, that's not true about Miss Nash and Mel Gibson is it?'

'No, Lieutenant, I made that part up.'

'Good, because my wife would be crushed.'

We both had oyster pan roasts. We ate at the counter. Always do.

As an appetizer I had nine blue points that I squirted with lemon juice and Tabasco sauce and washed down with a spicy Bloody Mary, which is my drink of choice whenever I eat raw oysters. I wore my pigskin driving cap so that I wouldn't have to explain my head wound to Tony, the counter man, who'd been there since VJ day and was just as delighted to see us as we were to see him.

When he asked me about Lulu's bandaged paws I explained that she'd tussled with a badger on Merilee's farm. 'And that was one sorry badger, let me tell you.'

'You don't have to,' Tony assured me. 'Lulu's *street* tough.'

'You bet she is.'

It was a bit after nine p.m. when I settled our tab and Lulu and I strolled our way out of Grand Central, me dragging on a Chesterfield that I'd lit with Grandfather's Varaflame lighter, the one that had helped save both of our lives. We caught a cab home, the night-time air in the city feeling uncommonly mild after being in the country.

I'd already taken care of business when we'd arrived home that afternoon. Unpacked my clothes and shaving kit. Deposited my baskets of apples and pears from Merilee's trees in the kitchen along with Mr MacGowan's jug. Parked my Olympia, my manuscript, notepads and that all-important wad of prescription pad notes on the Stickley library table in my office, gazing out the windows at my view of Central Park. I'd also scheduled appointments for later in the week to get the staples removed from my skull and have Lulu's paws checked.

It was my intention to resume my daily writing routine first thing in the morning. So when we got home from the Oyster Bar I turned out the lights, brushed my teeth, refused to floss, stripped down to my boxers and climbed into bed with Mrs Parker, listening to the comforting sounds of Central Park West sixteen floors below. Lulu's tail thumped as she lay sprawled out next to me on the huge bed. She was happy to be home, especially with an oyster pan roast in her tummy.

When the phone rang I lunged for it, hoping it was Merilee.

It was Colin Fielding. 'Sorry I wasn't able to touch base with you in Lyme earlier today,' he said in that slightly nasal voice of his. 'Just wanted to say thank you on the governor's behalf for the low-key way you handled everything.'

'I wish I could say it was my pleasure, but I'm afraid I can't.'

'I know you can't. This has been quite an ordeal for you. If I can ever lend a hand, don't hesitate to call, OK? Things happen. Unexpected things. I can be a valuable person to know.'

'I don't doubt that for one second.'

'I like the way you operate. If you're ever in the market for some freelance political consulting work . . .'

'I won't be.'

'Still, I'm going to keep your contact information in my Rolodex.'

'You do that,' I said before I hung up.

It rang again immediately. I was expecting it to be Colin Fielding pressing his case harder.

It wasn't. It was Merilee. 'Hoagy? My agent just called me with the news.' There was static on the line but the connection was strong. '*Annabeth* killed Austin and Michael? I can't believe it!'

'Believe it. And she would have killed me, too, if it hadn't been for your brave little girl.'

'I hope you let her know how grateful you are.'

'You bet. I just took her to the Oyster Bar for a pan roast.'

Merilee fell silent for a second. 'I don't even want to think that you almost . . .'

'That I almost what?'

'I'd just hate to lose you now that I've found you again.'

'That makes two of us. Or I should say three,' I said after a low moan from Lulu.

'Darling, why did I have to hear about it from my agent? Why didn't *you* call me?'

'Because I didn't want to distract you. Besides, I figured you'd hear about it soon enough.'

'It's just all so . . . so hard to imagine. Annabeth seemed like such a decent person.'

'She may have been a decent person once, but she wasn't one anymore. She was warped, twisted and incredibly dangerous. But enough about her. How's the film coming?'

'Well, I spoke to my director. Bluntly, just like Kate told me to.'

'And . . .?

'And he was thoroughly intimidated. He's terrified I'll bail if I don't get my way and that the picture will lose its financing. From now on I'm playing Brett the way I see her. So she feels real to me.'

'Good for you, Merilee. I'm proud of you.'

'I couldn't have done it without you, darling.'

'I think Kate had a little something to do with it.'

'Ix-nay on the Ate-kay.'

'Ah, your Hungarian sounds as if it's improving by leaps and bounds.'

'It was *you*, darling. You inspire me. I want you to be proud of me. Don't you know how much you mean to me? Oh, God, listen to me. It's the middle of the night and I'm babbling.'

'I love it when you babble.'

'I'm just so happy that you're safe. And you must be thrilled to be back in the city. You'll start working again?'

'First thing tomorrow morning. I've gone over those notes that I made on Dr Eng's prescription pad when I was still semi out of it and they're the real deal.'

'This would be your so-called Third Level?'

'I actually mentioned it out loud?'

'You did. I thought you were delirious.'

'I wasn't. It was a major breakthrough. So major, in fact, that I think from now on I should plan on getting a major whack on the back of my skull every ten years.'

'How about if we discuss that in ten years?' She yawned hugely. 'I have a six a.m. make-up call. Hanging up now. Love you.'

'Love you, Merilee.'

The line went dead. I lay there in total contentment for a moment. Thought about reading Mrs Parker, then decided to just say goodnight to Lulu, turn out the light, close my eyes and go to sleep.

I lasted there that way for all of thirty seconds.

Got up and went into the kitchen to put the espresso on. Rummaged around in the bedroom for an old T-shirt, torn jeans, my flight jacket and Chippewas. Returned to the kitchen and poured myself a steaming mug of espresso before I headed down the hall to my office. I cranked up my original vinyl *Rockaway Beach* by the Ramones on my stereo – not too loud so as not to annoy the upstairs neighbors. Sat down at my desk and sipped my espresso, gazing out the windows at the city that never sleeps. As I rolled a fresh piece of paper into my Olympia, Lulu wandered in and curled up in her Morris chair under that incredible Hopper painting of the craggy Maine coastline.

I took a deep breath and let it out slowly, pausing to savor this moment. And then, with a great big smile on my face, I went back to work.

I was *me* again.